PHOENIX ONE

Chase MacLeod

This is a work of fiction. Names, character, places, and incidents are the product of the author's imagination or are used fictitiously. Any Resemblance to actual persons, living or dead, events, or locales is entirely coincidental.

PHOENIX ONE (ASCENSION SERIES BOOK 1)
PUBLISHED BY
MARTIAN MALLARD PRESS, LLC
1603 CAPITOL AVE
STE 310 A462
CHEYENNE, WY 82001
WWW.MARTIANMALLARDPRESS.COM

ISBN-13: 978-1733946902

Third Edition. 2nd Printing

ii

DEDICATION
For Jose, my brother in arms

ACKNOWLEDGMENTS

Special thanks to Johnathan Perkins, Johnny "Admiral" Clagg, Joel Marsh, James Hudgins, and Daxton Newberry for your feedback and offering to be my beta readers. I also want to thank my parents and my wife, Kathryn, as well as my two children, Iris and Calvin. Without their continued support, it is likely that I would have given up at some point early on.

Prologue

"Well, we did it. We ruined our home. We took our planet for granted and now she's dying, officially. All our attempts to repair the damage we caused was too late. Humans, with our knack for adaptability, found a way to survive. Earth might be dying, but we will build a new home. It might not be better, and we may be stuck with some less-than-savory neighbors, but it is our only option. I only hope we don't ruin that world, too."

- Excerpt from the journal of Richard Dawkins, Phoenix One Project Lead, dated 1 August 2215.

As Earth lay dying, buried beneath mountains of trash and flooded by rivers of toxic waste, we took to the sky. Civilizations huddled together on floating platforms that were little more than large discs, approximately ten miles in diameter, with apartment buildings stacked on top of each other like a game of Tetris gone awry. The cities were kept aloft by powerful engines in the base that forced pressurized columns of air toward the ground, not too unlike the blades of a helicopter. Markets were mixed into the jumble of housing to provide what little sustenance was left. These floating cities hovered above the surface at just over five thousand feet when weather systems permitted, yet at that altitude, the wind made the walks to various destinations nearly unbearable. When storms rolled in the cities would ascend to a height of nearly thirty thousand feet, staying just above the worst parts. The only reliable source of food was grown synthetically in labs. Humans were one of only a few living creatures left on the planet. Almost anything that remained on the surface had become horribly grotesque mutations, which only added to the hostility of the surface. Most were variations of insects or reptiles. Few mammals remained.

Nearly a decade before the planet became virtually uninhabitable we sent a probe into space in orbit opposite our own and found a planet practically identical to ours that was also capable of sustaining life. We began communications with the denizens of the planet and as we learned their language, and they ours, it became clear that both our planets were heading for the same fate. Their planet had two equally dominant and sentient species, the Trooviians and Calvorans, who had shared their planet by residing in opposite atmospheres. The Trooviians found that becoming subterranean sheltered them from the toxic atmosphere while the Calvorans took to the air, much as we did. Our planets were dying and we, the dominant species of our respective worlds, were at fault. Their planet's condition was already fifty years ahead of ours, and we offered a home for them in the hopes that what we learned from them would prevent the death of our planet.

The first extraterrestrial ships landed as we launched our first floating city. They were too late. Our planet was beyond saving, but with their presence, we regained hope that our species could survive. With their unique technology and ours, there was finally a chance that we could build a new home that both species could inhabit and peacefully coexist. Mars was out of the question. While the planet may have been able to support life at one time, it would never be able to again as our efforts to terraform were a dismal failure, so we had to construct a planet of our own.

There were the Trooviians, a subterranean race who excelled at the more physical aspects of the project. They were easily two feet taller than the tallest human, and twice as wide. Their flesh had the appearance of a dried riverbed, cracked and dry. They had a froglike appearance, their eyes set on either side of their heads. Large, square teeth filled their wide mouths and a horizontal slit lay where a nose would be. Most Trooviians were darkly colored, and gender was nearly indistinguishable. We initially regarded them as a threat, but the Trooviians proved their trustworthiness by acting as guards and protectors.

The Trooviians' counterparts, the Calvorans, were tall and long of limb. They had long, eight-fingered hands, small black eyes set in their large oval heads. They resembled the "Greys" of human science fiction, but in truth, they had a bluish cast like that of a hypothermia victim. They were gentle in demeanor and seemed to glide when they moved. Their voices were the most unusual aspect, as it sounded like they spoke with more than one voice. All Calvorans were genderless, though some seemed more masculine than others. We often suspected that they were all lab grown.

On the surface of our derelict planet resided the outcasts. Humans who'd been shunned by the wealthier groups before The Human Collective had been formed to unite the entire Human Race. These outcasts had become divided into two groups, the Scavengers, and the more hostile Bandits. Both looked nearly identical, malnourished and badly sunburnt, but the Bandits chose to kill rather than coexist. Scavengers were often employed to maintain the floating cities as they had demonstrated an uncanny affinity for machinery. The Bandits were avoided at all costs.

Humanity, along with our Trooviian and Calvoran partners, banded together with a singular purpose: the construction of a new home. A manufactured planet capable of sustaining all three races in perfect harmony. A Utopia birthed from the ashes of ruin.

This project was deemed Phoenix One.

Chapter 1

12 June 2236: Hovering above Houston Ruins, Texas

In the dank, filthy bowels of Disc City 6, a figure moved with predatory grace along the service tunnels. It moved with undeniable urgency, but also with such stealth that the numerous service workers on duty never saw it. Any detection and the mission would surely fail.

It moved along the twisting tunnels as if it had traveled them many times before, which it had. There was little light and in some places no light at all, but the thing never slowed and never lost its way. Voices echoed in one of the tunnels ahead, and the shadow quickly changed direction, entering another tunnel and moving away.

In mere minutes the figure reached its destination. The engine compartment was massive and incredibly loud. The shadow of a creature no longer needed to tread quietly as the compartment was only occupied by the engine and nothing else. No engineers or maintenance technicians were present, thus making the mission easier to complete.

The thing strode toward the engine and immediately found its target. A large gray panel proved to be the perfect place to plant the explosive charge, as this was the flattest part of the fuel reservoir. The shadow gently affixed the charge, taking great care to avoid hitting one of the buttons on the keypad by mistake. It carefully punched in the activation code and set the timer, allowing just enough time to escape before detonation.

With the payload delivered, the unseen thing turned and raced through another series of tunnels that led back to the surface of Disc City 6.

***

Throughout Disc City 6, informally dubbed New Houston by some of the residents after the ruins they hovered above, people did their best to live a normal life. Several schools were erected along the thirty-mile expanse for the myriad of children on board; the future of the human race if Phoenix One was successful. It wasn't the only Disc City with schools and children, but it was one of the largest. Even with Earth's impending demise lurking in the near future, the residents of Disc City 6 tried to cling to normalcy.

The largest employer on the floating city was the major laboratory that housed most of the life support systems for Phoenix One, including the highly critical eco-generator prototype. Without it, the entire project would be useless. Even with the technology provided by the Calvorans and the Trooviians, an eco-generator would be necessary for humanity's very survival. The point was to create a viable ecosystem on the Phoenix One structure once the frame was sent into space and a surface constructed.

Atmosphere generators, which had already seen successful trials on Mars despite being unsustainable on that dead planet, were ready for deployment. They too were housed within the lab on Disc City 6. Some people feared that having all the life support systems in one area was a major risk, especially when a large group of the human population distrusted their alien neighbors.

Outside of the lab, there were other potential jobs for the residents. Grocery stores were available, even though the wares were purely lab-grown, and transit systems dotted the cluttered city. There were other, less savory jobs as well, but if people had a purpose and a distraction from the fear of extinction, there was little complaint.

The most unsavory jobs were left to whatever Scavengers could be found and "procured" from the surface. Most of these jobs were either sanitation or maintenance. The Disc City required diligent maintenance to stay afloat, and the Scavengers' knack for machinery was invaluable.

The working conditions resulted in the deaths of more than a few of the unlucky people enslaved for the task. Scavengers were also human, but their living conditions and the decision to stay on the surface made them outcasts, regarded as lesser beings and treated as such. They were the planet's new homeless population. Racism amongst humanity, since the introduction of the aliens, was near nonexistent except for the way Scavengers and Bandits were treated.

***

Dr. Joseph Weiss watched the slowly revolving image of a honeycombed sphere projected in the air above his desk before him. It looked more like a child's toy rather than the future home for all life on Earth. It was in the early stages of production, he knew, but time was quickly running out. Every able-bodied person, including the Trooviians and Calvorans, were working on this project; assembling the framework first and then the supporting equipment to keep the whole thing running.

Life could barely be sustained by the planet's atmosphere, and it was getting worse by the day. Forget trying to stay at ground level. The toxic fumes made traversing the surface next to impossible, even with the burdensome purification equipment the scavengers wore. Up here at ten thousand feet above sea level the winds were intense. The flimsy walls of the haphazardly stacked housing complexes did the job of blocking out the freezing wind, but nobody ever felt safe.

At any moment, it was feared that a building would be blown over. This project needed to be finished soon but creating a planet-like space station can't be done in a day. They'd been at it for over a year, but they still had several years' worth of work ahead of them. Years they didn't have.

Dr. Weiss sighed and turned away from the projection table located at the heart of his lab. The lab was small, lined with metallic walls and blinding white floors. He was the lead engineer tasked with creating life sustainment equipment, so there was immense pressure on him to succeed. The fluorescent lighting made his eyes hurt, but the lighting was necessary. Natural light wasn't bright enough anymore, not since the massive clouds of smog blocked much of the sun's light.

As Dr. Weiss crossed the room, he turned his attention to his tablet and scrolled through the numerous messages he had received from his engineering team. His team had been tasked with creating the machinery that would make the space station capable of sustaining entire ecosystems, yet the messages from his team ensured him that their task was near impossible. The machinery was massive and difficult to maintain. That he knew, but the scale wasn't the problem. They needed more than digital code to produce the atmospheric conditions that it would take just to make life possible on the space station. It would take massive amounts of organic material and fuel, which was not something they had in abundance.

All the organic materials left was being rapidly consumed by the millions of people crammed into their tiny apartments in the floating cities. They could grow some organic material, and in theory, let that material incubate in the generator. They were currently experimenting with the process in hopes that it would take. The process sounded so simple, but they still hadn't managed to get it to work.

It happened almost as soon as Dr. Weiss exited out of the messaging program on his tablet. A new message reached his inbox. He was ready to ignore the message, but the subject line caught his attention. The subject line said, "It Works!" and nothing else. He was confused for only a moment before he realized what it truly meant. He couldn't believe it! They'd finally gotten it to work! He opened the message only to confirm his suspicion. It was true. The machine had kicked on and was already showing readings that the implanted organic material was replicating. With the generator running, they could now create nearly an unlimited amount food and clean air, though not enough to repair the Earth's atmosphere.

Weiss's new concern was the limited fuel. Without more, the machine would shut off, and all their progress would be lost. He quickly responded to the message, only saying that he would make sure the team got the fuel they needed. He could barely contain his excitement as he video-called his supervisor.

"Dr. Weiss! What news do you have for me?" asked the image of a frail looking man with only several tufts of white hair adorning his otherwise smooth dome.

"Dr. Peterson," Dr. Weiss responded. "It works! The machine finally works!"

"Magnificent! Truly magnificent! Let's get it running at full speed, then!"

"Sir," Dr. Weiss quickly interjected. His expression turned somber. "We lack the fuel to keep it running. If it shuts off, everything that it has done will be lost, and we can only pray that it would work again. We need to pump more fuel into it before that happens."

"I see," Dr. Peterson replied, though he didn't seem too concerned about the problem. "I'll just make sure we have more delivered within the hour. I know we have the fuel stored for it in *this* city."

"Thank you, sir." Dr. Weiss ended the call and turned back to the hovering projection. Finally, the image no longer depressed him. They were finally on the right track.

An instant later Dr. Weiss started to feel the ground shake, and the last thing he saw was a flash of blinding light. Explosions pounded his ears, and he felt his flesh ignite as searing pain flooded his senses. All that remained of Dr. Weiss were ashes as flames swept through the facility.

Chapter 2

Devin Slade sat astride his headless mechanized steed on the remains of a ruined overpass. He'd been temporarily frozen in place as he watched the floating city crash in a blaze. The wind whipped at his protective clothing and the flying debris stung his exposed arms as he gazed out across the sun-scorched terrain. Skeletal concrete remains of skyscrapers that had once been Houston stood stubbornly against the elements, until now.

The disc city had been hovering quietly for an hour in the distance as Devin rode slowly over the barren landscape, and suddenly it had erupted in flames and dove sideways into the earth. Devin watched as the thousands of people, including hundreds of children and more than a few Scavengers like him, that inhabited the city were killed. What could he do? What should he do? Most of those people certainly felt no love for his kind, the barely human wraiths that everyone called "Scavengers," so why *should* he care? The dwellers of the floating cities had even begun calling his kind "Savages." Some people had even tried to kill his kind on sight.

Yet, Devin still felt an immense sadness as he watched the disc burn. There was always hope for the next generation. Hope that they would be more accepting, more progressive. He knew how close to extinction humanity was, and this catastrophe moved them even closer. Disasters almost never happened to the disc cities on such a massive scale. If one of the engines failed, the others would alternate between powering down and powering up to slow the city's descent. This was an unusual and rare occurrence, thanks to the Scavengers.

His people were often employed, or rather forced, to do repairs on the machinery due to their extensive mechanical knowledge. It appeared to Devin as though one engine was destroyed rather than the usual failure. When an engine failed on the hovering cities, all the engines would shut down gradually to slow the descent. Devin had a feeling it had been deliberate. He knew he shouldn't concern himself with it, yet he couldn't justify ignoring the tragedy. He'd been aboard Disc City 6 several times to maintain the engines and some of the other mechanical workings of the city. Each time he'd been regarded the same way: as a slave.

He wasn't the only Scavenger to be "employed" on the city, but he was one of the unlucky few who was dumped back on the surface after he'd done his part. Some of the others were fortunate enough to be given living quarters of their own and lasting employment. He'd certainly felt some degree of animosity toward the disc city residents, but the destruction of all life on board was never something he'd desired.

Devin didn't enjoy his life of scavenging small, meaningless trinkets to trade for basic sustenance and he did not enjoy having to wear the protective gear to survive in the toxic atmosphere. In truth, those who lived in the floating cities weren't much better off, but anything had to be better than what he had to deal with daily.

He was almost always alone, fighting off starvation, the occasional mutated wildlife or the clans of Scavengers that had turned to murder and thievery to survive. They were usually called "Bandits," though he thought the term was less fitting than the title of "Savage" that was usually applied to him. They were the savages, not him.

Devin was horribly malnourished, perpetually sunburnt and filthy. He may have been light-skinned, but the exposure to the elements left him permanently reddish brown. He refused to allow his hair to grow in great lengths like the Bandits, instead preferring to keep his hair shortly cropped. His face, which was always hidden behind a crude gas mask, was closely shaved as well. Stubble always clung to his jaw but removing the mask to shave was an unnecessary risk most of the time. His eyes held the only color different from everything else. They were a light shade of blue, though the yellowed lens of his mask tinted his eyes a sickly green.

Devin typically avoided any other person that came across his path, more for his own safety than theirs. The harpoon gun he carried was more for show than anything, which usually worked in scaring the Bandits away. Despite the deterrent nature of his weapons, he'd been forced to use them from time to time and had taken the time to become proficient with them. The Bandits sometimes carried conventional firearms but discharging one in the dangerous atmosphere so heavily choked by methane gas was almost always disastrous for the shooter. Some had eventually adapted and began using crude weapons instead.

The image of the wreckage was surreal. The large disc embedded into the ground sideways with buildings falling off it like a plate of food that had fallen off a table. Fire and smoke engulfed the disc and turned the sky orange.

Devin waited for a moment, grappling with the urge to turn and get as far away from the burning disc as possible, before spurring his mechanical steed toward the wreckage. His survival instinct nearly screamed at him as he moved toward danger, turning his stomach in knots and quickening his heart beat.

The steed, built to resemble a horse, was great at traversing the rough terrain and he didn't have to worry about feeding it, as it ran off the fumes in the atmosphere and expelled clean oxygen that was stored in oxygen tanks on its stomach. It carried him fearlessly at high speed across the broken asphalt of the ruined highways toward the wreckage.

After a half hour of navigating through the rubble and dilapidated buildings, he caught a glimpse of a shape running from the wreckage, obscured by the thick pillars of inky black smoke. A survivor? It didn't matter. Whoever it was would be dead in minutes, unless they wore the gear that Devin was currently shrouded in. Something seemed off about the fleeing figure. Even though it spotted Devin, it never changed course.

"Wait!" Devin yelled, but the thing kept running. "Wait! Are you okay?"

No response was forthcoming from the rapidly shrinking shape. He doubted whoever it was had heard him, as his voice was muffled by his mask. After a moment, the figure disappeared behind one of the few buildings still standing in the area. He could chase them down, but he'd be acting against his deeply ingrained survival instinct twice in the same day, and he doubted his body could handle the anxiety. He sighed and turned to explore the wreckage.

It was even worse up close. Devin approached as close as he deemed safe, avoiding the bulk of the heat and smoke. Even at a hundred yards away he could see the charred bodies of humans and aliens alike, including the tiny remains of children, scattered across the ground all around the wreckage. Buildings were reduced to their skeletal frames and embedded into the earth in a twisted jumble of metal and ash. Some of the buildings that had been constructed on the disc city had been thrown from their foundations and propelled into the ruined buildings in the area. He even saw the remains of a tall building jutting from the side of a skyscraper's skeleton as if it had been a spear.

Devin had little hope that there would be much to scavenge from the wreckage. He dismounted his mechanical steed and walked slowly toward the wreckage until the heat from the flames became unbearable. Was it possible that somebody else survived? If anyone had survived, the heat alone would kill them before long along with the toxic atmosphere and any injuries they would have sustained. There was little left of the remains, and anything that could have been of use was nothing but ash now He intently scanned each body, looking for any sign of life and fighting the urge to vomit. He tried to sort through what he was feeling at that moment. Shock? Sadness, perhaps? Relief that he wasn't among the dead? Or was he glad that some of the people who treated him as an outcast were reduced to smoldering piles of flesh?

Devin had allowed himself to be so distracted by the bodies and the jumble of his emotions that he didn't hear the two figures approaching from behind until it was too late. He heard the crunch of dirt beneath a boot, but a strike to the back of his head made his vision explode in color until everything went black.

***

Devin awoke in a dark space bound to a concrete pillar with a length of steel cable. The atmosphere was heavy and hot like it had been out in the open. The only relief he felt was the absence of the blazing sun and howling wind. It was slightly cooler inside, but only by ten degrees at most. Most of his gear had been removed, except for his protective mask, which made him feel even cooler, but also terribly naked and vulnerable. A small glowing light stick was suspended from the ceiling in front of him, bathing him in a dim green light. He could hear hushed voices somewhere off to his left, which stopped as soon as he turned his head to face them.

"It's awake," one of the voices said.

"You think it knows anything?" another voice asked.

"It was standing right in front of the wreckage like it was admiring its work," the first voice said. *Oh great!* Devin thought. *They probably think I caused the wreck. I'm going to die. They'll never believe I had nothing to do with it. They won't listen to me! I'm nothing to these people!* He heard the strangers approaching, but it wasn't until they were face to face with him that he noticed they weren't human. He felt his heart skip a beat, or two.

The face of the creature was, in his opinion, ugly. There was nothing where a nose should be, save for a horizontal slit. Its eyes were set on either side of its massive head and coal black, completely devoid of personality, making it impossible to tell what the creature was focusing on. Its skin was similar in complexion to a dried-up riverbed and blue-gray in color.

Then there was the mouth. Incredibly wide and filled with huge square teeth, making it look comical. The creatures almost looked frog-like. They were also incredibly huge. Both were easily over eight feet tall and nearly just as wide.

"What were you doing at the crash site, Scavenger?" one of the beasts questioned. Its breath was so horrible that Devin could smell it through his protective mask and had to fight to keep from gagging. "Did you do something to that city? Answer me!"

"Why do you care what I say?" he snapped back. He was frightened, angry, and a little embarrassed that he'd been caught. All because of his curiosity. "I'm nothing to you! Nothing more than a scapegoat! You don't care if I did it or not!"

The creature slammed its massive fist into his stomach, forcing the air from his lungs and causing him to nearly black out. He wouldn't have been surprised if the blow had ruptured one of his internal organs.

"You are in no position to be insolent, Scavenger," the beast said as it grabbed Devin by the throat and forced him upright. "Your life hangs in the balance. Anything you say can and will influence whether you live or die. As for whether I care what you say, the truth is that I do. Your kind has the mechanical knowledge and the ingenuity to cause the cities to crash. And your kind sure as hell have motive… but sabotage really isn't your style, is it?"

The last statement caught Devin off guard. It was true that he had a motive, but it was even truer that he didn't have it in him to commit mass murder. He was a survivalist, not a murderer, and while he did kill on occasion, it was always in self-defense.

"So, you don't think I did it?" Devin wheezed once the creature released its grip on him.

"I did not say that Scavenger," the alien replied sharply. "Listen, I don't wish to make unfounded assumptions. You're the only known witness, which also makes *you* our prime suspect. My species has just as much riding on the completion of Phoenix One as yours does and this incident has just set our progress back more than we can afford! You were the *only* living thing at the wreckage. My partner and I have been tasked with finding out who caused the catastrophe. So, if you had anything to do with it, I suggest you confess, because if I find out some other way…"

Devin had no idea what Phoenix One was, but he could tell by the creature's tone that it meant a great deal to a lot of people. He still wasn't sure if he could trust the creature to spare him, but he figured it would probably kill him either way.

Devin decided that giving the creatures what they were asking for would give him the best chance of survival, though he knew very little of what had happened.

"I watched the city crash from a long way off," Devin replied. "I've seen cities fall to the ground before, but this was different. It fell sideways, not straight down like the others. The whole city was burning, but the flames came from the side that was closest to the ground like something exploded and was taking the entire city down with it. I was curious, so I rode my steed toward it. By the time I got close, it was too late."

The alien creature seemed interested, but it was so hard for Devin to tell. It could have easily been considering how to kill him. The other beast grew more agitated by the second. Then, in his panic, Devin remembered the figure running the opposite direction.

"You said I was the only living thing at the wreckage," Devin continued hastily. "But before you arrived I saw someone running away from the crash. I think they saw me, but they didn't come close enough for me to get a good look at them."

This set the first alien back on its heels. It turned to its companion and said something in a language Devin had never heard. Both creatures seemed to get excited, and then the creature that was questioning him came back over to him.

"Did you see what it looked like?" the creature asked hastily. "Was it human?"

"I couldn't see it too well through the smoke, but it didn't look human to me. It was too big."

"Are you sure?"

"Like I said," Devin said. "It was hard to see through the smoke." *Keep it talking,* he thought. *Keep it from killing you. Maybe it'll get distracted long enough to let you slip your bonds and escape.*

"Who are you anyway?" he added.

"All your time scavenging across the surface, all those times of being forced to work as a laborer on the floating cities, and you've never met one of my kind?" the thing asked.

"On the surface, no, I've never met your kind," Devin replied. "On the cities, your kind avoided me as if I carried a plague!"

Now he'd done it. His mouth was going to get him killed. Instead, the creature snorted at that last remark, but Devin couldn't tell if it was from amusement or irritation. Damn these things were hard to read!

"My name is Deekin, and my companion is Ryve, Trooviians appointed as officers of the Order of Proper Justice, which is why we are questioning you about the destruction of Disc City 6." Devin had heard of the Trooviians from some of the other Scavengers, but he'd never been in such proximity to one before. He could see why the other Scavengers avoided them.

"Why would anyone want to stop Phoenix One from being completed? I mean, if this project is as important as you claim, what could anybody hope to gain?"

"That is the same question we've been asking. The only ones who could gain anything would be your kind or the Bandits. Both of your people have the mechanical know-how and the motive. So, I ask you again, are you sure the figure you saw wasn't human?"

Devin would have liked to have blamed the whole thing on the Bandits. He hated them, and this would bring some much-needed heat down on them.

"I can't be sure," Devin said, his frustration growing. He had no more information to give them, and he was sure they were aware of this as well. It would only be a matter of time before they killed him. He was of no more use to them, so why would they keep him alive? Sure, they could let him go, but that was a kindness rarely bestowed on his kind. One of the Trooviians, Ryve it was called, was speaking to Deekin and gesturing toward Devin. *Here it comes,* he thought. Deekin put up a hand to silence Ryve and then turned back toward

Devin.

"My partner thinks we should dispose of you," Deekin said. Devin's heart sank into his stomach. "However, I think there may be another use for you." Devin was shocked, but then his shock gave way to dread.

"What might that be?" he asked.

"You saw the direction the figure went, and you know the land much better than we do. You are going to help us track them down." Devin couldn't deny the logic of the statement. He'd been living in the areas surrounding the ruins of Houston for several years. He was familiar with the area and knew which parts of the ruins to avoid, but he still didn't relish the idea of being forced to track a fugitive for the Trooviians.

"I'm going to be your hunting dog?" Devin asked. "I can barely sustain myself, and you want me to try to chase something down? I don't even have my horse." The two Trooviians looked at each other and shrugged.

"'Horse'?" Deekin asked. "Are you referring to that machine that you were standing near?"

"Yeah, that," Devin replied. "How else do you think I get around? Do I look like I have the strength to walk more than a hundred feet?" There was no denying that he was weak. He was frail and barely had enough energy to stay awake for more than a few hours, especially while he was fully encased in his protective gear. These creatures would have to carry him after twenty minutes of walking.

"It's at the wreckage," Deekin said. "It is still intact, and we can take you to it. Until this figure you describe has been located, you are our prisoner, but we have something that will make you less of a burden."

Devin was relieved that his horse was unharmed. It was the only thing he had any attachment to. What was it they were referring to, though? What did they have that could help him?

"What would that be?" Devin asked. The creature tapped the rig strapped across its chest. It looked like a mechanical spider clutching the creature's entire torso with a glowing sphere in the center and hoses feeding into a pack on its back.

"This is a Biological Sustainment System," Deekin said. "It feeds us all the nutrients we need to survive and even reduces the need for sleep. With it, we can work for more than 48 hours straight."

Devin's interest had been peaked. The rig could improve his life drastically, and he could understand that it would make him a much more useful tracker for the Trooviians. It could also kill him, though he doubted they would suggest it if it meant destroying their tracker and prisoner. He reluctantly decided that he had no other choice. He could either help the Trooviians or die.

"Alright," Devin said reluctantly. "It's not like I have a choice."

If given a chance, he decided he would try to get as far away from these creatures as possible. He wouldn't get far until he got his horse. Once he reclaimed his steed, he could make his getaway. He didn't trust these Trooviians. Deekin was a little too polite, while Ryve seemed like he'd enjoy nothing more than to rip Devin's head off if an opportunity presented itself.

Chapter 3

Doctor Jacob Peterson sat at his desk with his face in his hands. He was one of several scientists heading up the entire Phoenix One project. His tasks were to create the eco-generator and life sustainment systems. They were so close! The eco generator was easily the most difficult piece of the Phoenix One puzzle, and they had finally gotten it to work!

The explosion and subsequent crash of Disc City 6 was the worst setback the entire team had ever experienced. It was foolish of them to only build one eco-generator, he knew, but it was a decision that he and the rest of the team leaders had made to save time. Now he regretted it. The only silver lining was that the blueprints and schematics were safe, stored on a high-security hard drive attached to his computer. The engineering team that had been working on it had been careful to document every new modification, which included the change in design and formula that had gotten the thing to work. He was thankful for that.

Dr. Peterson sat back in his chair and took a deep breath. He had to address the setback to the rest of the team leads, a panel comprised of humans, Trooviians, and their neighbors, the Calvorans. The idea made him feel sick.

The Calvorans most closely resembled humans, though the similarities were still minimal. The Calvorans were easily four feet taller than the tallest human, and their skin was so thin it was nearly translucent, though it held a blueish hue that shifted with their mood. They were gentle and kind in their demeanor, which helped the relationship between them and the humans, as well as making the delivery of the bad news more palpable.

It was the Trooviians that Dr. Peterson was more concerned about. They were gruff, aggressive, and he could barely read their emotions, which always made him nervous.

He grabbed as many of the hard copies of the documents that he could, which weren't many due to almost all the documentation being digital and prepared himself for the meeting. He took one more look at his office before heading out as he tried to make sure he hadn't forgotten anything. Confident that he hadn't (as confident as he *could* be) he headed out into the long, quiet hallway.

The hallway was more like a brightly lit tunnel, as it had rounded walls with a flat floor and equally flat ceiling. It made sense since the Trooviians had overseen the architecture and they had been a mostly subterranean race on their home planet. As he walked, he tried to go over in his mind what he would say. His heart rate quickened as he moved further away from the comfort of his office and closer to the conference room. Would the data be enough to salvage the project, or would this be the final nail in humanity's coffin? The Phoenix One project had already seen its share of setbacks, and it was entirely possible that this would be the one to do the whole project in, effectively dooming the entire human race.

Dr. Peterson fought to keep his anxiety at bay, focusing on breathing deeply and slowly while reminding himself that a panic attack would do little to delay the meeting. Despite his near-crippling anxiety and pessimism, Dr. Peterson approached the conference room door and strode into the room.

The room was relatively small, barely fitting the large table in the center of the room. The backs of the chairs that the council members sat in were pressed up against the walls. Doctor Peterson squeezed into his chair and began laying out documents detailing the progress of the eco-generator. He punched in a few commands on the virtual keyboard embedded in the table's surface, and a holographic image of the eco generator appeared above the middle of the table.

He remained silent as the councilmen sorted through the paperwork in front of him and examined the holographic image, occasionally manipulating it with commands entered in the virtual keyboards in front of them. There were only ten of them in the room, including Dr. Peterson, but it felt incredibly cramped, and he began to sweat as claustrophobia began to set in. At last a member of the council spoke. It was the eldest member and chief science officer, a Calvoran by the name of Professor Goordaiin.

"There is little doubt that the eco-generator was a success," Professor Goordaiin said in his celestial voice. His multitudinous voice was both unnerving and soothing at the same time. Dr. Peterson met Professor Goordaiin's beady black eyes detected something there. Sadness, perhaps?

"Judging by what we see here, the eco generator was

functioning just as we had hoped. The tragedy of Disc City 6 is unfortunate; however, and this setback is titanic. According to the records, the construction of the machine took over a year on its own to complete. As you know, we are under an enormous time constraint. We simply do not have another year to spare."

"P-professor," Doctor Peterson began, his voice shaking. Addressing the head of the project, and in turn, his boss, was deeply intimidating. "We don't h-have any other option. This machine *must* be created, or Phoenix One will be incapable of hosting life, which will render the entire endeavor useless. With the data we have and the knowledge we've gained, the construction time can be cut in half. I propose we build the generator at the heart of Phoenix One this time, as there is no need for laboratory testing to ensure its functionality."

"Phoenix One hasn't even reached completion of Phase 1," a Trooviian added. "Beginning construction of the eco-generator on board is entirely feasible." Professor Goordaiin raised a pale blue, eight-fingered hand to silence both Doctor Peterson and the Trooviian.

"This is true, but once again, the time constraint is harsh, and the machine would have to be completed in two months or less," Professor Goordaiin stated, his skin shifting to a darker blue. "This is the only way that Phoenix One will be completed on time. Our data shows that this planet will be completely uninhabitable in approximately fourteen months. The task before us is, in the simplest term, impossible. Yet, we have no choice. The orbiting space stations will only sustain life for a short period, and completion of Phase 1 will be impossible from space."

Everyone in the room nodded in agreement, including Doctor Peterson.

"Once Phase 1 reaches completion Phoenix One can ascend to its designated position, and Phase 2 can begin," Professor Goordaiin finished.

"I understand," Dr. Peterson said.

"No other setback can be allowed," Professor Goordaiin continued. "Therefore, I've dispatched a unit of the Order of Proper Justice to investigate the destruction of Disc City 6. I've received their initial report, in which they state that the crash was, without a doubt, intentional. They're searching for a witness as we speak and, if successful, they'll bring the perpetrator back to face justice. There is a chance that it was a suicide mission, in which case there will be no way to interrogate the perpetrator, but we still have hope. Whoever did this clearly aimed to harm the project. This alone narrows the scope of possible groups that could have orchestrated the attack. I have also ordered an increase in security around the labs."

"This is good news," Dr. Peterson replied, his voice shaking. "I do have one question, though."

Professor Goordaiin and the rest of the team stared at him. Dr. Peterson tried to keep his voice steady.

"How could the perpetrator survive? I mean, unless they're of Trooviian or Calvoran descent, no one can survive on the surface for long. Even the Bandits and Scavengers don't live long despite the protective gear *they* wear. Both of your species; however, wear that Biological Sustainment System, which has not been shared with my species. That rig allows your species to survive days longer than we can. So, unless the perpetrator is a Trooviian or Calvoran, who else could have done this?"

Everyone in the room stared at Professor Goordaiin, keenly awaiting his response.

"That is what we hope to find out," Professor Goordaiin said calmly. "As I've told you before, your species cannot handle the Biological Sustainment System, or BSS rig as many of us have taken to calling it. It would kill you. Your biological makeup is not supported by the rig. It would consume you rather than keep you alive. It is true the Bandits, and the Scavengers don't live long, but they do live on the surface, and they have a motive."

Dr. Peterson sighed and nodded. He had wished the answer would have been something more positive. The rig would give them more time for the project—time he knew they desperately needed.

"Trust me," Professor Goordaiin said. "If we could find a way to make the BSS rig work for your kind, we would. Humans are just not compatible."

Chapter 4

The BSS rig felt loose when Devin strapped it onto his chest. He had to remove his mask so that the rig wouldn't catch on the hose. He tried not to breathe in the foul air, taking shallow breaths until he could put the mask back on. A much larger creature must have worn this rig before him. He searched for a way to adjust it, but if there was one he couldn't find it.

After a moment of struggling with it, Deekin and Ryve both laughed and then Deekin walked over to him. He pressed a button near the glowing orb in the front. The rig cinched tighter almost immediately, and Devin managed a smile until he felt painful jabs in both pectoral muscles as if he'd been stabbed. Devin began clawing at the harness.

"Ouch! Shit!" he shouted as he tried to rip the rig off him. "What the hell?"

"Relax, Scavenger," Deekin said calmly. "That is how the rig feeds your body. Did you think your body would absorb the nutrients through osmosis?" Ryve laughed at that. It sounded more like a hacking cough to Devin.

"You could've warned me!" Devin shouted. He was still clutching at his chest. "That fucking hurt!"

"Trust me, it'll be worth it."

"I hope so," Devin replied under his breath.

Immediately he began to feel more awake and even a bit stronger as the rig began pumping a cool fluid into him. He no longer felt dehydrated, a sensation he'd only known a handful of times in his life. It was a vast improvement already. Devin stood more erect, and his limbs didn't feel nearly as heavy.

"Before long your body will get used to the rig," Deekin said. "Once that happens, the rig will work even more efficiently. You'll even notice a minor physical change."

Devin couldn't respond. He was lost in the new sensation. He was completely awake and full of energy for the first time in his life, and the feeling both confused and scared him. He felt as if he could run forever without tiring, though he knew better. The rig wouldn't push his body to superhuman levels, but he couldn't complain about his newfound strength and energy.

"Now," Deekin began. "Let's get your 'horse' and begin our hunt."

***

When the trio exited the twisted remains of an old parking garage, Devin nearly panicked. He wasn't wearing his mask, which he had forgotten about when he put the BSS rig on, and when he tried to run back inside both Deekin and Ryve stopped him.

"Where are you going?" Deekin asked.

"I need my gear!" Devin cried. "I can't survive out here without it!"

Deekin just laughed as he turned Devin away from the parking garage. Deekin tapped his own rig.

"You're wearing the BSS rig, remember?" Deekin said, clearly amused.

"What about it?"

"The rig filters out the toxins," Deekin replied. "Didn't you know that?"

Devin just shook his head, but Deekin could see him relax a bit.

"So, I don't need my mask?"

"Do you see us with one?" Deekin replied, pointing at his face.

Devin shook his head. It hadn't occurred to him that neither Deekin nor Ryve wore any protective gear on their grotesque faces when they emerged from the parking garage. It was strange that he could gaze across the landscape with the cloudy yellow glass marring his vision. Everything looked so much sharper as if he could see for the first time. For the entirety of his twenty-five years alive, he had had to wear gas masks and hazard suits. The change was both thrilling and terrifying.

The landscape was still a ruined wasteland, seemingly stained a yellowish-brown, but now he could see every depressing detail, though he wasn't sure if he was happy about that. He took a deep breath and gagged. The air was still foul. He'd be able to survive, sure, but the smell would drive him insane.

"You'll grow accustomed to it," Deekin said as Devin continued to gag. "It is unpleasant, but the stench will fade, and you'll barely notice. I suggest you take shallower breaths until then, though."

Devin nodded as he breathed shallowly through his mouth. His eyes were watering, clouding his vision, and for a moment he was worried his vision would stay that way. He wiped the tears from his eyes and felt relieved as his surroundings came into full focus once more. He scanned the area around him and realized that he had no idea which direction to go.

"Uh," he began. "Which way do we go?"

"North," Ryve said, pointing over Devin's right shoulder. Devin followed the extended digit and could see a plume of smoke coming from behind the skeletal remains of an old skyscraper. He began walking that direction but halted as Deekin cut in front of him. Deekin faced him silently, making Devin feel immensely uneasy.

"My harpoon gun," Devin gasped. "And my blade!"

"That cylindrical thing and the rusted shard of metal were your weapons?" Deekin asked as he drew a large, beautifully colored object from its holster on his back. The object looked like it could have been made of metal and had a groove for Deekin's massive hand near the end. It looked like Devin's harpoon gun in the way it was held, an opening at one end like the barrel of a gun.

"Well, yeah!" Devin replied, his anger tainting his words.

"How have you managed to survive this long?"

"I made do with what I had!" Devin retorted.

"I'll have Ryve retrieve them for you," Deekin said, chuckling. Then he suddenly became serious. "But know this: should you draw your weapons without my authorization, you will be killed on the spot. I'd rather you weren't armed at all, but out here that would be stupid." He muttered something to Ryve in his native language and gestured toward the parking garage. Ryve shook his head and growled something at Deekin, then pointed to Devin. After a few seconds of this exchange Ryve finally relented and turned toward the structure, visibly agitated.

"Ryve doesn't believe you should be armed either," Deekin said. "But I told him that we need you alive, and that means you should be able to protect yourself. I also asked if he wanted to be your personal guardian." Deekin laughed a bit and then continued. "He didn't seem too fond of that idea."

After what felt like an hour Ryve returned with Devin's harpoon gun and his blade in hand. He shoved the weapons into Devin's open hands and then forced him toward the skyscraper. Devin felt the weight of the harpoon gun in his hands and took comfort in the "cylindrical chunk of metal."

The harpoon gun certainly didn't look like much. Deekin's description was accurate, but it had saved Devin's life on multiple occasions. He didn't have to worry about ammunition for it, as the harpoon was tethered to the launcher by a length of thin metal cable. It didn't work against large groups of attackers, but Devin made it a point to avoid those situations as much as possible.

His blade was a length of sharpened metal that had come off a wrecked aircraft that he used when the harpoon gun was impractical. It had begun to rust, but this only served to make it a more dangerous weapon.

Devin slung the strap of the harpoon gun across his body, letting the weapon rest at his left side. His blade hung from his belt on his right, easily accessible should he need it in a hurry. Deekin lead the way through the wrecked building, navigating the rubble in the gloom as if the interior were brightly lit. The Trooviians must have superior night vision, Devin guessed. He had a difficult time following Deekin, and he would have lost him on several occasions if Ryve hadn't been forcing him forward.

"One more thing, Scavenger," Deekin said, holding up a small circular device. "If you try to flee I will disable the BSS rig remotely. I needn't explain what will happen to you once it's off."

Damn, there goes my escape plan, Devin thought.

"Once you've done your part and the fugitive is apprehended, I will give the remote to you, but until then I will hold on to it," Deekin added. There was no malice in his voice.

Devin had begun to like Deekin, who had been kinder to him than anyone else he'd ever met. Ryve, on the other hand, was a dick. Ryve's disposition toward him was just like that of everyone else, which only made him dislike the brute even more.

The exit of the ruined building shone in the dark like a beacon. Daylight forced its way through the murky gloom of the skyscraper's dusty bowels. It was a welcome sight for Devin, who had to squint as he stepped out into the open air. Once his vision had adjusted he could see the wreckage of the disc city in the distance. He was immediately assaulted by visions of the burned corpses scattered around the burning city when he had first approached it.

Devin suddenly felt the desire to turn away from the wreck and just run as far as he could. It would mean leaving his steed, and with that, his decision was made. He would force himself to endure the grisly sight of the mangled bodies once more. After he retrieved his steed he would never come back to that place for as long as he lived, and with the aid of the BSS rig that could be a very long time.

Chapter 5

It was as Devin had feared. He could not fight the urge to vomit as his gaze fell upon a horribly charred corpse. Deekin and Ryve didn't appear to be bothered by the catastrophe, and Devin reckoned that was something they were relatively accustomed to in their line of work. What had they called it? The Order of Justice? It sounded like law enforcement to him. Deekin shook his head as he gazed at the burning remains of the disc city. The flames were low now, and Devin figured it had been several hours since he saw it crash. The heat was still intense, and he figured the city would continue to burn for some time still.

"We need to make this quick," Devin said. "The fumes in the air could set this area off like a bomb at any moment. Bandits may be nearby, too. I won't be the only one that saw the city go down." Deekin was looking at a small, beeping handheld device. It was odd that the area hadn't yet erupted in a massive fireball, though, but Devin figured it would soon.

"I need to find my steed," Devin added. It wasn't in sight, and he didn't relish the thought of staying in the area any longer.

"We found you on the opposite side," Deekin said as he slid the handheld device into its holster on his belt. "It should still be there. If this place is about to go up in flames, then we should probably hurry." As if on cue, a flame shot up from the burning wreckage nearly a hundred feet into the air. This spurred all three of them into motion. They ran to their right, along the flat of the disc to its edge and nearly ran into an ambush. The ambush wasn't intentional, but the Bandits that swarmed over the dead bodies would have capitalized on the opportunity. Deekin had approached the edge of the disc city first and halted as soon as he could see the other side. Ryve stopped immediately, and Devin nearly slammed into his broad back.

"Damn scum," Deekin said under his breath. Devin gave him a puzzled look. "Bandits. Twenty, at least." Devin gritted his teeth. He had expected as much. To make matters worse, his steed was with them.

"Shit!" Devin balled his fists. "What do we do?"

"I say we let the city explode and kill them all," Deekin said. "I do apologize about your steed."

"To hell with that!" Devin shot back. He would not leave the only companion he'd ever had. "There must be another way."

"To rush in, there would be suicide!" Deekin hissed through gritted teeth. Ryve growled something, and Deekin nodded. "That thing is not worth our lives. Maybe it'll survive the blast." Devin had never subjected the robotic horse to that kind of punishment and had never intended to, but the thing was very well built, and some of the materials he'd used weren't even manmade. Alien technology was not something he'd become too familiar with. The entire exoskeleton, with exceptions to the saddle and hoses, was made of alien material. It could very possibly stand up to intense heat. He shook his head. It may not have been worth Deekin and Ryve's lives, though Devin thought otherwise, it was worth his. Without it, he'd be completely alone and without decent transportations. Besides, the steed had saved his ass on many occasions. It was the only friend he'd ever had.

"I don't want to risk destroying it," Devin said in a firm voice. "Maybe we can frighten the Bandits away. Your weapons would do the trick, I'm sure."

"Our weapons could also set off a chain reaction that could kill us all," Deekin retorted. "One stray blast could have devastating effects."

"Well," Devin said. He had to throw his only card on the table. "I'm not leaving without it. You need me to find the suspect, and I'll do you no good dead." Ryve growled, and Deekin nodded.

"I'm sure we could manage," Deekin replied. Devin was taken aback. He hadn't expected that response. Instead of responding; however, Devin just stared at Deekin. He would call his bluff and hoped that Deekin would break first. What seemed like ten minutes, but was more like thirty seconds, passed before either of them made a move. To Devin's relief, Deekin relented.

"You are going to get us all killed," Deekin spat. "From here I can see two areas to take cover where the bandits are least likely to see us. We can begin to circle them. I will make for the farthest one, and Ryve will follow to the other. Once this is done, I want you to get their attention. If done right, and if we are incredibly lucky, they'll go down before they get a chance to react. Let us hope that we don't cause an explosion in the process. I suggest you ready your weapon."

Devin was not pleased with the idea of being a diversion, but if it would help him get his steed, he'd do what was needed. He felt entirely dependent on the robotic horse, though he needn't be now that he wore the BSS rig.

Ryve growled at Deekin, but Deekin just shook his head and growled back. Ryve slung his weapon off his massive shoulder and took up a defensive position just at the edge of the smoldering remains of the disc city. The heat didn't seem to bother him much. Deekin crouched down as low as he could without crawling and quickly made his way to his designated position a hundred yards away, behind a massive slab of concrete which was no doubt a wall of a building at one time. The bandits didn't seem to notice and then it was Ryve's turn. He made his way over to another slab of concrete about twenty yards from the disc's edge.

It was Devin's turn to make his move, and though he was relieved by how smooth the first part had gone off, he was not comfortable with bringing attention to himself on purpose.

Devin swallowed a lump in his throat as he slid his weapon from his shoulder and steadied his breathing. He had one shot, and he hoped to score a kill with it, although a harpoon flying in the middle of the Bandits would no doubt get their attention all the same. He crouched at the edge of the burning disc - damn it was hot! – and took aim at the nearest Bandit.

The man was frail in appearance, and Devin found himself second-guessing taking the shot. No doubt that was how he had looked before donning the BSS rig. He'd already gained nearly fifteen pounds since putting the rig on, and his skin felt tight against his swollen muscles. He was still quite thin, but a great deal healthier in appearance compared to his target.

To shoot someone in the back when they already had little chance of defending themselves was not something Devin liked to do, though he had needed to from time to time. This moment seemed different, though. They were completely oblivious and doing nobody any harm. He could easily sneak past them, but they had his horse. He hung his head a moment, took a deep breath, and then took aim again.

The harpoon fired with a pop and buried itself in the back of the Bandit's neck. The cable that was attached to the harpoon hadn't even extended its entire length. The dead Bandit fell forward with a thud, getting the attention of five Bandits nearby. Devin retched as the Bandit died.

As the Bandits moved to investigate Deekin moved out from his hiding spot and fired. The weapon made a hissing noise, and Devin saw a faint streak of light before one of the Bandits dropped, clutching at the new hole in its chest. Ryve fired next and hit two more of the Bandits before Deekin's target hit the ground. Devin could do little more than stare in awe as the pair fired several more shots in rapid succession, hitting their mark every time.

The Bandits began hooting and hollering as they noticed their companions falling dead around them. Devin had to move away from the edge of the disc before his flesh charred, and he had no choice but to draw his blade when a Bandit nearby spotted him. The Bandit charged at him with what looked like a length of rebar with the end filed to a point.

Devin sidestepped his attacker's thrust faster than he'd expected and almost stumbled. The Bandit did stumble, and Devin took the opportunity as it presented itself. His opponent looked back at him just in time to catch a sideways swipe of Devin's blade in the face, cutting its head off just below the nose. Devin was in awe. He didn't think he'd put that much force into the swing, but the decapitated corpse of the Bandit said otherwise.

Devin grabbed the dead Bandit's makeshift spear, fastened his blade back on his belt, and moved to free the harpoon from his first target. He liked the makeshift spear and silently applauded the Bandit's ingenuity. He struggled to free the harpoon and nearly broke it before it finally came out with a crunch and a wet sucking noise. He felt his stomach churn.

He loaded the harpoon back into the gun and slung it over his shoulder. Devin turned just in time to see another Bandit bearing down on him. The Bandit's head disintegrated, along with most of its upper torso, before it got to him and Devin knew that either Deekin or Ryve - though he figured Deekin was more likely - was responsible.

Devin grabbed his new spear and made his way toward his horse, which he could now see standing alone several yards from the fighting. He could make a dash for the horse, but he decided a more cautious approach was necessary. He didn't want to get hit by a stray shot from either Deekin or Ryve's weapons.

***

Ryve killed two more Bandits and had to drop his rifle to meet a third that was approaching from his rear. How the Bandit had gotten behind him, Ryve couldn't tell, but the Bandit proved to be little more than a nuisance. The crazed man leaped at him wildly. Ryve caught the man in his left hand and, in a quick motion, crushed the Bandit's windpipe while also simultaneously snapping his neck.

The Bandit dropped his weapon, a club made of burnt wood and a chunk of metal, and Ryve tossed the corpse over his shoulder. He grabbed the fallen club, turned it over in his massive hand, and then threw it with all his strength at another nearby Bandit. The force of the throw nearly took the Bandit's head off and would have if the club hadn't broken apart. The Bandit was dead before he hit the ground. Ryve scanned the area and saw five, maybe six, Bandits ducking behind whatever cover they found. They were all that was left of a raiding party of twenty, their numbers cut down in less than five minutes.

***

Deekin peered from behind cover to see Ryve throw the club, hit his mark and then charge at a hiding Bandit. Deekin fired before Ryve could reach the hiding figure and smiled as Ryve turned to look at him, displeased at having the kill taken from him. The distraction almost cost Ryve his life as a daring Bandit tried to sneak up on him. Deekin took aim, but the Bandit froze as a piece of rebar burst through his chest. As Deekin's attacker fell, Deekin could see Devin standing behind it, still holding the length of rebar. Deekin couldn't help but feel a little impressed. He hadn't expected the Scavenger to be any use in a fight and found that he had misjudged the man.

He was more dangerous than Deekin had anticipated and couldn't help feeling a twinge of fear. Had he made a mistake in trusting the Scavenger? More importantly, was giving the man the BSS rig a mistake? What would he do when he got his robotic horseback?

Before Deekin could reach a decision on how to deal with his newfound dilemma, another Bandit was running toward him, a makeshift spear of wood and what appeared to be glass in its hand. The Bandit threw the spear and nearly hit Deekin in the chest. He tried to sidestep and caught the spear in his right shoulder. Deekin tried to yank the spear free, but the Bandit leaped at him and buried the spear deeper. Deekin howled in pain and reached up to throttle the Bandit, but Devin's rebar spear reached the Bandit first, lodging itself in the Bandit's throat and sending it tumbling off Deekin's prone form.

He looked at Devin and nodded in thanks. Devin sprinted over to him and began trying the pull the Bandit's spear out of Deekin's shoulder. Deekin pushed him away and yanked it out himself. The pain was agonizing. He stood and nearly fell over again. His vision was blurring, and he realized with a shock that the spear tip had been coated in poison of some kind.

The BSS rig would cycle the poison out, but it would take the time that Deekin didn't immediately have. His knees buckled, and he dropped to the ground.

***

Devin watched as Deekin fell over and then moved to help him. He heard the familiar hiss of Ryve's weapon and turned around in time to see a Bandit drop only a foot away from him. He looked at Ryve and nodded, then pointed at Deekin. Ryve looked at his fallen comrade and sprinted toward him.

"What happened?" Ryve asked in an incredibly thick accent. Devin found he couldn't respond. Ryve could speak English? Since when?

"Poison," Devin said hastily. "I think." Ryve helped Deekin to his feet and looked into his comrade's eyes.

"Yes," Ryve said. "It's poison. He'll be okay." Devin could tell that Ryve was struggling with the words. So, he spoke English, but not much.

"How long will it take?"

"A minute. Maybe two," Ryve replied, although he didn't sound confident. Devin scanned the area, looking for any remaining Bandits. He saw over a dozen, but none alive. He yanked the rebar spear from the dead Bandit's throat and made his way toward his robotic horse. He was almost to the horse when a Bandit leaped over it at him.

Devin slammed the Bandit in the face with the butt-end of his spear, knocking the Bandit to the ground with a heavy thud. The Bandit clutched at his mouth, blood gushing between his fingers. Devin planted his right foot and thrust the point of the spear into the Bandit's face, catching it in the eye. Devin felt the spear burst through the Bandit's skull. He tried to yank the spear free, but the Bandit leaned forward with it. The spear was stuck.

"Damn it!" Devin yelled as he planted his foot on the dead Bandit's chest and pulled again. The spear began to pull free, and after a couple harder tugs, it finally came out. He almost gagged when he saw the chunks of brain matter clinging to the tip of the spear. After he scraped the spear tip across the ground, removing most of the gore, he moved toward his horse. The headless robot seemed to sense him and lowered itself to the ground in response. Devin hopped into the saddle, constructed from parts of an aircraft seat, and felt whole again.

Chapter 6

Doctor Jacob Peterson slumped into his chair behind his cluttered metallic desk. He released an exasperated sigh as he tried to sort through the events of the meeting. Two months? The task was grossly impossible. How could Professor Goordaiin expect the eco generator to be completed in such a short amount of time?

Almost as if in answer to his question, Professor Goordaiin stood in the doorway to Dr. Peterson's office, flanked by Peterson's assistant, Elaina Perry. She was young and attractive, with auburn hair, fair skin, large brown eyes, a round face, and pixie-like nose; but it was her incredible brilliance that Dr. Peterson enjoyed most about her. She'd been newly assigned, but he felt as if he'd known her forever.

There was something familiar about her, but he couldn't place it. His memory had been going, and without the help of the Calvorans' medicinal technology, he would have completely succumbed to Alzheimer's. Some of his memories were intact, but others were gone.

He may have known her, but he couldn't remember.

"Doctor," Professor Goordaiin began before Elaina could speak. "Are you capable of sparing a moment?"

"Yes, professor," Dr. Peterson replied, standing abruptly. He waved Elaina away so that they could speak in private. She threw a sideways glance at the Calvoran before briskly walking away.

"It is my understanding that the task that we have set for you is - how should I put this? - Beyond your ability, which is why I have assembled a team of engineers who will use your information on the eco generator to build a working replication. We will be using a great deal of the technology and materials, but we Calvorans still must improve on its design, of course, and you will be tasked with ensuring that the technical specifications are followed exactly as they are written. Any deviation would spell disaster, as I'm sure you know."

Dr. Peterson sat in silence while he tried to process this new information. He tried to decide if Professor Goordaiin's reassignment of the project was meant as an insult, or if the professor was doing him a tremendous favor. He didn't particularly relish the thought of babysitting engineers. It was his experience as a scientist that had made the eco generator possible in the first place. It was a project that he had overseen and directed. Now he was expected to ensure that a group of engineers followed instructions? He felt as if he were being demoted.

"Professor," Dr. Peterson began. "I really don't know what to say. Is this team really capable of meeting the two-month deadline?"

"They should be," Professor Goordaiin replied. "They are my people, after all. With your schematics, they should have it completed in mere days."

***

Professor Goordaiin sat behind his desk, which was constructed from a transparent material that shimmered and changed color every passing hour and listened as the Captain of The Order of Proper Justice gave the most recent report on the search for Disc City 6's saboteur.

The Order of Proper Justice, Professor Goordaiin thought. *Such a silly name, but nobody has yet questioned their validity.*

In truth, The Order of Proper Justice was no more than a bunch of Trooviian bounty hunters and mercenaries that he had rounded up and passed off as law enforcement. It was a clever ruse, really, and effective as well. He'd decided to keep the name, as the irony amused him. None of the humans could tell that the attire the Trooviians wore were once prison garbs and their ignorance of Trooviian culture only aided in keeping the ruse going.

Simple minded creatures, these humans, but hardworking and expendable. The latter was most important to Professor Goordaiin. It was better to put the humans to work on the dangerous aspects of Phoenix One than one of his own. Besides, Calvorans weren't meant for hard labor. They were far more superior and far too intelligent for slave work. The Trooviians had filled the role of laborer quite nicely until they became too difficult to control.

Everyone wanted compensation and justification. They all wanted to be treated as equals. Ignorant fools. The Calvorans had no equal.

The report that the Captain gave was less than promising, which should have upset Professor Goordaiin, but he found that it hardly mattered. Phoenix One was now under his complete control, and he intended to use the entirety of Richard his focus on its completion. The hunt for the supposed saboteur was meant only to calm the humans. They demanded justice, and he had promised exactly that, but he didn't have to deliver it. Better if the saboteur stays hidden, at least until after Phoenix One was completed. The destruction of Disc City 6 only helped cement Professor Goordaiin's hold on the entire project. Without the eco generator, which his people would create and ultimately hold sole ownership, the entire project would die.

Professor Goordaiin sent the Trooviian away after the full report was given.

Finally, Professor Goordaiin thought. *Peace and quiet.* He sat in his chair with his long hands folded in front of his face and his eyes closed.

How long would it really take to get the eco generator finished? With the technology that they had at their disposal, it shouldn't take more than a few days.

Securing the blueprints was the critical part, and Dr. Peterson had given them over willingly. The man had done what he had thought was the best course of action, and it helped that he was afraid of Professor Goordaiin as well. He certainly had cause to fear the Calvorans, though he didn't yet know why. It didn't matter. That fear had worked in Goordaiin's favor, and he began to formulate a plan to fully exploit that fear.

Any additional information the human scientist had could be of some use to the project. These humans, simple as they were, were truly capable of amazing feats of engineering and often stumbled upon designs that made their creations capable of more than their fragile minds could possibly imagine. Calvorans, as intelligent as they are, lacked the imagination that the humans enjoyed.

Professor Goordaiin hadn't always been the head of the project. In fact, due to the arrogance and distrust of the humans, the President of the Phoenix One project was once a man named Richard Dawkins. He was quite intelligent, as far as humans go, but he was frail and passive. The project was his brainchild, but Professor Goordaiin had supplied the knowledge needed to turn a dream into reality. When Richard Dawkins had suddenly expired, the project had been passed to the next in line. Professor Goordaiin knew that the humans distrusted him, but that no longer mattered. He was in control, and they were entirely dependent on the completion of the project.

A prototype of the eco-generator was nearing completion already. Now that he had all the information he needed, Professor Goordaiin could finally move it into the final phase of construction and begin testing. He'd planned every detail and was growing increasingly pleased as everything fell perfectly into place. Once completed, the eco generator would be *his* accomplishment and he would finally gain complete control of Phoenix One and its future.

Chapter 7

Nearly ten minutes passed since Deekin was struck by the poisoned spear, and for some reason, his BSS rig hadn't managed to filter the toxin out of his system. Ryve began acting agitated, and Devin knew something was terribly wrong. Deekin could no longer move or speak. Ryve began barking at Devin in his strange guttural language, and all Devin could do was stare blankly back at him. After a moment Ryve finally calmed down enough to speak in English.

"We need to go," Ryve insisted. "This place is not safe. Blow up!"

Devin looked at Deekin, who was in no way capable of moving on his own.

"Well, we can't carry him out of here," Devin said. "And he's not going to walk out of here on his own any time soon."

"Not us carry him," Ryve said, and then pointed at Devin's steed. "Robot horse will do it." Devin wanted to argue. He wanted to take his horse and leave, but if he tried, Ryve would shoot him before he got the chance. He sighed and then nodded.

"You're right," Devin said reluctantly. It was amazing how much it sickened him to say those words to Ryve. "My horse can carry him."

For the next five minutes, both he and Ryve struggled to heave Deekin's girth onto the robotic horse. They had to strap him across the back of the steed after realizing there was no way the massive Trooviian would fit into the seat. Once Deekin was safely harnessed to the horse they began to scour the surrounding area for the tracks left by the mysterious figure Devin had seen fleeing the scene. After twenty incredibly uncomfortable minutes, they found shallow indentations in the dirt and began to follow them away from the ticking time bomb that was the smoldering disc city. They fled the area as rapidly as they could, wanting nothing more than to put as much distance between them and the wreckage as possible before it inevitably detonated. They were nearly ten miles away when they heard, and after a moment felt, the blast from the exploding city.

"I wonder how far our mysterious stranger managed to run," Devin wondered aloud. Ryve hadn't spoken a word since their escape, and Devin doubted he would get a response. "Unless they had the rigs you guys wear, they'll be dead before we find them." Ryve snorted at this, but, as Devin had expected, he didn't say a word.

This is going to be fun, Devin thought bitterly.

***

They walked for nearly an hour in the unrelenting heat before Deekin showed signs of recovery. He had regained consciousness and tried to carry on a conversation with Devin, but the attempt exhausted him, and he fell silent once more. He had fallen asleep, but at least he was breathing deeper, and some color had returned.

Devin wasn't sure what he was searching for, but it was his role to track the fugitive, and he knew failing would mean he had exhausted his usefulness. He hadn't found any noticeable tracks, no doubt due to the wind and the dust that was sweeping around the surface in waves of filth. How could anyone expect to track anything in this environment? His frustration grew as Ryve complained.

"Why we haven't found something?" he grumbled. "This taking too long." Devin gritted his teeth and remained silent. He didn't want to goad the Trooviian into shooting him. Devin doubted that much instigation would be needed for that anyway.

"You are trying to help us, right?" Deekin asked as he awoke. "I would hate for the effort in getting your horse to be for nothing."

"I *am* trying!" Devin barked. "There aren't any tracks out here! I'm *looking*!"

"Careful, Scavenger," Deekin seethed. "I have half a mind to order Ryve to shoot you where you stand. We took a huge risk in getting you your horse, and I got poisoned doing it. You need to hold up your end now."

"I understand that," Devin replied. "I am as frustrated as you are. This terrain is just not suitable for tracking." The words were barely out of his mouth when he tripped over something. He looked down and examined the ground. He'd stepped in a rather large footprint. It was too large to be human, and too deep. He stared for a moment and then felt his stomach drop. The print belonged to a Trooviian. Of this Devin had little doubt. He glanced at Deekin's boot, confirming his assumption.

"What is it?" Deekin asked.

"I tripped over a hole in the ground," Devin replied. He decided that it would be safer to keep the observation to himself. At least they had a track to follow now. "I think I know which way our fugitive headed."

They began moving west, following the sparse tracks in the terrain. The tracks would be difficult to follow if the fugitive used concrete pathways and broken asphalt, but now the fugitive had been running through the dirt. They had their heading and Devin hoped they would reach their quarry soon.

"So, you mentioned Phoenix One," Devin said, attempting to make conversation and keep Deekin awake. "What is it exactly?"

"Phoenix One is the name of a massive space station that is projected to house every living human, Trooviian, and Calvoran. It is a replacement for Earth and the only hope any of our races have for survival. Without it, everyone will perish."

"What about the BSS rigs, though?" Devin asked.

"True, the rigs would sustain every species in the current atmospheric conditions, but that is going to no longer be the case as the atmosphere continues to decay. Before long, no rig we could hope to create will sustain anything on your planet. It is imperative that we leave Earth soon."

"Oh," Devin said. "Then why would anyone want to stop it from being completed?"

"I don't know. I've been pondering that for some time now. The motives behind the sabotage of Disc City 6 are a mystery to me. I was originally guessing that it was based on jealousy or revenge, but I am beginning to doubt that. Destroying the city could very easily be a death sentence for every living person on the planet."

"How could the destruction of one city doom then entire planet?"

"It was on Disc City 6 that an eco-generator was being constructed. Are you familiar with what an eco-generator does?"

"I don't have too much experience with them," Devin replied. "I've seen them on some of the cities, but they were tiny and were only powerful enough to create an ecosystem in a terrarium. How does that fit into the Phoenix One project?"

"Imagine that the eco generator that you saw was the size of a house. That was what was being constructed. It was projected that it would create an ecosystem large enough to sustain every living creature we know, and it would be aboard the space station. Now it is destroyed, and without it, we can't hope to live very long."

Devin walked in silence for a while, considering Deekin's words. The information he now had only made understanding the fugitive much more difficult. Why would someone want to do such a thing? Then another thought struck him.

"What about us? The Scavengers? The Bandits? Are we going to be left behind?" he asked.

"I don't know what is planned for your people, but I assume that we would be bringing your kind along as well, for your mechanical expertise. We need someone to maintain the space station, after all. As for the Bandits, well, they've been deemed unworthy and will be left behind. You can't tell me that this would upset you."

"I don't suppose so," Devin replied. He felt no love for the Bandits but leaving them to die with the planet seemed cruel all the same. "Wouldn't there be another way, though? Janitorial duties or something?"

"What you fail to realize is that we've already attempted to civilize the Bandits. They act out, get violent, and people start dying. They don't follow the rules and they don't seem to know how to do anything besides kill and steal. They're beyond our aid."

Devin could almost feel the hatred in Deekin's words. Whenever Scavengers were mentioned, the attitude had been condescension and distaste, but with Bandits there was only pure hatred. Devin had once shared the same feeling toward Bandits, but now he felt pity. The massacre at the wreckage and the emaciated forms of the Bandits had surely sparked his change in attitude toward them. He began to wish that there had been another way.

Devin looked across the landscape and then toward the sky, which had lost its blue coloring many years ago and had now taken on a dusty grey. Devin longed to see any color besides brown, red or orange. Grey wasn't much of an improvement, nor was black. He wanted most to see blue and green. Plants no longer grew on the surface, and almost all the water was heavily polluted. Finding water that was safe to drink was always immensely difficult. Fortunately, Devin's steed could filter most of the water he found, though it wasn't much.

There wasn't much left of the city that had once been built in the area. Most of the buildings had crumbled as the temperature had risen and earthquakes had become more common. Twisted mounds of concrete and metal reached for the sky, but it appeared as though the remains had grown exhausted as the years passed and the temperature rose.

Devin could relate. He had only spent between four to six hours awake at any given time before he donned the BSS rig. The heat combined with dehydration and malnourishment had sapped all his energy. He found it amazing that he had managed to live as long as he had, which had been nearly twenty-seven years. Most of the surface dwellers rarely lived past seventeen, yet he'd survived a full decade longer. He had to thank his mechanical steed for that.

How many more years would he live now that he had the BSS rig? Twenty? Thirty? He hoped that those years would be spent somewhere other than the surface of Earth.

He peered toward the west and could see the remains of a massive freeway, jutting out of the earth like broken ribs. He was still getting used to the clarity of his sight and found he could see quite far with ease. At the base of a column that had at one time supported the freeway was a thin trail of smoke.

A campfire? In this atmosphere? Devin wondered. *Who would be foolish enough to attempt that?* Then it struck him. Scavengers and Bandits knew better than to attempt a campfire in the highly combustible atmosphere, but a fugitive who'd never spent much time on the surface may not know better. Devin was willing to bet that their quarry had built a fire and was taking cover for the night. The sun was sitting low on the horizon, and the surface would be blanketed in darkness before long.

"Ryve," Devin called out. Ryve turned his gaze his direction. Devin jerked his head in the direction of the campfire. Ryve followed his gaze and then stared back at him.

"I'm betting that's our fugitive," Devin said. Ryve just continued to stare at him. Devin let out an exasperated sigh and began to explain.

"Listen, our quarry isn't a Bandit, nor is it a Scavenger. Bandits aren't allowed aboard the floating cities and Scavengers are always under extreme supervision. The saboteur was most likely someone who could wander without suspicion. Anyone who can do that is not someone who would be familiar with the surface conditions." Ryve continued to stare at Devin. "A campfire is too dangerous. The air could ignite and kill anyone in the vicinity. Surface dwellers know that, but the floating city dwellers wouldn't, and neither would our fugitive."

Ryve seemed to catch on because he suddenly looked out at the campfire again with wider eyes. He nodded at Devin and then turned to Deekin, speaking in that strange language that Devin couldn't understand. Deekin nodded after a moment and then spoke.

"Then let's go and get them," Deekin said. Devin looked out at the horizon and saw the sun rapidly disappearing. He shook his head.

"It will be too dark soon," Devin said. "It would be smarter to find somewhere to hold up for the night. There are too many things that come out in the night, and the temperature is going to drop down to nearly freezing. Our prey isn't going anywhere."

The thinning atmosphere made the surface temperature fluctuate drastically from blisteringly hot during the day to nearly freezing at night. A campfire would be desirable, but that was out of the question. There was no point in taking the risk. If their quarry didn't perish in a fiery explosion from its campfire during the night, they'd be able to catch up in the morning.

"They could flee while we hide in there," Deekin said pointing toward a gutted skyscraper. He was getting agitated again.

"I'll keep watch," Devin offered. "I don't think I will be sleeping tonight anyway." It was true. He had more energy now than he'd ever had before. He genuinely believed the fugitive wouldn't be going anywhere soon, but he found that there was no point arguing with Ryve.

"Shifts," Ryve offered. The suggestion surprised Devin. It always surprised him when Ryve spoke. Deekin was quiet for a moment and then nodded. He was still weak from the poison and would no doubt like to rest. Devin nodded as well.

They ducked inside the ruined building and made their way to the third floor. They couldn't go up any further, as the stairways up to the next level had either collapsed or were covered in massive piles of debris. A large hole in wall existed where a window had once been, offering them a perfect vantage point to keep an eye on their quarry.

***

Devin had taken the first shift. After five hours, Ryve had relieved him, though Devin was still completely awake. He was thankful for the reprieve and walked over to where Deekin and the mechanized horse lay. The horse had been put in standby and was completely quiet. Deekin rested against the horse, looking more alert and in increasingly better health. Devin sat across from him and found he had nothing to say. He suddenly felt incredibly awkward and was about to get back up when Deekin spoke.

"Ryve hates you," he said.

"Yeah, I figured," Devin replied. He looked over at Ryve and frowned. "Why, though?"

"He doesn't really care for humans. Though, he really despises you. You see, he believes you killed his brother." Devin jumped to his feet, rage immediately coursing through him. He'd never harmed a Trooviian in his life. Hell, he'd hardly seen them until now!

"Why?!" Devin seethed. "Why is he blaming me for that?"

"His brother was on board the city that crashed. And, since he thinks you are the one who sabotaged it, he is accusing you of murdering his brother."

Devin suddenly understood Ryve's initial hostility and why the Trooviian had insisted on killing him. Devin obviously hadn't killed anyone on the city, and he certainly hadn't killed Ryve's brother, but another thought occurred to him. The figure that had fled the wreckage, along with the large footprint Devin had found, began to take form. Devin was starting to put together a picture, though Deekin and Ryve (especially Ryve) would adamantly disagree. It would be safer to keep his theory to himself, for now.

"Ryve's brother didn't have the best luck," Deekin continued. "He was a member of the Order of Proper Justice for a time. He'd gotten himself into trouble and got bumped down to security detail for Disc City 6. Ryve was saddened by this, but he always felt that his brother could, and eventually would, redeem himself. But, the crash took any hope for redemption away. We Trooviians live by a code of honor, and Ryve's brother had brought dishonor to his entire family."

"So, he is going to hate me right up until the moment we find who sabotaged the city," Devin grumbled. "Fantastic."

"Perhaps not," Deekin said. "He has become less intent on killing you, especially since the attack at the crash." Devin gave him a puzzled look.

"You could have tried to flee," Deekin explained. "You could have left us to fend for ourselves when the attack started, but you didn't. You even gave up your steed for me."

"So, he doesn't want to kill me?"

"Well, I never actually said that. He is just having an easier time holding himself back."

Devin hung his head. He was still on Ryve's hit list. He was beginning to wish that his theory had never formed. If it proved to be true, Devin believed he wouldn't survive the fallout.

Chapter 8

Elaina Perry watched as Dr. Peterson slumped in his chair after Professor Goordaiin left the office. She had stood outside the office during their conversation and had heard nearly every word that had been said. Dr. Peterson, as smart as he was, didn't seem to see what she thought was obvious. The Calvoran didn't appear to be doing the doctor any favors. If anything, it appears Dr. Peterson was being used.

When she took the job, Elaina had dreams of seeing the new "planet" in its full glory, but as time progressed she began to see that dream fade. Too many setbacks had occurred, delaying the project and seemingly sealing their doom. Elaina was Dr. Peterson's assistant, but she was also his security detail. After the mysterious death of the project's original leader, The Human Collective Government (or just The Collective) felt it necessary to assign secret security details to the rest of the Human project leads.

Her cover was quite effective, as she obviously didn't look like a bouncer or an agent of The Collective. She was attractive and, at 23 years old, unassuming. This gave her the ability to move about without garnering too much scrutiny. She was a junior agent, and this was her first assignment. She was required to observe and report.

The Collective distrusted the Calvorans and the Trooviians. She was tasked with keeping an eye on the project and everyone involved. With Professor Goordaiin seemingly in full control of Phoenix One, her job would be more important than ever.

Elaina left Dr. Peterson in his office. Though he would need protection, she doubted that anything would happen to him until the Calvoran got what he wanted first. She figured Dr. Peterson would be safe until the completion of the replacement eco generator. If Professor Goordaiin was correct in his estimation, she had two months to find out what was really taking place.

Hopefully, she would be able to find something and expose the Calvoran. Dr. Peterson's safety would no longer be in question, and the fate of humanity would be better assured.

As she walked down the hall, she felt increasingly anxious.

What if she was wrong? What if something happened to Dr. Peterson while she was gone? She shook her head. If she didn't find something to prove the Calvoran was up to no good, she would find that protecting the doctor would become an impossible task. She was well trained, but that would do no good against a myriad of would-be assassins.

Professor Goordaiin strode past his office and continued down the bright white hall. Elaina stayed back as far as she could while keeping the Calvoran in her sight. She ducked into a doorway when he stopped at a large metal blue door at the end of the hall. She peered into the hall and watched as the professor looked around before entering the room.

What's in there? She wondered. *Where is he going?* Elaina checked the hallway to make sure nobody was around and then quickly, but quietly, approached the door. The sign said that the door lead to a chemical lab. What could Professor Goordaiin be doing in a lab? He would never do experiments himself. He had a slew of scientists for that.

Something felt wrong, though Elaina couldn't pinpoint why. She checked the door. It was locked. Well, she would find no answers standing at a locked door. There had to be another way into the lab.

Elaina checked the hall and found a ventilation duct in the ceiling. As clichéd as it seemed, the duct would most likely be her only option. She sighed and looked around the nearby rooms for a chair or a stool of some kind. She found a chair with wheels and nothing else.

Terrific, she thought. *I'm going to break my damn neck trying to climb into a freaking vent!* She wheeled the chair under the vent and slowly climbed on top of it. The chair shifted under her weight, and she nearly lost her balance. She steadied herself and then reached up to pry the cover off the ventilation duct. The cover wouldn't budge, and she noticed it had been secured to the ceiling with many small rivets.

Elaina may not have been able to enter the ductwork, but that didn't stop sound from traveling to her. She was about to step down from the chair when she picked up a fragment of conversation.

"It's under control," a voice said. She identified it as Goordaiin's. "My agent will be found and eliminated. Nobody will know that we orchestrated Disc City 6's elimination. As far as the council knows it was committed by some rogue agency. Relax."

Elaina gasped. She fucking knew it! Goordaiin *was* up to something! It was far more than she'd expected, but this was everything she needed to remove Goordaiin, protect Dr. Peterson, and return control of the project back to the humans.

As Elaina began to climb down from the chair a pair of Trooviians rounded the corner at the far end of the hall. They looked almost identical, their skin the same shade of blue-grey and cracked. Their hide was incredibly thick, Elaina could see, and she began to wonder if anything short of the weapons they carried would do any damage. Matching black, shark-like eyes stared at her from their amphibious heads, their massive square teeth bared.

Elaina knew she looked horribly suspicious crawling off a chair in the middle of a hallway. She also found it difficult to remove the expression of shock that seemed permanently affixed to her features.

The Trooviians bellowed in their strange guttural language, and her heart sank.

***

The sun sank behind the horizon and took all the heat of the day with it. The temperature dropped below freezing as Devin, Deekin, and Ryve took refuge in the ruined building. The walls did little to buffer the bone-chilling wind that found every opening in their desolate shelter. Devin sorely missed his protective gear, which had served as little relief against the cold. He was nearly bare to the waist now, and though the BSS rig had aided him in many ways, it did not help now. He began to shiver horribly and began to fear that he wouldn't survive the night.

"How do you manage to survive out here?" Deekin asked.

"The gear I used to wear helped a little," Devin replied. "I normally wouldn't choose a place like this for shelter, either. The only reason we're here is to keep an eye on our fugitive. I would have preferred to find a smaller building or something underground, if possible."

"I envy the fugitive," Deekin said as he tried to brace himself against the frigid air. "The fire seems like a very good idea right now."

"It does, but the risks aren't worth it. We'd likely explode."

"At least we'd be warm!" Deekin growled, his agitation getting the best of him. "I'd rather risk it than freeze to death!"

Devin found that he couldn't disagree. His mechanical steed fed off the combustible fumes, so it was likely that after several hours, the atmosphere in the building would be slightly cleaner. Blocking the openings would help cut down on the wind, and the steed could continue to act as a filter. They could either take the risk or die.

"Fine," Devin relented. "But we need to seal the room up as best as we can."

Deekin pushed himself off the floor and tried to steady himself. The poison had mostly run its course by now, and his strength had been gradually returning. He found that he was still dizzy, but he decided to manage it. Devin searched around for anything they could use to block the openings and found pieces of cardboard and even a large sheet of clear plastic. They fastened the plastic over the largest hole in the wall with pieces of rebar that Deekin had managed to shear into inch long pieces. The cardboard proved more challenging, as most of it had been soaked and started to decay.

After struggling for a bit to get the cardboard to stay, they decided to give up on the smaller openings and use as much of the cardboard as they could to block the larger gaps with more rebar pieces than they felt should have been necessary.

Devin found chunks of wood that had been furniture at one time and after what seemed like an hour managed to get the wood to ignite by striking the side of his harpoon gun with his blade until the sparks began feasting on the wood. Devin and Deekin held their breath, waiting for the room to erupt in a massive fireball, but the explosion never came. Ryve continued to stay at his post to keep an eye on the fugitive's camp in the distance, though he managed to cast a glance their way every now and then.

Deekin eventually relieved Ryve of his post and Devin sat in silence by his steed, never taking his eyes of Ryve. He didn't trust the Trooviian, especially after Deekin told him how much Ryve hated him. Fortunately, Devin was wide awake thanks to the BSS Rig, so he didn't have to worry about being murdered in his sleep.

***

Elaina climbed off the chair and raised her hands as the Trooviians marched toward her with their weapons drawn. The weapons were no bigger than a pistol, but the exteriors were sleek and bluish in color. Even though she'd been acting suspicious, she doubted the Trooviians would attempt to kill her or even apprehend her.

The risk of causing a rift between Humans and the alien species working on the Phoenix One project was too great. Tempers flared frequently and the project leaders, as well as the Collective Human Government, did their best to quell the anger before the three races fought each other.

Elaina expected to be barraged by a flurry of questions, but the Trooviians took her by surprise by aiming their weapons at her face. Her doubts disappeared, and she suddenly realized that these Trooviians didn't care about ruffling the feathers of the project leaders.

Their uniforms were emblazoned with the Order of Proper Justice's emblem. It was a globe with a large fist superimposed on it with flames around the edges and a blade piercing the top. She'd seen them around and had even seen a few humans wearing the uniform as well, though it was incredibly rare. She always figured they were a police force or security. These two Trooviians acted more like thugs.

The Trooviians looked at each other, and, after seemingly listening to something, both prepared the weapons to fire. She had no idea what they were saying, but their intent was clear. They intended to kill her. She heard the tell-tale whine as the weapon charged.

Elaina moved just as the shot went off. She pushed the weapon carried by the Trooviian to her left away from her as she ducked under the other's, simultaneously pulling what appeared to be a pen from her belt. The pen was, in fact, a blade that was made of hyperactive plasma coursing along a metallic alloy core. The blade was the same length as the handle when it was fully extended, which she thrust as far into the Trooviian's lower back as she could. The Trooviian howled in pain, but her blade had severed its spinal cord, and it dropped to the floor, its legs now completely useless.

The second Trooviian had been trying to aim at her, but she

managed to stay half a step ahead of it. She ran around the Trooviian and leaped briefly onto the wall before propelling herself toward the Trooviian's now exposed right side. She stabbed her blade into the side of its head, and it quickly dropped to the floor, quite dead.

Elaina glanced at the closed door in which Professor Goordaiin had disappeared behind, and a thought occurred to her. The hostility of the Trooviians was unusual, and the behavior of the Calvoran made her uneasy. They were planning something, and she wasn't meant to know anything about it, which she didn't at present. There was no way anyone knew that she'd found out about Goordaiin.

She looked down the hall in the direction that she and later the two Trooviians had come. Panic struck her as she thought about Dr. Peterson.

The partially paralyzed Trooviian had managed to regain its weapon and twisted to face Elaina. She heard a hissing sound next to her head and turned to face the fallen Trooviian. The next shot would have hit her if she hadn't dropped to the floor. She rolled to her right, toward the dead Trooviian and grabbed the beast's fallen weapon mid-roll. She continued to roll as she took aim at the second Trooviian. It was having trouble following her, and she had just enough time to fire off a shot before it could shoot at her again. The beast's head disintegrated.

Elaina realized she'd been holding her breath and exhaled. The weapons were quiet, which was fortunate. She would have time to flee before anybody found the bodies. She scrambled quickly to her feet and sprinted down the hall, keeping the dead Trooviian's weapon. She may need it again.

Chapter 9

Devin sat in silence for some time after his conversation with Deekin. He glanced over at Ryve constantly, fearing to keep his eyes off the Trooviian for too long. Deekin had tried to reassure him that Ryve wouldn't make an attempt on Devin's life, but he refused to let down his guard after all that Deekin had told him. Devin tried not to stare or make any obvious signs that he was watching Ryve, but he let his gaze linger every occasionally, and caught himself just as Ryve stirred. Had the Trooviian been sleeping? Devin couldn't tell since Ryve's back was facing him.

Ryve jumped to his feet in a flash and Devin thought for a split second that Ryve was about to make his move, but that idea fled from his mind the moment he heard the explosion. Their quarry's campfire must have finally ignited the toxic fumes. Devin rushed over to the opening to look, taking special care not to get too close to Ryve. In the distance, he could see the residual flames from the explosion. Their quarry was most likely dead, but Devin felt uncomfortable waiting to find out. The fugitive could be terribly injured and dying, which would make any attempt at gaining information more futile with every passing moment. Braving the cold would be incredibly dangerous, though. The nocturnal wildlife presented an immense hazard as well.

Deekin must have been thinking the same thing because he got to his feet and began retrieving his gear. Devin thought about the risks they would be taking and wanted nothing more than to cuddle up next to his mechanical steed. He wanted to sleep, to escape the world for an hour at least, but the BSS Rig was keeping him wide awake.

"We need to leave," Deekin said. "We can't let the fugitive get away or die."

"If we go out there now, we'll die," Devin argued.

"We'll risk it," Deekin retorted. Devin could tell by the Trooviian's tone that he had no choice in the matter. He was their prisoner after all. He was going to die a prisoner and all because of his damned curiosity! Devin gritted his teeth and could feel himself tremble with frustration. Deekin must have noticed because he drew his weapon and pointed it straight at Devin's face. That made Devin retreat several steps.

"We. Will. Risk. It," Deekin repeated. Devin put his hands up in surrender.

"Ok, ok," Devin said. "I get it."

Ryve had moved from the opening during their exchange and was already making his way down the stairwell to the second floor. Deekin and Devin snatched up their equipment and led the steed hurriedly toward the stairs. Devin had to slow to ensure that his steed didn't tumble down the stairwell. Deekin rushed ahead, his energy fully returned, and tried to catch up to his partner. Ryve had nearly made his way to the first floor before Deekin caught up. Devin lost sight of them as he led his steed down the second stairwell. He could hear their voices, but they spoke in that guttural language again. He still could not trust them, and the constant debates in that foreign language did nothing to ease his distrust.

Deekin rushed back up the stairs toward Devin, and for a moment Devin feared for his life. But Deekin lifted the mechanical steed and began trying to carry it down the stairs. The steed had to weigh several hundred pounds, and Deekin lifted it as though it weighed no more than a few pounds. Devin hadn't realized how incredibly strong the Trooviians were, and this only made him fear them more.

Ryve waited on the first floor for them and then took off out into the freezing night. Deekin sprinted after him, and Devin climbed atop his steed. He hesitated a moment before finally urging his steed out into the dark. The icy wind slammed into him immediately, and he once again regretted leaving part of his protective clothing in the garage where he first met the Trooviians. He skin was covered in gooseflesh, and he began to shiver uncontrollably within less than a minute. This wasn't going to work. He would end up with hypothermia long before they reached the fugitive's camp.

Devin looked around in desperation, but the darkness covered everything, and his eyes had yet to adjust completely. Perhaps running instead of riding the steed would help fight off the murderous chill. He dismounted reluctantly and began running, his steed moving independently to keep up. He had programmed the steed to be partly automated and self-sufficient, but it was still far from sentient. He tried desperately to avoid tripping over debris in the dark, but he stumbled several times. His lungs ached from the frigid air, and his body temperature hadn't raised much.

Devin decided that running wasn't working, nor was it worth the risk. He mounted his steed again and spurred it into motion. The wind whipped at his face and exposed flesh, making his skin feel as if it were peeling off. He tried his best to ignore the pain as he rushed toward the campsite. After what felt like an eternity he finally reached the ruined campsite, but he must have passed Deekin and Ryve, for neither of them was in the area. He dismounted and fumbled for his new makeshift spear with numbed fingers before exploring. He immediately knew something was wrong.

Several bodies were strewn about. They looked like Bandits, though some of them were badly burned or missing body parts. Bandits? Why would they risk a campfire? Devin felt the hairs on the back of his neck stand on end and whirled around to face his rear. Deekin and Ryve had caught up and were beginning to search the area as well, but Devin hadn't heard their approach.

"Bandits," Deekin spat. "This was a damned Bandit camp!"

"Something about it doesn't feel right," Devin said. He looked at the bodies again and could tell something was off, but he wasn't sure what.

"You're right," Deekin said as he turned to face Devin. "This doesn't. You know what I think?"

"What?"

"I think you made up all that shit about a fugitive to save your own skin! I am starting to think you've been lying to us the whole time!"

"I haven't been lying!" Devin yelled as he began retreating. He tripped over a body, and then he realized what had seemed wrong. The body was missing its left arm and the head, but the body parts hadn't been sheared off in the explosion or by a sharp instrument. They'd been disintegrated. The stumps were cauterized and almost rounded.

"The Bandits didn't own the camp!" Devin shouted when he made the discovery. "They were attacking somebody! Look!" Devin pointed at the ruined body and pointed at the stumps. Deekin paused to look. He shook his head after a moment.

"Those wounds were made from a Trooviian weapon,"

Deekin said, his black eyes widening. "This makes no sense."

***

Elaina rounded a corner, putting herself out of sight of the dead Trooviians and slowed her pace. She slid the firearm she'd taken from one of the dead beasts into her waistband and grabbed a shiny silver lab coat from an open room to help conceal the weapon. She would need to make her way back to Dr. Peterson, but she desperately wanted to know what Professor Goordaiin was up to. She'd been tasked with keeping an eye on the Calvoran by The Collective, and she had a strong feeling that Professor Goordaiin had a hidden agenda. Going back the way she'd come would be too great a risk, as it was incredibly unlikely that the two dead Trooviians had evaporated. She would need to find some other way to spy on the Calvoran and whomever he was most likely meeting with.

After several moments, Elaina decided to double back. No alarms had sounded, and nobody had come sprinting to investigate the deaths of the Trooviians. If she hurried, Elaina could duck into an adjacent room and wait for Professor Goordaiin to leave the chemical lab. If someone left the lab afterwards, she would follow them and try to get them alone. She hadn't done much interrogating during her time as an agent of The Collective, but she knew how to get information if she needed to.

Elaina carefully walked down the brightly lit circular hallway and fought to maintain her pace when she saw the corpses where she'd left them. Professor Goordaiin would see them and raise the alarm, which would make it nearly impossible to find out what he was up to. She would likely get caught as well. Talking her way out that situation would be quite a challenge considering she was carrying the murder weapon. She would have to move the bodies, and quickly.

The corpses were massive, easily three hundred pounds each. Elaina had no idea how she was going to move them on her own, but the rolling chair was where she'd left it, and this gave her an idea. She struggled to move the first corpse onto the chair and found herself near fainting from the effort. She couldn't drag the corpse and lifting it was out of the question. Another idea came to her. It was grotesque and the last thing she wanted to do, but she was getting desperate.

Elaina drew the weapon she had stolen and fired at the corpse, blasting it into smaller and more manageable pieces. She then reluctantly grabbed each piece, fighting the urge to vomit the entire time, and moved them into a storage closet nearby. She did the same thing with the second corpse and was preparing to leave the closet when the door of the chemical lab opened. She hurriedly closed the closet door, trapping herself inside with the dismembered corpses.

Elaina heard Professor Goordaiin's voice as he stepped into the hallway and then heard another voice she couldn't place. The voice sounded like Goordaiin's, which led her to believe the second speaker was also a Calvoran. She slowly opened the door, so she could peer out into the hallway and caught a glimpse of Professor Goordaiin's opalescent jacket as he strode down the hall and out of sight. She rushed out into the hallway and forced her way into the lab before the door shut.

When her eyes adjusted, and she could see what sat in the center of the room, her blood froze.

Chapter 10

Devin watched as Deekin and Ryve searched to site. There were residual flames from the explosion, and he welcomed the heat. The explosion had consumed the toxins in the atmosphere, and it would take several minutes before the area was flooded again. It wouldn't take long, though, and Devin wanted to be far from the area when it ignited again. He was surprised that the area hadn't ignited almost immediately after their fugitive had made the campfire. Perhaps the atmosphere in this area wasn't as combustible as he'd thought.

Deekin was grumbling to himself as he shifted corpses and scanned the ground for prints. Devin wasn't sure what he was looking for and was growing impatient. Ryve had stopped rifling through the destruction and had begun staring at Deekin. Deekin's persistence was making Devin anxious, and he found himself gripping the handle of his makeshift spear. Deekin finally stopped and turned to face him.

"The only bodies here belong to Bandits," Deekin grumbled. "If our fugitive is a Trooviian, they are not here. Either they fled or…" Deekin trailed off, not wanting to finish his thought. Devin knew how vicious the Bandits could be and if any had survived the blast, it was likely that they had overwhelmed their victim. If this was the case, the Bandits had probably carted the fugitive off. Devin dared not think what the Bandits would do after that.

"Scavenger," Deekin barked. "There must be tracks to follow! If the fugitive fled again, I mean to find them!"

"I don't know what to look for," Devin said. "Our fugitive may not have left tracks. They might not even be alive."

"I suggest you look anyway," Deekin said through gritted teeth. Devin decided not to argue. The Trooviian was on edge, and understandably so. To find out that the person they were hunting was one of their own was likely to upset Deekin. Devin found it hard to dispute Deekin's suspicion, especially after the track that he'd found earlier and the unfamiliarity of the fugitive with the environment. All the evidence pointed to a Trooviian suspect.

Devin began to scour the area for any sign of tracks that

could belong to a Trooviian, and after several minutes he found some. They led further west, followed by smaller tracks that no doubt belonged to the remaining Bandits. Devin mounted his mechanical horse and began following the tracks until the Trooviian's tracks disappeared. He dismounted once again to search more closely.

The tracks belonging to the Bandits were deeper, indicating that the source had increased weight. They must have overwhelmed the Trooviian and had begun carrying it. If this was indeed the case, the Trooviian was likely dead. Devin hoped so, for the Trooviian's sake. The Bandits could be incredibly cruel and more than once Devin had run across the remains of their torture victims. Sometimes they were still alive.

Deekin came up behind Devin without much sound, startling Devin when he spoke.

"What did you find?"

"I think the Bandits caught up to our fugitive. If you look here," Devin pointed at the footprints set deep in the dirt. Deekin knelt to examine the prints. "The Bandits leave deeper impressions from here on. Either they put on an incredible amount of weight suddenly, or they started carrying someone very heavy."

"So, they overwhelmed a Trooviian and then started to carry it? Why" Deekin asked. Devin didn't want to answer the question, but he knew that Deekin would continue to press until he did.

"They took it, prisoner," Devin replied. Deekin didn't respond. Instead, he stood and marched toward Ryve. They spoke hurriedly, and Ryve began to grow agitated. Devin wished he could understand them. He didn't like being left in the dark when dealing with these two. Deekin had begun to soften until they discovered that the fugitive was a fellow Trooviian, and Ryve still wanted to kill him.

"Let's go, Scavenger," Deekin called. "If the bandits took our fugitive prisoner, I intend to get them back before any harm can be done." Devin nodded, but he knew the chances of finding their quarry alive and unharmed were incredibly low. Bandits were incredibly cruel and surprisingly imaginative. He climbed astride his steed and began to follow the trail once more. After several moments, they crested a small hill and stopped dead in their tracks.

***

The chemical lab had been stripped of any apparatus used to mix volatile substances and was instead home to a massive machine. The chemical lab had a catwalk, which was where Elaina now stood, overlooking the lab and the machine in the center. The machine itself looked very much like the eco generators some of the wealthier Disc City residents owned to keep their living quarters filled with clean oxygen and a supply of food to supplement the rations everyone was given. However, this massive version would have needed far more organic material to make it work, and the organic material the machine's owner had chosen were human beings.

She watched as a Bandit, still technically human, was forced into a chamber kicking and screaming. The creatures loading the Bandit were Trooviians, both much stronger than the panicked creature fighting to escape the chamber that was attached to the oversized eco generator.

One of the Trooviians shoved the Bandit against the far wall of the chamber with enough force to knock the Bandit unconscious while the other Trooviian shut the vault door, sealing the Bandit inside. With what appeared to be a smile, the first Trooviian threw a switch on the panel outside the chamber.

Elaina had to stifle a cry as the Bandit regained consciousness with renewed panic before being rent limb from limb by the force of the vacuum that drew it into the machine. The Bandit nearly disintegrated from the force before disappearing completely. The machine hissed and whirred as it used the organic material to try to create the start of a brand-new ecosystem within the room.

The machine began to buzz loudly, and a crackling sound emitted from within, sending everyone in the room into a frenzy as they tried to shut the machine down.

Apparently, they haven't worked out all the kinks, Elaina thought bitterly. *The Collective is going to hear about this, too!*

Elaina turned and made her way to the exit as quietly as she possibly could; hoping that nobody below would spot her. She made it to the door when she heard a guttural voice call out in alarm. She quickly rushed out of the room and slammed the door before sprinting down the hall, back toward Dr. Peterson's office. If the Calvorans, especially Professor Goordaiin, had decided to use human beings to power the eco generator for Phoenix One, everyone who wasn't Calvoran or Trooviian was in danger.

***

Professor Goordaiin paced in his office, seemingly floating above the floor. Two of The Order had not reported back to him, and now the eco generator had failed its first test. The eco generator, which he had had his team begin building long before the other one had been destroyed in the explosion that crashed Disc City 6, had just been completed shortly before his meeting with the team.

It was expected that the eco generator would take several test runs before being completely operational, and organic material was plentiful. The unexplained disappearance of his two Justice Officers troubled him, though. Trooviians were as dependable as they were simple-minded, and it was completely out of character for them to shirk their duties. He'd given strict instructions, and now they were late in reporting back.

As he paced, Professor Goordaiin mulled over the multiple possibilities and scenarios that would lead to the disappearance of the two Trooviian Officers. The humans were not strong enough to overpower the much more physically superior Trooviians and nobody, but the Order carried weapons within the facility. Had the simple-minded fools gotten lost in the halls? This, too, seemed unlikely as the Trooviians were adept at navigating winding passages, as they had spent most of their time subterranean on their home planet.

Something else must have happened. Could they have deserted the Order? Betrayed their oaths? Did he need to worry about dissension within the Order? These also seemed unlikely. What could it be? He knew he would arrive at the answer soon. But would he like what he found?

Professor Goordaiin stopped pacing and decided to sit in his chair, allowing himself to relax enough to enter a meditative state. Calvorans had some degree of psychic ability, and Professor Goordaiin was certainly no exception. As he settled into his meditation, he let his mind expand, probing the offices and halls outside his own office. He caught snippets of thoughts and flashes of images as he explored the thoughts of every living thing within 300 feet of his office. Nothing stood out. Most of the thoughts and images were pointless, and he never lingered more than a millisecond on each.

He kept searching until something caught his attention. Images of a Bandit being loaded into the eco generator, dismembered limbs, shadowy figures, and even Doctor Peterson flashed before his eyes. Someone had seen more than they should have, he deduced, but whom? He followed the source of the thoughts, probing deeper.

Images of a training facility entered his vision, filled with human trainees. So, the owner of the thoughts was a trained individual. A special agent, perhaps? How would one of The Collective's agents be within his facility? He'd screened everyone before admitting them. Now his interest had been peaked. Who was this individual? They were obviously well trained because nothing personally identifiable had been made available to him just yet. Doctor Peterson kept appearing in the owner's thoughts, however.

Professor Goordaiin had spent enough time probing his target's thoughts that he was able to create a psychic link. He moved away from the target's thoughts and began probing their emotions. The individual was panicked and desperately trying to get somewhere. Fear, disgust, despair, and even a shred of hope flooded his target. So, the sight of the eco generator consuming the Bandit was causing the disgust, the fear, and possibly even the despair. That wasn't the only source, Professor Goordaiin deduced. Something else was causing the emotions. He recalled the images of Doctor Peterson. Could this be the source of hope and fear? Who would care enough to feel this way?

Finally, Professor Goordaiin arrived at the identity of the mystery figure. Doctor Peterson's pet: Elaina Perry. Probing further he discovered a recent memory containing his voice.

She knew.

Chapter 11

Devin held his breath as he surveyed the area. Bandits were everywhere, circling a figure that Devin couldn't make out in the dark. They were jabbing at the figure, which had been strung up to a massive circular object, though he couldn't determine what the ring was made of. There was little light in the area, produced only by small light sticks carried by some of the Bandits. Deekin and Ryve seemed to be able to see in the dark better than he could because they growled and pounded the ground with their fists.

"What is it?" Devin asked as quietly as he could.

"They're torturing a Trooviian," Deekin snarled.

"So, we *were* looking for a Trooviian," Devin said, more to himself than to Deekin.

"Yes," Deekin said, his voice dropping along with his gaze. "It would appear so. But that isn't the worst of it."

"Then what is?"

"We know him. He's Ryve's brother." Devin stared at Deekin with his mouth hanging open. He dared not look at Ryve. He couldn't imagine what Ryve might be feeling, but the last thing he wanted to do was to provoke the Trooviian.

"Ryve's brother? Are you sure?" Devin whispered.

"Without a doubt. I just don't understand why." Deekin slid away from the peak of the hill, turning his back on the commotion. Devin noticed that Deekin wasn't looking at Ryve either. "Why would his brother kill all those people and sabotage the Phoenix One project? What could he have hoped to gain?"

Just then Ryve charged over the hill, roaring as he went. Devin looked up in surprise and heard cries of pain from the congregation of Bandits. Deekin quickly jumped up and raced after his partner. *Oh shit!* Devin thought just as he, too, sprinted toward the Bandit camp. The scene was chaos. Bandits were dropping from cauterized wounds as they were trying to figure out what was going on. Ryve was frenzied, shooting in all directions and smashing his weapon into any Bandit that got to close. Deekin was more controlled as he picked off any Bandits who were trying to circle his partner. Devin had to duck several times as Ryve pointed the barrel of the gun his direction and Devin could almost swear that it was intentional.

Deekin was too preoccupied with keeping his partner safe that he didn't notice the small group of Bandits approaching from his left. In an instant, they were upon him, and he fell as they began stabbing him with their rebar spears. Ryve had yet to notice, but Devin cried out in alarm as he charged with his spear and tried to help his fallen companion. This seemed to get Ryve's attention, though, and in seconds Ryve was tearing into the Bandits who were mercilessly spearing his partner. Ryve attacked with such ferocity that he had begun tearing Bandits limb from limb, but it wasn't enough. Deekin was already dead.

***

Elaina rushed through the halls as quickly as she could without arousing suspicion. Her mind was swimming. Why were humans being used as fuel for the eco generator? The Calvorans and Trooviians had been working with humans toward a common goal, hadn't they? She felt betrayed and now understood why The Collective had planted her here. They had never trusted the aliens, and it seemed they may have known more than they'd let on. She hoped she could get back to Dr. Peterson before anybody else. She didn't know if the workers in the Chemical Lab had seen her, but she didn't want to take that chance. If she could tell Dr. Peterson about what she had seen, perhaps he could spread the word to the other scientists while she contacted The Collective.

She found herself in the wrong corridor more than once, even though she'd traveled these halls over a thousand times in the past. She was distracted and panicked, which was disrupting her concentration. She finally found herself down a familiar hallway and knew she was close to Dr. Peterson's office. The hallway appeared deserted, which gave her some hope, but also filled her with dread as her mind wandered toward the worst possible scenarios she could imagine.

Elaina picked up her pace, nearly running now, as Dr. Peterson's office door came into view. She was ten feet away when everything went black.

***

That was close, Professor Goordaiin thought. Elaina had nearly made it to Dr. Peterson. Fortunately, the psychic link he'd been trying to establish took hold.

It always seemed to take longer to establish a link between Humans and Calvorans. This allowed him to send a surge of psionic energy into her brain, rendering her unconscious.

He called in several of his officers from The Order and instructed them to retrieve Elaina and Dr. Peterson. Word of his involvement in the destruction of Disc City 6, not to mention the thousands of lives extinguished, and of the eco generator couldn't be allowed to get out. He was too close now to take any chances. Dr. Peterson was no longer of any use to him, now that he'd fully relinquished control of the eco generator project to Goordaiin. It had now become necessary to remove Dr. Peterson and Elaina from the picture.

***

Dr. Peterson was sitting at his desk going over the details of the destroyed eco generator when he heard a knock at his door.

"Come in," he called as he stood. In walked a pair of massive Trooviian Officers. He was taken aback as he had fully expected to see Professor Goordaiin standing before him.

"Professor Goordaiin would like to see you in his office," one of the Trooviians said.

"Yes, of course," Dr. Peterson said as he grabbed the tablet with the schematics for the eco generator. No doubt Professor Goordaiin wanted him to begin overseeing the construction of the new machine.

He walked behind the Trooviians as they led him down the hall and through several winding passages. He began to grow confused. He knew where Professor Goordaiin's office was, but they were walking the opposite way. Where were they going?

The trio walked for nearly five minutes before the stopped outside the Chemical Lab. Why were they stopping here? What could Professor Goordaiin need from him in the Chemical Lab? He noticed that the door had now been fixed with a biometric lock with a fingerprint scanner, which one of his escorts was now using. The lock clicked, and a light at the top of the door turned green. The Trooviian pressed a button on the lock, and the door swung inward with a hiss. Dread suddenly spread over Dr. Peterson as he was led inside.

Chapter 12

Devin swung his spear at any Bandit that dared to come close, catching one in the side of the head and another across the belly, the pointed end of the spear ripping flesh. Ryve had gone berserk and was tearing Bandits apart as he howled with rage. He tore a Bandit's head off and smashed the head into the face of another Bandit, crushing both skulls.

Another Bandit got too close and found itself in Ryve's powerful grasp. With another howl, Ryve ripped the Bandit in half. Devin never realized just how strong the Trooviians were and now feared Ryve more than ever. He hesitated, questioning whether he should move any closer. Ryve would likely take his rage out on him as well. Devin looked at Deekin's bloody corpse and felt a massive wave of grief grab hold of him.

Deekin had been the only living thing who'd ever shown him any kindness, and now he was gone, leaving Devin alone with Ryve.

***

The Bandits began to flee after they watched most of their clan fall at the hands of the Trooviians and the strangely aggressive Scavenger. One Bandit took a bite out of the leg of the Trooviian they'd captured before running off into the night.

The Trooviian prisoner made a pathetic sound; something close to a moan. Blood poured out of the prisoner's thigh as he struggled against his bonds. He was too weak to fight anymore. The wounds the Bandits had inflicted had taken their toll as he felt himself begin to fade from consciousness.

***

Devin decided it was best to stay as far from Ryve as possible, as much as he wanted to tend to his fallen friend, and instead ran over to the Trooviian that the Bandits had taken as their prisoner. The damage they'd inflicted was immense. Chunks of flesh had been carved off the Trooviian's limbs and chest. His teeth had been yanked out, and the teeth that remained were all broken.

It appeared as if the Bandits had gotten access to acid because some of the Trooviians fingers were melted off, along with one of his eyes. The worst of it, however, was what they'd done to his abdomen. He'd been cut open, and his intestines were nailed to each side of the ring that held him in place. Blood pooled at his feet, and Devin wondered how the poor creature was still alive.

He slung the spear across his back and walked toward the Trooviian with his hands out in a gesture of peace. He didn't want to set the creature on edge. The panic would only make the Trooviian bleed out faster. Devin felt pity for the creature, even though the Trooviian had caused the deaths of all the people on Disc City 6. Regardless of his crimes, the Trooviian didn't deserve the amount of torture he'd been subjected to.

"I'm not going to hurt you," Devin said quietly. The Trooviian looked at him weakly. Devin saw defeat in the Trooviian's remaining eye. "The Bandits are gone. We drove them off." The Trooviian didn't respond. He just continued to stare at Devin.

"What's your name," Devin asked.

"Tor," the Trooviian managed to say, his broken teeth chattering as he shivered.

"Tor," Devin repeated. "Are you Ryve's brother?"

"How do you know Ryve?" Tor asked weakly. Devin got his answer. He'd hoped that Deekin was mistaken.

"Ryve found me outside of the wreckage of Disc City 6," Devin said. "He was with another Trooviian, named Deekin."

"I don't know Deekin," Tor said. "Where's Ryve? Where's my brother?"

"Ryve is fine," Devin said. He pointed behind him where he'd left Ryve and Deekin, but he couldn't see anything. "He's here."

"Why?"

"We were looking for whoever caused the massacre of Disc City 6," Devin answered. "We wanted to know why the city was destroyed."

"I didn't want to," Tor said as he tried to look away, tears welling up in his remaining eye. "I was ordered to."

"Ordered?" came a growl behind Devin. He turned and saw

Ryve stalking toward them. "Who order?"

"I was told the humans were building a bomb," Tor protested. He was becoming distraught at the sight of his brother. "I was told that they were going to try to kill us!"

"Who order?" Ryve repeated forcefully.

"Professor Goordaiin."

***

Dr. Peterson gazed at the machine. It looked like the original eco generator, but it had obviously been modified with Calvoran technology. It looked sleeker, with smooth edges and the color of an abalone shell. It was pearlescent and multicolored, which shifted as he moved. The machine almost appeared to breathe. It was beautiful, but somehow it also seemed sinister. The massive translucent chamber attached at the far end seemed out of place. His original design did not have the chamber. The organic material it had needed was loaded in a metal tube and inserted in a port near the controls. He couldn't see anything like that on this new design.

"You - you already completed it?" he asked. "How?"

"With the technology of the Calvorans at our disposal," Professor Goordaiin's voice echoed. "It took far less time to construct."

"But, I only gave you the schematics this morning!"

"Yes," Professor Goordaiin said as he strode into view. "This made assembling the machine much simpler. We had been building a back-up in case anything happened to your prototype, and it is fortunate that we did. But now we need your help with the final piece of the puzzle. You see, the original method of supplying organic material was inefficient. With my improvements, the eco generator will be able to work more efficiently with less effort. Now, if you'd be so kind, I'd like you to be the first to inspect it. You designed the machine, after all. You know best how the machine should absorb the materials provided."

Dr. Peterson stared at Professor Goordaiin, confused. How was this possible? Before he could speak, his Trooviian escorts grabbed him by the shoulders and led him toward the massive collection chamber.

***

Elaina regained consciousness and found herself back in the Chemical Lab, tied to a support beam. Panic overwhelmed her as she tried to flee, but she couldn't budge. She was tied with a length of rope made of a material she'd never seen.

She looked around; trying to get an idea of the amount of trouble she was in. She saw several Calvorans, the Trooviian workers she'd seen earlier, and several other Trooviians as well. She continued to scan the room and let out a scream as she looked at the eco generator. Inside the clear chamber attached to the machine where the Bandit had been disintegrated was Dr. Peterson, beaten and bloody.

"What are you doing?!" she screamed at the creatures around her. "He hasn't done anything to you!"

"I know that to be true," came a voice from behind her. She turned her head as far as she could to look behind her. Professor Goordaiin floated into her peripheral vision and positioned himself directly in front of her.

"What I wonder," he continued. "Is what you planned to tell him? Were you planning on telling him about the eco generator? About the Disc City? Were you going to tell him to run away? Or perhaps you wanted him to help you inform The Collective."

"How?" she began.

"How did I know that you are affiliated with The Collective?" Professor Goordaiin asked. "How did I know what you knew?" Goordaiin lightly pressed two long fingers against Elaina's temple. "I saw it in your mind as you ran away from this room after you killed two of my Officers. The Collective trained you well, I must admit. It took me far longer to retrieve that information from you than I had expected, but you couldn't hide for long."

"I figured The Collective had planted *someone* amongst us, but somehow I'd never suspected you. I must say, Dr. Peterson, is quite taken with you. He fought with more passion than I expected when he saw you, but of course, he was no match for me or the Trooviians. I don't believe he knew you were working for The Collective, either."

"Please," Elaina said. "Please leave him out of it. He doesn't know."

"Oh, I know that," Professor Goordaiin chuckled. It sounded more like notes from an accordion than a laugh. "But you brought him into it. You were going to tell him everything. I couldn't have that. Not with everything I've fought so hard to achieve. I must thank him, though. As much as I despise to admit it, the eco generator wouldn't have been possible without him. That took a bit of creative thinking on his part. It only fits that he should help me test the new eco generator, to ensure that it works properly."

With that Professor Goordaiin turned and signaled to the Trooviian standing by the generator's switch. The Trooviian nodded and flipped the switch, and Dr. Peterson screamed.

The machine hummed as it powered up, buzzing softly and punctuated by mechanical clicking. Dr. Peterson seemed to regain his strength as he began banging on the clear chamber wall. His eyes went wide as blood began to ooze from his pores. The machine hummed louder, and within seconds Dr. Peterson exploded into a spray of gore, and seconds later his remains were consumed by the machine.

"No! Dad!" Elaina screamed. She hadn't meant to scream that, but the terror and the grief overwhelmed her senses. She was no longer fully aware of her actions as she thrashed violently against her bonds. Professor Goordaiin stared at her, his beady black eyes widened in surprise. He hadn't known the truth of her identity. She'd been able to hide that much, until now.

"Oh, this *is* interesting," Professor Goordaiin said. "So *that's* why he fought so hard when he saw you! You're his child! How cruel of The Collective to plant you as his secretary, knowing that the compromise of your mission could get him killed. Though I suspect that's exactly why they did it. A guarantee of sorts."

Elaina continued thrashing and screaming. She didn't know how, but she'd managed to break free and kicked Professor Goordaiin in the face. He fell backward, and she took advantage of the opening to sprint toward the door. She had to get as far away from the machine as she could.

Elaina fought the reflex to vomit as she ran out into the hall. Where was she going to go now? She decided that she needed to leave the facility as fast as possible. From there she would figure out what to do next. The Collective had to know.

Chapter 13

Devin and Ryve tried to free Tor from his restraints, but the effort caused Tor too much pain, so they had to stop. Tor wasn't going to survive much longer. The only reason he hadn't bled out already was that the cold had caused his heart rate to slow, but his time was rapidly coming to an end.

Devin left Ryve to console his brother and walked over to Deekin's body. The sight made tears flood his eyes. The Trooviian had taken over a dozen stab wounds from the Bandits, but the wound that had killed him was a spear taken in the throat. The spear still jutted from his torn trachea. Blood had started pooling from his mouth, but the freezing temperature was making it congeal rapidly.

Devin knelt beside his fallen friend. He had no idea what to do now. Ryve would likely be enraged once his brother finally died and Devin knew it was only a matter of time before that rage would be directed back on him. He didn't want to be anywhere near Ryve when that happened.

He closed Deekin's eyes and crossed his massive arms over his chest. He regretted that he wouldn't be able to bury his friend, but there wasn't time. The chill was seeping into his body, and he'd begun to shake uncontrollably. He reluctantly began searching Deekin for the remote to BSS rig. He needed to get as far away from Ryve as possible.

"Running?" Ryve growled. Devin's heart pounded with fear. He'd taken too long with Deekin.

"I need to find shelter," Devin protested.

"You not run," Ryve said, holding the BSS remote in his massive hand. "You stay with me."

"But- "

"We must kill Goordaiin," Ryve snapped. "Kill Goordaiin for killing Tor."

"Who's Goordaiin?" Devin asked, surprised by the turn of events. He'd been expecting Ryve to try to kill him now that Deekin was gone.

"Was boss," Ryve said as he tore the badge that marked him as an Officer of The Order of Proper Justice from his uniform. "But no more. The Order is a lie. Got Deekin killed. Goordaiin doesn't care about humans *or* Trooviians."

"If we don't find shelter before morning we won't be able to avenge your brother," Devin said to reason with the vengeful Trooviian. They were likely to develop hypothermia if they hadn't already. He couldn't tell as his adrenaline was still pumping like crazy.

"We go at light," Ryve said. Devin was confused for a moment until he realized that Ryve agreed with him.

"That building we were holed up in should still work," Devin offered. Ryve only nodded in reply. With that, they hurried off back toward the skyscraper that had been their shelter before Tor's camp had exploded.

***

Professor Goordaiin raged. The human woman had knocked him on his back, something he should have been able to predict and avoid and had stripped him momentarily of his dignity. He rose gracefully to his feet and rubbed his face. The blow had been strong enough to cause soft tissue damage to his delicate flesh.

Calvorans weren't physically durable, at least compared to their Trooviian counterparts. The mind had been the focus of their evolution, so physical power and resistance to damage were sorely lacking.

The Trooviians had evolved the opposite direction. They were an incredibly physical race. Immensely powerful and incredibly thick-skinned, the Trooviians were adept to subterranean life, though they lacked the same level of intellect.

Professor Goordaiin barked orders in the Trooviian language, ugly as it was, to his officers. Elaina must be caught before she could reveal anything to The Collective or any other human aboard the flying city. The Trooviian officers bounded out of the room with single-minded purpose. The Calvorans used to despise their subterranean counterparts, but that hatred had since been turned toward the humans.

Professor Goordaiin found that he appreciated the efficiency of the Trooviians in the execution of the various tasks he'd assigned them. They were simple but followed directions exactly and without question. Humans were stubborn and opinionated. They carried an air of entitlement, even though they were far inferior to the Calvorans, as well as the Trooviians. They were expendable, which made them useful for a time. Eventually, they would exhaust their usefulness, but Professor Goordaiin had found another use for them: as fuel.

***

Elaina sprinted through the winding halls of the complex toward the exit with renewed vigor. No doubt Professor Goordaiin's lackeys would be hot on her tail.

Let them try to stop her. She'd gotten her first taste of battle and found that once she moved past the queasiness, she'd felt at killing another creature she had partially enjoyed it. The thought worried her, though. She shouldn't enjoy combat, and she certainly shouldn't enjoy killing another living thing, but she couldn't help it.

The training she'd received from The Collective had made her an incredibly efficient combatant. Combine that with the weapons she'd retrieved from her fallen enemies, and she would be an even bigger threat. That thought alone made her smile.

Elaina rounded a bend and saw the hatch that exited the building. On the walls, next to the hatch were several environmental suits with special breathing apparatuses. The height in which the city hovered made it difficult to breathe. The oxygen levels were low, so special breathing apparatuses were necessary to survive. She debated for a minute; however, whether she should take the time to don the suits before going outside. Should she risk it? Probably not.

She took a moment to slip into one of the smaller suits as quickly as she could. She heard the Trooviians approaching behind her and rushed to put on the mask just as she opened the hatch. She didn't manage to get the mask on correctly and could feel the change in the atmosphere almost instantly. The mask wasn't providing enough oxygen, as she hadn't created a proper seal, and began to black out.

The Trooviians weren't faring well, either. Only two had followed her, and both had collapsed to the floor. She took the opportunity to fix her mask and dash outside before any more Trooviians could come for her. Once the seal had been created, she found she could breathe easy once more.

She hadn't been outside the research complex often. All the staff had living quarters inside the complex, so venturing outside was rarely necessary. She'd forgotten how horrible everything looked. The buildings were in terrible shape. They were slapped together and appeared as though they would collapse under the slightest breeze, but somehow, they could stand up to the incredibly powerful wind.

She realized she'd been standing near the opening of the complex, leaving herself vulnerable. The air was icy and thin, and Elaina triggered the hood to protect her ears. The suit didn't have a full mask, and she could feel the chill begin biting the tip of her nose.

Elaina immediately started off in a run, winding between buildings and bracing herself against the ever-present wind. Behind her, she could hear the thudding footsteps of her Trooviian pursuers. Elaina dared to glance behind her and saw she now had five pursuers, all of which were wearing their own protective gear. She fought a laugh. The Trooviians looked like bizarre, green Armadillos in their segmented armor, except for their frog-like heads.

Elaina zipped around a corner and found herself at a dead end. The road had been barred by massive steel fencing with corrugated tin roofing fixed to the sides to help block the wind. There was no way she would be able to scale it. She looked around the alley for a place to hide and found a door to her left that stood ajar. She quickly ducked inside the building, trying to be as quiet as possible. Her eyes took a moment to adjust to the gloom and what she saw saddened her. People were huddled together, filthy and obviously hungry.

She determined that she must be in the slums of this Disc City. The wealthier neighborhoods had their own personal eco generators. These were only the size of a microwave, of course, and only produced enough resources for a single family. The poor neighborhoods didn't fare so well. They were lucky if anyone in the building had an eco-generator, which would then be communal and never had enough fuel. The people huddled inside the doorway paid no attention to Elaina as she slowly moved down the hallway.

Elaina expected someone to go on alert or at least react to her presence in some way. The environmental suit was a deep blue, segmented at the joints and waist, and topped with a retractable hood that folded into a collar. There was a breathing apparatus linked to the collar, which had small oxygen sacks that pulled oxygen out of the wind via vents in the suit. She certainly looked frightening to anyone unfamiliar with the suit, but these poor people barely glanced at her. She found a stairwell and debated about going up to the next floor. If she climbed higher, she would effectively be pinning herself in, but if she tried to enter one of the living quarters she'd likely be met with screams that would immediately give away her position.

She looked back the way she came, hoping that she'd lost her pursuers, but this hope was dashed as the first Trooviian appeared in the doorway. The presence of the imposing creature managed to elicit screams from the impoverished residents. She no longer had time to weigh her options. She immediately ran upstairs, the screams of frightened people following her as she ascended.

Elaina scrambled up two flights of stairs as quietly as she could, but the suit was bulky, and every movement made noise. Rather than continue to climb she decided to step out into the hallway. She was on the third of maybe fifteen floors and hoped that her Trooviian pursuers would continue the climb, giving her an opportunity to slip behind them and back down to the first floor. She hoped to be out of the building before the Trooviians ever realized she'd given them the slip. The hallway seemed empty and quiet, leaving Elaina far too exposed. She could hear the heavy thudding footfalls on the stairwell coming fast.

She tried the first door to her right. It was locked, as she'd expected. The door to her left was as well. She tried several more doors, growing increasingly frantic at each locked door. She reached the end of the hallway and found herself at a T-junction. She could go either direction, but she doubted either would link back up to the stairs. She elected to go right, trying the doors as she went. Five doors down she finally found a door that opened for her. Without hesitation, she ducked inside.

As Elaina closed the door, she took in her surroundings. The apartment was cluttered with trash and debris, but nobody appeared to be home. She slowly searched the bedrooms to make sure and then hid in what appeared to be a child's room. She heard the Trooviians barking at each other through the paper-thin walls. They had stopped on this floor as well, she realized. Her heart began to race again. So much for her initial plan! She crouched by the bedroom door, trying to hear over her thudding heartbeat and the sound of each exhalation, which seemed louder than they should.

She heard the Trooviians voices growing louder as they came down the hall and arrived at the T-junction. She held her breath, even though they couldn't possibly hear her. The voices began to fade, and she realized they'd gone left, moving away from her. She breathed a sigh of relief and rose to exit the bedroom, but she froze when she heard heavy footsteps right outside the front door of the apartment. How could they possibly know that she'd hid in this apartment? It didn't seem fair.

The door slammed open, and Elaina heard the Trooviians as they strode into the apartment. She drew the pistol she'd taken from one of the Trooviians she'd killed. She was going to have to shoot her way out, and she didn't like her chances. Then she opted to holster the pistol and instead draw her blade. If they split up, she could catch one by surprise and silence it before it could alert its partner. She held her breath as the Trooviians began searching the apartment.

They weren't quiet about it. Doors crashed open and things shattered as Elaina crouched in the dark. The door across the small hallway of the apartment slammed open, and she knew her door would be next. She readied herself, preparing to use all her training. The door flew open, crashing off its hinges as one of the Trooviians strode in. It hadn't seen her, and she took the opening to strike.

She rushed the Trooviian from its left, getting behind it before it could register the movement. She jumped onto its back and plunged the blade into the base of its skull. The Trooviian let out a grunt as it dropped to the floor. Elaina sprang off the falling Trooviian's back, spinning in the air to face the open doorway and the second Trooviian, who had its back to her as it searched to room across the hall.

The Trooviian turned when it heard the crash of its partner's body hitting the floor, but Elaina had already pounced and slashed the Trooviian across the face as she flew past it into the room. The Trooviian clutched its torn face as it howled and turned to face her. She'd caught the beast across the right side of its face and had sliced open its eye.

The Trooviian tried to fire its weapon at her, but Elaina

hadn't stopped moving. She ran around the room, staying just ahead of the Trooviians aim as she rushed back at it. The Trooviian fired at her and hesitated when she disappeared. She had slid beneath the shot and between the Trooviian's legs. The Trooviian's remaining eye widened as it realized what had happened. Before it could turn around Elaina had drawn her pistol and fired, catching the Trooviian between the shoulder blades.

The Trooviian turned, clutching the hole in its chest. She fired again, hitting the Trooviian square in the face and blasting a hole where a nose should have been. The Trooviian stood for a moment and then dropped back through the doorway and into the room.

Elaina dashed out of the apartment and back down the hall toward the staircase. She needed to get as far from the dead Trooviians as possible. More would arrive to look for their missing comrades, and when they found the corpses, the search effort would double. Members of the Order would start to swarm the city. Her only hope was to get off the floating city and out into the wasteland.

Chapter 14

Professor Goordaiin paced in his office, waiting impatiently for any development in the hunt for Elaina Perry. She'd managed to kill several of his guards on her way out of the facility; a feat he'd previously thought impossible. He'd made the mistake of underestimating the human woman, and he vowed he wouldn't make that mistake again. Elaina had not only killed two Trooviians single-handedly but had also stripped them of their primary firearm.

The Trooviian rifles and pistols were simple in appearance but effective, much like their designers. It was believed that the rifles fired a concentrated laser, but in reality, the Trooviians had discovered a way to harness and discharge pure UV energy in concentrated bursts. The blasts wouldn't ignite the fumes that filled the toxic atmosphere of Earth, making them invaluable to Professor Goordaiin's ground troops.

Once Elaina had escaped with the weapon, Professor Goordaiin immediately commissioned the construction of specialized armor designed to defuse the blasts on impact. Unfortunately, the first group of Trooviians he'd dispatched wasn't adorned in this new armor, but any further deployed troops would be. He hoped it wouldn't be necessary, but Elaina had been well trained, and Goordaiin harbored some doubt that she would be eliminated easily. She had likely dispatched his second contingent of Trooviian guards and another more heavily armed contingent would be needed.

Tracking her was simple, now that he'd established a psychic link to her. If uninterrupted, the link would strengthen, and distance would no longer matter. Currently, the psychic link was like chewing gum: the further it was stretched the thinner it would become before finally breaking.

After thirty minutes of radio silence, Professor Goordaiin ordered a squad of five Trooviians to begin the search, ensuring that each troop was fully equipped in the protective armor and given the Calvoran counterparts to the Trooviian rifles. These rifles were more complex in appearance and design but were more powerful and used not only concentrated UV but also excited plasma. He didn't worry about the atmosphere of the city, as it floated thousands of feet above the combustible fumes on the surface. If these troops couldn't eliminate the human woman, who he'd concluded was an agent of The Collective, then more drastic measures would be needed.

He didn't care about human casualties but destroying the entire city would mean he'd have to evacuate his crew and the eco generator. It would be like dropping a grenade in an anthill to kill one ant. Such extreme measures seemed unnecessary. He would do it if he needed to, though, unless he could come up with another plan.

***

Elaina ran toward the nearest edge of the disc city in the hopes of securing transport to the surface. Her protective suit would suffice temporarily on the surface, but she knew she'd need to secure more appropriate equipment before long. The streets were crowded with people trying to go about having normal lives, frequenting shops that sold anything that could be considered useful and trying to hold conversations of the howling wind.

Elaina caught sight of several Trooviians among the crowd, but none seemed to be wearing the uniforms of The Order of Proper Justice. These looked like regular citizens, but she kept her head down anyway. She didn't want to take the chance that none of them had been planted by Goordaiin. Elaina had to slow to a brisk walk to navigate the mass of bodies milling about. If she rushed through the crowd and knocked people over, she'd be drawing unwanted attention. The protective suit she wore stood out enough on its own.

Elaina had never been to the surface, but she'd known people who had and had heard about the small vessels they'd used to fly down from Disc City 9. The vessels weren't heavily guarded as almost nobody wanted to brave the lethal surface conditions. Those who had to go to the surface often fought to try to get out of it, though not always with success. The survival rate of those who were unlucky enough to set foot on the surface was less than twenty-five percent. If the toxic atmosphere didn't kill them, the mutated wildlife or the psychotic tribes of Bandits did.

It was a massive risk, Elaina knew, but it was also the only chance she had. Staying aboard the city was tantamount to suicide, as she would eventually be caught, and no doubt put to death in the most imaginative way possible if she stayed aboard the city. At least she had a slim chance on the surface.

As Elaina made her way through the crowd, she caught sight of several more Trooviians walking through the crowd. These Trooviians wore white protective gear, like hers, but these suits were plated with what appeared to be plastic over the chest, abdomen, and limbs. On the shoulder, which she could now see as one of the Trooviians turned, was the symbol of The Order. It was a red circle with alien lettering around the face of a Calvoran.

Elaina wanted to turn around and run, but she was caught in the current of people and moving against them would be difficult without pushing people aside. She had no choice but to continue forward with her head down. At this point, she could only hope they didn't spot her.

Her anxiety worsened as she drew nearer, and it was as if the Trooviian soldiers could smell it because they immediately turned to look at her. They didn't immediately spot her, but within seconds one of the Trooviians began pointing and barking at the others. They drew their weapons and began forcing their way through the crowd.

How had they known she was there?

She'd ducked down so that she was below their line of sight, letting the taller citizens block the Trooviians' view, but they'd spotted her anyway. Could they smell fear? She'd never heard of such a thing about the Trooviians, but much was still a mystery about both alien races.

There was no longer any point in trying to remain hidden. Elaina began forcing her way through the crowd, knocking some people down in the process. She didn't have time to apologize. The Trooviian guards were hot on her trail.

The edge of the city was only five miles away or so, but with an active pursuit, it may as well have been fifty. Elaina didn't dare try to escape into any of the buildings as doing so would leave her trapped. She needed to keep moving. If she could at least get clear of the innocent civilians, she'd be able to try and defend herself, but she couldn't right now. She didn't want to harm any of the people around her.

She hadn't really wanted to harm the Trooviians, either, but that wasn't a choice she'd been given. The Trooviians in pursuit seemed to have the same reservation, as they hadn't attempted to fire a shot either.

The wind whipped at her face as Elaina navigated her way through the sea of miserable people. If only the hood of her suit had had a mask! Her face was beginning to sting as bits of debris hit every inch of exposed flesh. She brought her arm up to shield her face as much as possible, but it did little to protect her. She squinted, which had less to do with the bright sun and more to do with keeping the debris from her eyes and saw a break in the crowd.

Elaina accelerated toward the opening as much as she could, but this didn't go unnoticed by her Trooviian pursuers. They'd noticed the opening as well and, instead of charging forward, had stopped to raise their weapons. Elaina glanced back and felt her heart jump into her throat. They would open fire at any moment, and Elaina knew she'd be completely exposed with nowhere to hide. Buildings were flanking the streets, but ducking inside any of them would pin her in. She still didn't know exactly where she was going or where the shuttle might be.

The pursuit had only taken her a third of a mile, thanks to the mass of people blocking the walkways at every turn. She'd begun to feel claustrophobic as the crowd had seemed to thicken, but the opening had become a disadvantage. Instead, Elaina ducked and began weaving through people, staying at chest level with everyone else.

Someone screamed nearby, and Elaina knew that the Trooviians had opened fire. They must have decided that the collateral damage was worth keeping her from escaping. A man who was no more than thirty years old fell in front of her, clutching his throat and trying in vain to stem the flow of blood from the opening. Tears welled up in Elaina's eyes as she muttered "sorry" and stepped over him.

The crowd had erupted in a panic as more people fell around her. She tried to keep from crying out as a woman clutching her child dropped to the ground, both very dead. This was her fault and more than once Elaina almost stood up to surrender, but she knew that more people would die if she didn't contact The Collective. Instead of surrendering, Elaina turned and fired her weapon at the Trooviians. They'd advanced slowly toward her, but she still had fifty yards between them. She expected the blast from the pistol to drop her target, but it only sizzled when it hit the Trooviian's armor. A small black scorch mark indicated where the blast had hit. The Trooviian looked down at its chest and then looked back at her, smiling.

Several blasts streaked past Elaina's head, and it was then that she noticed that they were carrying very bizarre weapons. The blast was a streak of electric blue light that sizzled as it passed through the air around it. Elaina could smell burning hair and realized that it was her own.

One of the shots had barely missed her, but it had been close enough to singe hair. She abandoned her current course of action and broke into a sprint. People parted, wanting no part of the death that seemed to encircle her. She could have run straight ahead when the crowd finally broke, but to do so would mean her death.

She decided, instead, to cut across the walkway to her right and then back to her left, hoping that the zig-zag motion would make her a harder target. More blue steaks flashed around her, narrowly missing her. She felt the left side of her face start to burn as a shot missed her head by mere centimeters.

She hazarded a glance back toward her attackers. The Trooviians were trying to steady their aim, but the panicked crowd jostled them as people ran by. One man ran straight into one of the Trooviians, a brute with a missing eye, and ended up being shot square in the face as he bounced off the massive creature. The Trooviians were become enraged by the difficulty they were facing in killing their target. Innocent bystanders started to catch the brunt of their rage as the Trooviians began firing at the people around them.

The distraction afforded Elaina an opportunity to put as much distance between her and the Trooviians as possible. She abandoned the zigzagging motion and broke into a sprint. She heard at hiss as a streak of light flashed past her and then a searing pain shot up from her left elbow. The pain caused her vision to flood with white, and she thought her head would explode. The pain had traveled up her arm and into the base of her skull. She cried out and dropped to the ground, all the strength leaving her legs. Elaina tried to catch herself, but her left hand seemed to be completely numb. Instead, she slammed into the ground, bouncing her head off the pavement.

Elaina's vision had begun to clear, but the pain was still agonizing. Her entire left arm felt as though it were on fire, except below the elbow. Everything below the elbow had gone numb. A sudden, horrible realization struck her, and she forced herself to examine her damaged arm. It was as she had feared. Her arm had been amputated beneath the elbow. She let out another cry.

The Trooviians began howling, and Elaina figured they were cheering. She closed her eyes as she expected to hear another hiss before she died. Instead, Elaina felt strong, cold hands grab her roughly under the arms that hauled her to her feet. She tried to break free, but the hands had too strong a grip on her. She shot a look over her shoulder and saw a blank, steel face staring back at her. Panic overwhelmed her, and she began thrashing wildly.

The faceless creature began dragging her from the open street toward a derelict building on the right side of the road. Elaina continued thrashing, despite the searing pain in her damaged arm, and this seemed to aggravate the faceless thing because it let go with one hand and struck her in the back of the head, knocking her unconscious.

***

The Trooviians that had been pursuing the fugitive woman found themselves face to face with faceless metal men. The new development confused them. They'd never seen anything like these things before. One of the Trooviians, the squad leader, howled in rage as the fugitive was hauled out of the street and into cover.

The squad leader had expected to finish the mission once the woman collapsed, but the metal men were standing directly in his line of sight. He raised his weapon and fired at the nearest metal creature. The blast tore through the creature's torso, but it didn't seem to notice. A second later the metal creatures all raised their arms directly in front of them, hands replaced with open cylinders.

The metal men fired blasts of bright green light at the Trooviians. The Trooviians, including the squad leader, expected to hear the blasts singe against their armor, but the armor seemed to do nothing. The Trooviians fell, clutching holes in their chests as they died staring into those blank metal faces.

***

Professor Goordaiin screamed in rage as the psychic link with his latest task squad had been broken. He knew his men had died. What angered him the most was Elaina's escape and the appearance of those damned metal men! Where in the hell had those things come from? He'd never seen the creatures and had never heard of sightings, either! How had they come aboard the city? He had spies all over Disc City 9, and not even one of them had seen these metal creatures. How could that be?

To make matters worse, his psychic link with Elaina had been severed. She was within range, he knew, so something else was blocking him. This only made him angrier. He called out to his secretary, a rather squat looking Trooviian woman, and ordered that she bring him one of the human scientists remaining on the Eco-Generator team.

Professor Goordaiin paced impatiently while he waited, his anger turning his pearlescent skin a shade of red. His secretary led a young, handsome (by human standards) man into Professor Goordaiin's office. He cast his secretary an icy look, telling her to leave him with so much psychic force that she dropped to the floor. This frightened the scientist.

"What's happening?" the scientist asked, his voice beginning to tremble.

"A mere taste of what's to come," Professor Goordaiin shot back.

Before the man could try to run, Professor Goordaiin began to force his way inside the poor man's mind. It took less than a second and then he directed all his anger into the man's brain. The scientist began seizing, but he remained standing. Goordaiin approached the man and, still psychically holding him aloft, began tearing into the soft flesh with his bare hands. He would normally find the act appalling, but his anger needed to be sated. The scientist was being assaulted mentally and physically at the same time. Professor Goordaiin regained control of himself and stared at the mess before him. The man was clearly dead, a gaping bloody wound in his abdomen that was so deep light could be seen on the other side.

Professor Goordaiin turned his attention away from his

victim, letting the man's body crumple to the floor, and turned his gaze inward. He would need to find another way of keeping Elaina from contacting The Collective. He could try to lock down all of Disc City 9, but The Collective would no doubt come to investigate. Anger began filling him once again. How had they managed to slip an agent under his nose? If he'd known about Elaina, he'd have dispatched her ages ago. Furious and desperate, Professor Goordaiin found himself without a plan. He'd never been without a plan, and the new development frightened him.

He also knew that he would have to conduct a fair amount of damage control. The body in his office, and Dr. Peterson's death would not go unnoticed. He ordered more of his officers to clean up the mess the scientist's body had made. He would have to explain Dr. Peterson's disappearance to the council.

Goordaiin summoned his secretary and ordered her to contact the council. All they were to be told was that there had been a development in the project and an emergency meeting would be required.

He swiftly exited his office and made his way back to the conference room that the council had convened in previously. Dr. Peterson had been the last human on the council, which made convincing the rest of the council even easier. Goordaiin would play on their prejudices, as buried as they may be, and make the death of Dr. Peterson appear as a massive step forward.

"My fellow councilmen," Goordaiin began as everyone found their seats. "As you have no doubt noticed, Doctor Peterson is not among us. I regret to inform you that there was an unexpected function of the eco generator."

Murmuring began to fill the room. Professor Goordaiin knew he'd be immediately bombarded with questions, so he spoke up again to cut them off.

"During testing of the machine, Doctor Peterson was unfortunately trapped inside the fuel chamber. The machine detected the introduction of organic material and immediately absorbed him."

Gasps erupted around him, though the Calvorans in attendance didn't seem too deeply affected.

"As tragic as the accident was, it has also revealed that the eco generator is capable of far more than previously expected. Within minutes the entire lab was covered in plant life, and within an hour an entirely new ecosystem had formed. You see, Dr. Peterson's accident may have saved the entire project. The biological makeup of human beings is much more efficient than any source of fuel previously tested."

Goordaiin was pleased to see the expressions on the council's faces change. They no longer looked concerned. Hope had crept into their features.

"As we know, humans reproduce at an extraordinary rate. By using the savages on the Earth's surface, we can sustain the Phoenix One project nearly indefinitely, if we were to breed them and use them as fuel. It is no secret that we've tried to make them useful in some form or another, and now we have. I know that what I am proposing seems barbaric, but we would be ensuring the survival of three species at the expense of the castaways, who'd surely perish soon anyway."

Nods of agreement and further murmurs filled the room. Goordaiin had to work incredibly hard to hide his elation. He concluded the meeting and immediately hurried back to his office. There was only one loose end left to tie up.

Chapter 15

Devin and Ryve ran back toward the skeletal remains of the skyscraper they had initially taken refuge in. The chill was worsening, and Devin could no longer feel his fingers or his face. If he stayed outside any longer frostbite would surely set in. Ryve didn't seem to be bothered as much. The mechanical steed moved autonomously beside them, following Devin's vocal commands. He wished he could communicate telepathically with the machine, but that bit of technology was guarded by the Calvorans.

It seemed that they were withholding quite a bit from humans. He'd never seen another human wearing the BSS rig and figured they'd probably been told they were incompatible. Humans always seemed to be carrying inferior tools and protective clothing, while the Calvorans, which Devin had seen in abundance while working on the Disc Cities as a laborer, were adorned in exotic clothing and used items that were completely foreign in nature. Their technology had clearly been far beyond that of humans, and it didn't appear to be shared.

Devin had been lucky to have gotten the parts for his mechanical steed. Most of the parts had been scavenged from the remains of man-made machines, but he'd found pieces of Trooviian and Calvoran technology in the wreckages they'd left behind when they first arrived on Earth. Not every extraterrestrial visitor had landed safely on the surface, which had been fortunate for Devin. He'd managed to scavenge quite a bit from those wreckages, which had unfortunately brought unwanted attention from both Scavengers and Bandits alike. He hadn't been lucky enough to scavenge weapons from the wrecks, but he had had enough material to trade for basic sustenance until recently.

He now carried Deekin's rifle, which Ryve had reluctantly allowed him to take from their fallen friend and had even been kind enough to explain the basic operation to him. The weapon was surprisingly light, and Devin was thankful for it.

The dilapidated skyscraper was finally within reach. They were only a quarter mile away from the building, and Devin was thankful for that. His arms were going numb, and his legs were on fire. The BSS rig had given him more energy and increased his stamina, but he was still getting used to it. He was still human and would need to rest soon. Ryve was even beginning to tire, though it was more likely caused by the harsh weather rather than the actual act of running.

Devin's lungs felt as though needles were filling them as the icy wind entered. He knew he couldn't take much more and would need to resort to his steed to carry him the rest of the way. He didn't want to ride his steed while Ryve was forced to continue running. It didn't seem fair, but Devin would be of no use if he collapsed. He relented and quickly mounted his mechanical horse. The steed almost seemed grateful to have him aboard. Devin decided that he would need to give it a head of some kind when he had the chance. It would need a way to emote, which would make his loneliness more tolerable when he and Ryve eventually parted ways.

They arrived at the entrance of the skyscraper and quickly ducked inside. They made their way upstairs carefully, as the steed didn't seem to do to well with, and finally arrived in the room that they'd been camping in before the Bandit attack on Tor's camp. The lack of icy wind was greatly appreciated, and the fire that Deekin had helped Devin make was still burning, though it was quickly running out of fuel. The thought of Deekin made tears well up in Devin's eyes. He didn't realize how much he'd grown to appreciate the Trooviian's company and unique attitude toward him, or how much he was going to miss it. Ryve was less hostile now that the true culprit behind the attack on Disc City 6 had been revealed, but he was still cold toward Devin.

Ryve was driven purely by revenge. Devin was just a convenience, a way to get aboard Disc City 9, within which Professor Goordaiin resided. Devin didn't know which city that was, but Ryve seemed to know or would know how to find out. The Order of Proper Justice had been founded by Professor Goordaiin, after all. This was practically all the information Ryve had felt was necessary to share with Devin.

Devin dismounted from his mechanical steed and began scrounging for more material for the fire. Ryve sat at the window that looked out toward the broken overpass where Tor had set up camp, gazing soundlessly at the landscape. He was no doubt mourning the loss of both his brother and his partner in his own way, and Devin decided to leave him alone. Ryve didn't need him to intrude. Devin managed to find scraps of paper and even some wood from some broken furniture on one of the lower levels to feed the fire. He tossed some of the tinder and the paper into the hungry flames before settling down on the floor next to his steed, soaking up the warmth from the fire. The feeling was beginning to return to his limbs, and before he knew it, he was asleep.

***

A loud crash woke Devin, and it had sounded incredibly close. He could see light streaming in through the myriad of cracks and holes in the walls, but he couldn't immediately see Ryve. He sat up with a start as another explosive crash assaulted his ears. Devin spotted Ryve by a window on the far side of the building. Had Ryve kept watch all night? Devin jumped up and grabbed his weapons before rushing over to Ryve's side.

"What is it?" Devin asked as he looked out the window. So far, he couldn't see anything, but that was more because his eyes hadn't yet adjusted to the light.

"Not sure," Ryve said. His attention was trained outside and had not answered Devin's question right away. "Big, though."

"I can't see anything!" Devin complained. His eyes had begun to adjust, but nothing seemed to be outside. There was yet another crash, and it sounded like it was right outside the window.

"It is hitting the building," Ryve said. "Knows we're here."

"Where is it exactly?"

"There," Ryve said as he stuck his arm out the window and pointed directly downward. Devin slowly inched his head out the window and then ducked back in so quickly he hit his head on the side of the opening. His heart had skipped several beats, and sweat immediately broke out.

"What is it?" Ryve asked.

"I don't have a name for it," Devin managed. He was panicking, and he'd begun to hyperventilate. "But I've heard some people on the disc cities call them Millipedes."

The name wasn't too far off. In truth, the massive creatures were related to millipedes, but the cocktail of toxic waste and radiation had caused the creatures to mutate until they were the size of a bus. These still bore a resemblance to their ancestors, but instead of insect-like mandibles, they had massive jaws, like a wolf. They were eyeless and had razor sharp forelimbs, nearly a hundred legs, and even had smaller forelimbs with claws capable of grabbing. The Millipede was also a lighter color than their ancestor, usually a dusty red or light brown.

Devin dared to peer outside once more. The Millipede had ceased slamming its girth into the building and was now scratching at the wall. Why hasn't it tried to climb through one of the openings in the walls? There was a huge hole in the wall ten feet above the creature's head, but it hadn't yet noticed. Devin couldn't help staring at the thing. It was the first time he'd ever seen one in its entirety, and he had never noticed just how massive they were. He immediately regretted staring at the creature, as it seemed to take notice and turned its enormous head upward, seemingly staring right back.

"Shit!" Devin yelled as he pushed away from the window and sprinted toward his steed. Ryve echoed him as he, too, ran from the window. Outside they could hear the Millipede begin scaling the wall as it slammed its legs into the building in its ascent. It was incredibly fast. Devin had just reached his steed when the Millipede appeared in the window. The window was too small for the Millipede to fit through, and for a moment Devin thought they might be safe after all. That may have been the case had the Millipede not reared back and slammed into the window, exploding through the opening and rushing toward them.

"Run!" Ryve bellowed. Devin hesitated as he thought about leaving his steed once again. He doubted that it would survive this time, but he needn't have worried as the steed seemed to sense the danger and bolted down the stairway past Devin and Ryve. Devin's hesitation nearly got him killed as the Millipede nearly caught him as he descended the stairs. The Millipede crashed into the wall and Devin thought it may have fallen out of the building, but the creature's horrifying visage appeared directly above him.

Ryve and Devin continued their descent at breakneck speed, the Millipede quickly following. Devin worried that he was about to fall, and nearly had more than once, but Ryve had been quick enough to grab him and keep him upright. Devin had lost sight of his steed as it continued to race ahead. He didn't know the mechanical horse could manage the stairs so well. He also hadn't expected it to exhibit a self-preservation instinct. This would be something to investigate if he survived.

The Millipede was gaining on them as they were one floor above the ground floor. The Millipede, exhibiting more intelligence than seemed fair, decided to forego the stairs and jump over the railing, crashing to the floor below them. Ryve and Devin stopped in their tracks. It would be slower to try to ascend the stairs, and the creature would no doubt catch them. Ryve slung the rifle off his shoulder and fired three rounds in quick succession at the Millipede's head. The first two rounds seemed to have no effect on the abomination. The third shot, however, managed to hit it in the mouth as it tried to catch Ryve in its nightmarish maw. The Millipede reared back and emitted a sound much like a scream; seemingly more from anger than pain. This only afforded Devin and Ryve seconds as they began their climb.

Devin pulled his harpoon gun from his back and fired the barbed projectile at the beast. The harpoon stuck, but Devin immediately regretted his decision as the harpoon was attached to the weapon. The Millipede reared again and yanked him from his feet. Devin landed painfully on his chest directly beneath the creature and had to roll out of the way to avoid being skewered by one of the creature's hundred pointed limbs. The attention was now on him, allowing Ryve the opportunity to escape. Devin half expected him to take the opening but was surprised when he saw Ryve leap from the stairs onto the Millipede's back. He began firing at the nearest break in the Millipede's exoskeleton as one segment ended, and another began. The Millipede bucked, but Ryve managed to stay on its back. He continued his relentless assault and Devin could see the barrel of his weapon start to glow red from the increased heat.

Ryve was gritting his teeth as he fought to keep his balance and focus his shots on the same location. The blasts finally cut through the armor, and the Millipede gave another piercing shriek, and the blasts tore through its organs. The Millipede changed tactics as it scaled a wall and crawled onto the ceiling, finally dropping Ryve off its back. The Millipede twisted to face Ryve and tried to lunge, but its weight made the ceiling give way, and it was buried under the rubble. Devin held his breath as he waited for the beast to explode from under the debris, but after a moment he managed to exhale a sigh of relief. The weight of the concrete seemed to have crushed the mutated insect to death.

The harpoon, at some point, had dislodged from the beast's hide and was lying near the rubble, still attached to the harpoon gun. Devin snatched it up and reloaded the harpoon. He was relieved that the weapon wasn't lost to him.

Ryve stirred, dust falling from his shoulders as he tried to push himself to his feet. The impact had taken its toll on him, rendering him nearly unconscious, and the dizziness from the blow forced him off balance. Ryve fell back to the ground in a heap. Devin debated leaving the Trooviian behind, but he couldn't bring himself to do it, as Ryve hadn't abandoned him when the opportunity presented itself.

Devin helped Ryve to his feet, and they both limped out of the building. Devin's steed was standing in the glaring sunlight, almost as if it was completely oblivious of the danger it had just left behind. Ryve and Devin exchanged quick glances before Devin jumped astride his steed. With the threat seemingly eliminated they could begin formulating a plan to reach Professor Goordaiin. Devin wanted no part of Ryve's vendetta, but he couldn't shake the feeling that something sinister was going on. Why else would Tor be sent to sabotage the eco generator?

Devin and Ryve began trying to lay out the foundations of a plan when the ground rumbled beneath them. They looked down and saw the ground push upward. Devin shot forward on his steed and Ryve ran to his right just as the ground exploded upward. The Millipede shot out of the ground like a breaching whale and began spinning as it searched for its prey. Devin turned his steed toward Ryve and managed to grab ahold of the Trooviian's massive hand before the Millipede locked on to their location and raced toward them. Ryve jumped aboard with more grace than Devin had expected, but there wasn't much room on the steed. He held on with all his might as the steed raced ahead, squeezing Devin around the midsection and cutting off his oxygen. Devin slapped at Ryve's hand, and he let up just enough for Devin to resume breathing.

They raced for another quarter mile before the Millipede changed its mind and gave up. The creature's wound was no doubt what had saved them as it had not been fast enough to catch them.

Ryve finally loosened his grip as they began to slow down. Neither of them exchanged a word as they continued east toward Disc City 9.

Chapter 16

Elaina faded in and out of consciousness as she was hauled off the main street and into one of the buildings nearby. When Elaina was conscious, though only for seconds at a time, she'd caught glimpses of her captors. Their faces were blank and made completely of metal. They were almost like mirrors. The faceless things moved with a singular purpose and had remained completely silent. They terrified her. They also intrigued her. What were they and what did they want with her?

After what may have been an hour, or maybe only mere minutes, the faceless things released her. Elaina dropped to the ground and slammed her injured arm. The pain made her lose consciousness once again. When she awoke again, she saw several of the faceless things, which she now saw to be entirely made of metal, flanking a silhouette of a man (or maybe a woman, she couldn't tell) dressed in a large coat with a hood that helped conceal the figure's face. A large length of cloth was wrapped around the figure's face, and goggles hid the eyes. The figure wasn't terribly tall, at least in comparison to the faceless robots, and carried an old-fashioned assault rifle.

Elaina felt panic welling up inside her as the figure raised its weapon, but the panic subsided as she saw the figure sling the weapon over the opposite shoulder, letting it rest across the figure's back. The figure moved toward her, keeping its hands out in front with the palms out, obviously trying to reassure her that she was safe for the moment.

"That's a rather nasty wound you got there," the voice, obviously male, spoke. "You're lucky to be alive. It's a good thing their weapons cauterize the wounds, or you would've bled out by now."

"Who are you?" Elaina managed. The pain in her arm was still intense and had made breathing difficult.

"An ally," the voice said. "And no friend to the Troglodytes or their masters."

"Troglodytes?"

"The big ugly fellas that were trying' to kill ya," the voice answered. "Good thing they didn't succeed. The Collective would've been mad to lose an agent."

Panic gripped Elaina once again. How did this man know she worked for The Collective?

"You know me?" she asked.

"Sure do," he answered. "You're Agent Elaina Perry, assigned as security detail for Doctor Jacob Peterson and as an Intel unit to keep an eye on the Phoenix One Council."

"And just who the hell are you?" Elaina snapped, trying to keep the fear out of her voice.

"I'm Agent Kyle Mathis," he answered. "My job is, or was, to manage a secret task force trusted with providing security for the entirety of Disc City 9. We weren't supposed to be seen, but that's a bit too late now."

Elaina looked around at the faceless metal automatons and shook her head.

"Secret task force?" she asked incredulously. "Are you serious? Do you really expect me to believe that?"

"Ah, yes," Kyle said, nodding. "I expected that kind of response. Let me prove it." He produced a badge that stated his identification number and the seal of The Collective. Elaina looked doubtfully at it. She had a badge as well, but that did little to prove anything.

"Might be a fake," she said through clenched teeth as a new wave of agony washed over her.

"Hmm…" Kyle had stuck a pensive pose which could have been comical had Elaina not been in so much pain. Then he snapped his fingers. "I know!" Kyle turned toward the automaton on his left.

"Unit 16," he said as he addressed the faceless metal robot. "Identify yourself."

"Unit 16FF, Human Collective Sentron, serial number 33685528-Alpha," it said, its featureless face pulsing with blue and green light at each word.

"Is that proof enough?" Kyle asked Elaina.

She would have spoken, but the pain in her arm made it impossible for her to speak as her throat seemed to make her throat close. Kyle noticed the intense grimace on her face as she grabbed her injured arm.

"We really need to get you fixed up," he said as he moved closer.

He removed the goggles from his eyes and pulled down the cloth covering his face. He had a dark complexion and strikingly handsome features that had been weathered by the elements. His eyes were a rich brown, and Elaina found she couldn't look away. Something about his eyes set her at ease. There was a kindness in them that she'd not seen in many other people.

"Unit 16," Kyle said over his shoulder. "Dispatch medical sentrons to our location." There was a buzzing sound, almost like the static on an old radio station, coming from Unit 16.

"Medical units dispatched. ETA 5 minutes," Unit 16 said in its monotonous voice. Elaina couldn't help but stare at the featureless robots. She'd never seen anything like them. Robots had been a major development for humanity before the entire human race had to ascend in the disc cities, but the manufacturing of robots had ceased afterward.

Kyle crouched in front of Elaina to get a better look at the wound. The blast had indeed cauterized the wound, but there were lines of blue stretching up the injured limb that seemed to glow faintly. The blast of the Trooviians' weapons seemed to have not only cauterized the wound but also filled the limb with a strange chemical or even remnants of electricity that continued to surge through the entire limb. He tried to examine more of the arm, but Elaina pulled away. Whatever the Trooviians had done, it was obvious the injury was meant to worsen if it didn't kill the target outright. He shook his head at the idea. It was almost too cruel.

Kyle had met several decent Trooviians, so he knew they weren't all bad, but the ones employed by Professor Goordaiin seemed to be completely evil. Why else would they create such a weapon?

He looked at Elaina's pained expression and found himself feeling desperate to help her. He was enthralled by her beauty, though her face was a mask of pain. She'd managed to fight back for a while, which he'd watched from the safety of cover, and he greatly respected her for it. The degree of bravery she'd shown was becoming incredibly rare as more and more people seemed to fear everything.

As he looked at Elaina, he felt a mixture of pity and anger. She didn't deserve this.

"Where are those medics?" Kyle barked.

"ETA two minutes," Unit 16 replied. Kyle closed his eyes and shook his head. Elaina may not have that long.

"Agent Perry," Kyle said, trying to get her attention. "Elaina!"

"What?" she managed, though it had only come out a whisper.

"What were you doing? Why were you running?" He asked in quick succession. "Where were you going?"

"Have to warn The Collective," she wheezed. "Have to get off this city." This did little to answer Kyle's questions, but it was more information than he'd had.

What did she need to warn The Collective about? He almost asked, but she'd lost consciousness again. For a moment, he feared that she was dead, but he saw her chest rise slightly as she continued to breathe. She was fading fast.

True to Unit 16's word, the medical unit arrived two minutes later. The unit was also comprised of automatons, but these were painted completely white. They moved past Kyle as he stood to get out of their way. He watched as they crouched on either side of Elaina and took hold of her gently. A thin, horizontal line of red light emitted from their featureless faces and moved over Elaina's wound as well as the rest of her body. The unit crouched on her wounded side pressed its right hand, which had changed to resemble a syringe of sorts, into her shoulder. Elaina didn't even flinch. The other unit crouched on the opposite side placed both hands on either side of her head as it emitted a faint blue glow from its palms.

Kyle continued to watch as the medical units worked on Elaina. He could see the glowing blue lines on her injured arm flare for a moment and then fade to nothing. Elaina's face, which had grown incredibly pale, was beginning to fill with color once again. She began to stir, but the medical unit that had been working on her injured arm stuck her with the syringe again, and she immediately relaxed. After nearly ten minutes the medical units released their gentle grasp on Elaina and rose to face Kyle.

"Patient stabilized," the medical automaton on the left said. "The patient must be transported to a nearby medical facility. We must transfer the patient off Disc City 9 and take her to The Human Collective main medical facility on Disc City 12."

"I'm going with her," Kyle said. "She's under my protection."

"Negative," the automaton on the right said. "Agent Kyle Mathis is not authorized to accompany the patient to Disc City 12. Order 3382, issued by Director Clavin. Agent Mathis must remain on

Disc City 9.”

"Bullshit!" Kyle shouted. The automatons repeated the message in unison, clearly not dissuaded. "Agent Perry is my responsibility. She is now under *my* protection!"

"Under order 3382, this is not permitted," the robot on the left said. "Agent Perry is now in the care of The Human Collective Medical Unit 3. She will be accompanied by a security unit to initiate and secure the transfer." Kyle's shoulders dropped as he realized that there would be no way to change their minds. If he tried, they'd likely resort to force to stop him.

Kyle had dealt with enough of the sentrons to know they possessed powerful weapons. He'd be dead before he got close, as any movement against the orders they'd been given would be perceived as a threat.

I just need to remain unseen, he decided. He would follow them to the transport ship and try to find a way on board without detection.

He couldn't explain it, but he felt a strong need to stay close to Elaina. Kyle planned to follow the medical unit from the shadows, but then another idea occurred to him.

"Fine," Kyle relented. "But my detachment will provide security up until Elaina reaches the transport. You've got to allow that much, at least."

"Affirmative," the medical robot on the left said. "Agent Kyle Mathis has been temporarily assigned as security escort. The assignment will end once the patient is on board the transport vessel."

Kyle didn't argue. He knew the way the automatons' protocols worked. They were programmed in a specific way, and he'd figured out how to circumvent the trickier protocols.

The two medical units carefully lifted Elaina and carried her on a makeshift stretcher that had been created from a pair of circular rods that the units produced from the medical kits on their backs. The rods held by one unit extended and connected to the rods held by the other, and an invisible barrier, much like a force field, was created between the rods.

Elaina was breathing deeper now that the medics had stabilized her, which brought Kyle a modicum of relief. If she were kept away from the danger, she'd survive the trip to the medical facility, where she'd likely make an expedient recovery.

Kyle and his detachment of sentrons flanked the medical units as the left the cover of the building. Kyle looked for the Trooviian guards that had been sent to kill Elaina, but the sentrons that he'd dispatched to handle them appeared to have eliminated the threat thoroughly. The bodies of the Trooviians still lay where they'd been killed, and the crowd that had been nearby had vanished. All that remained were the bodies of the dead. Kyle saw that the Trooviians, in their fury, had killed at least a half dozen people. He'd never seen that level of ferocity in the Trooviians before today. He continued to scan area as they headed west toward the nearest edge of the city.

They walked for nearly two miles before they were presented with another threat. Kyle had been watching for Trooviian soldiers, so when he saw a pair of Calvorans, he'd casually dismissed them. It wasn't until the Calvorans turned toward them that he realized they were in trouble. Calvorans weren't known to get their hands dirty. Kyle figured that whatever Elaina knew, Professor Goordaiin was desperate to keep The Collective from finding out. The Calvorans were garbed in black robes that draped over their frail bodies and each carried what looked like a communication device. He had guessed incorrectly as one of the Calvorans pointed what he'd assumed was a communication device at them and fired. The blast was little more than a thin beam of red light, but the blast tore through one of his sentrons' head with no effort. The blast obliterated the sentron's head, and it dropped to the ground, taken completely out of commission. Kyle hollered at his sentron unit to open fire.

Kyle could hardly believe his eyes as the Calvorans simply vanished when the sentrons began firing. He whirled around and spotted them on the opposite side of the street. They had access to short range teleporters! He couldn't believe it. He barked out another order, and half of the security detail turned to face the new threat, while the other half continued facing the Calvorans' original location. The sentrons fired again and, as Kyle predicted, the Calvorans disappeared. He heard the blasts before he could turn around. Another sentron fell, but this time the sentrons had found their mark as one of the Calvorans fell to the ground. The other barely regarded the dead Calvoran as it continued to fire at them.

The sentrons, now cut down to half their original number,

fired in return and completely obliterated the Calvoran. What had started as a unit of fourteen sentrons had been reduced to seven. Kyle had managed to avoid being hit, and he was relieved to see that Elaina and both medical sentrons were unharmed.

The remainder of the trip to the transport shuttle was uneventful, and Kyle was thankful for that. Unfortunately, he was approaching the most difficult part of the plan. How was he going to sneak on board? The shuttle was not very large. It looked as though it would barely accommodate the medical unit along with Elaina. He found an opening in his plan as the medical sentrons loaded Elaina in the transport and then hooked themselves in specialized stations made specifically for them. He watched as they appeared to go into hibernation and quickly jumped on board. Elaina had been laid on a bed suspended above the floor, and Kyle crawled underneath it. The sentrons he'd had with him had formed a perimeter around the transport, facing away from the interior. He sighed as the door rotated shut like a camera shutter and the transport lifted off.

***

Elaina blinked, trying to clear her vision. The pain in her left arm was still horrible, but it was no longer the blinding pain that had caused her to blackout in the first place. As her vision cleared, she found herself completely disoriented as she didn't recognize where she was. It didn't look like the foyer of the building she'd taken cover in.

Kyle was nowhere to be seen, nor were the robots that had accompanied him. She looked around and realized that she was inside a vehicle of sorts, as no normal room would jostle and shake. To her right, she noticed two robots painted white, but they were each confined in a small chamber.

Where was she? Where was she going? She started to panic as her mind wandered toward the worst-case scenario. Had Professor Goordaiin finally captured her? Had Kyle been killed? Why was she still alive?

She waved those questions away as she looked at the hibernating robots. Professor Goordaiin didn't have robots, as far as she knew. She'd been nearly everywhere in the laboratory and had never once seen any sign of a robot.

Elaina attempted to sit up but found that she was strapped to a

105

small cot. As she looked around, she noticed the cot seemed to be suspended in mid-air. Her vision whirled as she lifted her head. She'd been drugged, of that she was certain. Elaina laid her head back down and tried to sort through what she knew.

She was in a vehicle of some kind, pumped full of drugs and strapped to a cot. She was accompanied by two robots painted white, and on further inspection, she noticed a small red cross on each robot's shoulder. Elaina figured she was most likely in a medical transport, which meant she was no longer on Disc City 9! She'd made it off!

Elation flooded her as she started to feel safe for the first time since Professor Goordaiin had dragged her to the room where her father had died. The memory pained her, as she saw the light of recognition in his eyes just before he was disintegrated. He had finally remembered who she was.

Tears began to roll down the sides of her face as Elaina recounted the horrid memory. She hadn't had a moment to properly grieve and now seemed as good a time as any. It was her father who had encouraged her to join The Collective, and it was her father who had helped her continue through the difficult training with his frequent video messages. She had been nearing graduation day when his Alzheimer's began to eat away at his memory of her. When she saw him again, he had no idea who she was. The doctors who were caring for him managed to stop the disease's progression, but not before it had taken memories of his daughter from him. Now he was gone, and she was completely alone.

"Are you okay?" a voice asked. Elaina recognized the voice, but it took her a moment to place it.

"Kyle?" she managed as she stopped herself from sobbing.

"Why are you crying?" he asked. Elaina watched as he crawled out from under her cot and knelt beside her. What was he doing under there?

"What are you doing?" she asked.

"They weren't going to let me come with you," he said as if that explained everything.

"What?"

"The medical units," he replied. "They were going to leave me in that city while they took you away. I couldn't let you out of my sight. Two medic sentrons weren't going to be able to protect you by themselves."

"But," she began. "I don't understand. Why does that matter?"

"You're a fellow agent," Kyle said. "You're important."

She noticed he'd begun to blush a little, though it was difficult to tell with his dark complexion.

"But why are you hiding under my cot?"

"Well, once they started to cart you away I convinced them to let me escort you to the transport ship. After they loaded you inside, I slipped in. I…uh… I was under orders to stay on Disc City 9 by Director Clavin."

"You disobeyed an order? What were you thinking?"

"I know," Kyle said, lowering his eyes. "You're the first person I've had contact with in a long time. I've been surrounded by sentrons for several years, and you have no idea how lonely that is. They don't feel. They don't care. There just… there."

"But you don't even know me," Elaina protested. He was acting irrationally. He had jeopardized himself to ensure her safety, but he had absolutely no obligation to do so.

"I know that," he said, looking her in the eyes. "But there is something about you that I can't explain. You're important, that's for sure. I just can't shake the feeling that you're the most important person I've met. What was Professor Goordaiin after?"

"I… I know what he's really up to," she said after a moment of hesitation. "He doesn't want to save us. I'm sorry, but I can't say any more than that."

"And he wants to keep you quiet," Kyle said, nodding slightly. "It must be something really damaging. Something really, really bad."

"It is," she said. She didn't want to say anymore. Tears began to well up in her eyes as her thoughts returned to her father.

"Well," Kyle said as he stood up completely. "Then we'll just have to make sure you tell The Collective. I never really trusted the Calvorans anyway. They always seem to know what you're thinking."

Chapter 17

Devin and Ryve slowed down after an hour without incident. They'd lost the Millipede and figured they were safe, or as safe as they could be in that hostile environment. They had decided to take turns riding Devin's robotic horse. Despite wearing the BSS rig, the both of them had started to fatigue after running for as long as they had. Devin had never run for longer than five minutes, and they had run for over an hour straight.

At the moment Ryve was astride the mechanical steed, leading Devin further east. It had occurred to him that he hadn't eaten in over twenty-four hours. He'd gone longer without food before, but he wasn't feeling the pangs of hunger. He marveled at the BSS rig's capabilities. He would need to eat at some point, he was sure, but for now, he only needed to worry about getting some water. He may not have been hungry, but he was certainly thirsty.

"We need water," Devin called to Ryve. Ryve looked over his shoulder at Devin and gave a slight nod.

"No water here," Ryve said as he looked around. They were walking through the streets of Houston's ruins. The dilapidated buildings seemed to be pressing in closer as Devin began to contemplate where to find water. He'd built in a filtration system in his horse, but he still needed to fill it with water. It couldn't filter water out of the air.

"There should be a river nearby," Devin said. He tried to recall where he'd seen the filthy body of water, but it seemed like an eternity since he'd last been there. He then remembered the bay to the east that opened into the ocean.

"If we keep going the same direction we'll reach the bay. There'll be plenty of water there, and I can filter it," Devin said. Ryve nodded in apparent agreement.

As the pair continued through the heart of Houston, they began to feel as though they were being watched. Devin knew Bandits liked to hole up inside the ruined buildings, and more than one hapless wanderer had stumbled straight into an ambush. He began feeling claustrophobic as the buildings seemed to press in on both sides. His heart began to race as he scanned the buildings, looking for any sign of movement. He drew the Trooviian rifle when he detected a flicker of movement in a blasted-out skyscraper on his right. Ryve took notice of Devin's action and drew his weapon as well.

Devin and Ryve slowed their pace as they continued to search the surrounding area. Devin was hoping his eyes had played tricks on him. Perhaps the local Bandit tribes had fled after Disc City 6 crashed and subsequently exploded. The Bandits, while barbaric and primal, weren't inherently stupid. They knew the dangers that fire presented on the surface and would have certainly vacated the area when the disc city began its fiery descent. Devin hoped that was the case, anyway.

Out of the corner of his eye, Devin saw movement in the building to his left. His heart raced faster. Were they surrounded? He didn't like that possibility. If they were indeed surrounded, then they'd managed to walk straight into an ambush. Their odds of survival would be slim if this were true. To his dismay, Devin caught sight of a Bandit in the window where he'd first spotted movement. He didn't hesitate, which was unusual for him, as he leveled his weapon in the Bandit's direction and opened fire. The Bandit screeched as the blast tore a hole through its gut. A second shot tore off half of its face. Chaos erupted seconds afterward.

Ryve immediately jumped off the robotic horse and fired as Bandits poured out of the surrounding buildings. There was at least a dozen in all. Devin ducked behind a massive slab of concrete that had embedded itself in the street. A rebar spear glanced off the concrete mere inches from his head. He ducked out and fired as he saw a Bandit racing toward him, no more than ten feet away. Ryve was trying to dodge spears and even a crossbow bolt. Devin saw as a thrown spear caught Ryve in the upper thigh of his right leg. Ryve barely seemed to notice.

The noise from the Bandits was deafening as they screeched and hollered. Devin fired several more times into the throng of Bandits that had tried to surround Ryve. Ryve had taken down three Bandits who'd gotten too close with the side of his rifle, bludgeoning them to death. He'd left his flank exposed, and a Bandit took the opportunity to jab its spear into his thick hide. Ryve roared in pain as he whirled toward the creature. The Bandit was still holding the spear when Ryve turned and had been thrown off its feet. Ryve stomped down on its head before it could roll out of the way, crushing its skull like an egg. He grabbed the spear protruding under his right armpit and yanked it out.

Devin dropped his rifle when a Bandit hit him across the side of the head with its rebar spear. He hadn't noticed Bandit as it had approached from his right, circling around the slab of concrete Devin had adopted as cover. Devin barely had time to roll out of the way before the Bandit slammed the spear down into the ground, having meant to skewer him. He struggled to free his blade from its holster as the Bandit stabbed at him again. He rolled the opposite direction and managed to free his blade in the process. His vision was doubled from the blow to the head, and he had only nicked the Bandit's leg when he swung his blade at it. The Bandit hesitated as it looked at the superficial wound, giving Devin a chance to swing again. This time the blade connected solidly against the Bandit's other leg, cutting through the bone and coming out the other side before sinking into the leg he'd initially nicked. He got to his feet as the Bandit fell over, howling in pain. Devin slashed its throat as it clutched the amputated limb.

Ryve had killed two more Bandits, firing several shots and connecting on every one of them. The Bandits fell to the ground, riddled with massive holes. He and Devin had narrowed the Bandits' numbers down from a dozen to less than a handful. He spotted at least three that had backed away across the street and another near Devin just before it had its head cloven in two by Devin's rusty blade. Devin picked up his rifle and aimed at one of the remaining Bandits. He fired, but nothing happened. The Bandits stopped their retreat when they noticed the weapon's failure. Ryve knew what it meant. Devin had expended the energy cell within the rifle and hadn't known it. Ryve knew by the flashing red light on top of his own rifle that its energy cell was also nearly depleted.

Devin dropped his rifle and ducked back behind the concrete slab. He missed his harpoon gun, which was still attached to the Millipede that had attacked them that morning. It was shaping up to be another terrible day. He was reduced to his rebar spear and the rusty blade, neither of which would do much against the Bandits as they were out of throwing range. Ryve solved the problem by charging directly at the Bandits, taking their attention off him.

Devin took the opportunity that Ryve had given him and began moving to flank the Bandits. Ryve reached them first and bowled over one Bandit before slamming straight into another. Devin was there seconds later, his spear catching the last Bandit standing right in the throat. Ryve tore the Bandit under him to pieces as the only surviving Bandit struggled to get back on its feet. Ryve noticed and turned on it before it could get away. He grabbed it by the back of the head and smashed its face into the side of the building.

Devin yanked the spear out of the dying Bandit's torn throat and, after running back to retrieve his dropped rifle, walked back toward his mechanical steed. He did his best to block out the gurgling sounds the Bandit was making, but he still felt as though he was going to vomit. Devin did not take any pleasure in the killing, and everywhere he looked he could see the ruined bodies. It was necessary, as the Bandits would surely have killed him, but Devin felt a mixture of nausea and guilt anyway.

As he approached his horse, Devin noticed something odd about the Bandits that had attacked them. The Bandits he had encountered in the past wore baggy clothing over their emaciated bodies and donned gas masks. The ones that had just attacked wore strips of cloth and leather, punctuated by rusty shards of metal, and not even one wore a mask of any kind. For the first time, Devin could see the Bandits' faces. They were barely even human anymore.

The mutations caused by the mixture of toxic fumes and radiation were extensive, as were the tumors that protruded from nearly every inch of exposed flesh. The most noticeable mutation, however, was their faces. Their noses were flatter than a typical human nose, and there were six nostrils on either side, more closely resembling gills. Their eyes also appeared to have a protective layer over them, much like a crocodile. They'd adapted grotesquely to the harsh environment, and Devin wondered if they could even be considered human.

Ryve came up alongside Devin, clutching at his side and the wound on his leg. Devin pulled his gaze away from the bodies littering the ground and noticed that the wound on Ryve's side was bleeding profusely. They would need to stop the bleeding quickly. He watched as Ryve pulled a wad of material from a pocket on his pants and stuffed it into the wound. Ryve then pulled what looked like dust from another pocket, spat on it, and then smeared it over the wadded material. The bleeding seemed to stop almost instantly.

"How long is that going to work?" Devin asked.

"Not long," Ryve grunted. "Need to make a fire to harden the paste. Paste will seal wound and speed healing."

"You're not going to be able to make a fire down here. Not with the fumes. It'll blow up in your face."

"Don't need big fire," Ryve snapped.

"Fine," Devin said, his hands held up in surrender. "But if it blows up it's your fault."

Ryve ignored Devin as he began to scrounge up dry, flammable material from the filthy street. There was plenty of debris, and it hadn't rained in weeks. After a moment of striking two rebar spears together, he produced a spark that instantly caught and grew into a small fire. Ryve quickly scooped up the burning debris and pressed it against the paste covering his wound. He hissed in pain as the fire did its job. Devin just stared. Ryve noticed his gaze, grunted and then climbed back on the horse.

"Well, ok," Devin said as he followed Ryve, shaking his head.

Chapter 18

Professor Goordaiin stormed out of his office, a mixture of rage and (as much as he hated to admit it) panic flooding him. The human bitch had managed to escape, again! Three squads of Trooviian enforcers *and* a pair of Calvoran assassins hadn't been enough to stop her!

How could one human woman get away from him? To make matters worse, Professor Goordaiin now had to contend with the sudden appearance of humanoid robots that had taken down his most powerfully equipped Trooviians with ease. Where had they come from? He had to know, and he suspected that The Collective was behind it.

He'd grossly underestimated the woman *and* The Collective.

As he stormed through the tunnel-like hallways, Professor Goordaiin nearly slammed into several scientists and laboratory technicians who'd exited one of the nearby labs. He ignored them as they collided with one another to avoid him. He was clearly emanating rage as his skin took on a reddish hue once again. He was completely lost in his thoughts, oblivious to the stares of the people around him.

The path he'd taken had led directly back to the room where his new eco generator prototype was located. He had that, at least, but for how long? If The Collective found out that Professor Goordaiin intended to use humans as fuel to keep it running, they'd flood the city with their entire military force. The mass homicide wouldn't help matters, either.

He didn't fear the humans, but he knew that they still outnumbered the Trooviians and Calvorans on Disc City 9, and he intended to avoid an all-out war if he could. He needed to figure out a way to stop Elaina and fast.

To make matters worse, Professor Goordaiin's psychic link with Elaina had been broken. The distance hadn't been too great, so he knew something else had interfered. How it was possible, he couldn't begin to fathom.

Had The Collective devised a way to block psychic signals? How could they? Human beings were only capable of the simplest psychic abilities, which was purely subconscious and unintentional. "The collective human consciousness," they'd called it. Unfortunately for them, Professor Goordaiin had managed to tap into this subconscious telepathic link and found he could, in most cases, move along the threads of psychic connection like a spider as long as he maintained contact with an initial link. From there he could climb into the minds of anyone nearby who knew the first point of contact with relative ease.

Professor Goordaiin's contact with humans was minimal, and thus made traveling along the collective subconscious difficult. Most of the humans he'd dealt with had no contact with the outside world. He knew what everyone inside the laboratory was thinking and what everyone was up to. He hadn't been able to control these people beyond minor suggestion, but he knew he'd succeed eventually. The human mind was weak compared to a Calvoran's, and they would eventually succumb to his will. When they did, he'd have nothing to fear from the inferior species, as their superior numbers would no longer matter. None of it would matter if he didn't stop Elaina, though.

The eco generator hummed as it continued to run, though it was in standby mode. Professor Goordaiin absent-mindedly ran his eight-fingered hand along its exterior as he walked over to the desk in the far corner of the room. He sat and let the hum of the eco generator lull him into a trance-like state. He let his mind wander as he tried to puzzle through his current conundrum.

Elaina had likely been taken to a transport shuttle, as her last reported location was very near the edge of the city. If she was on board, she could already be out of reach. It was a shame that the city didn't have any anti-air weapons. He could send out a detachment of aircraft to shoot down the transport shuttle, but The Collective was no doubt monitoring the airspace and would react. Let them, he decided. Why not let The Collective shoot down his aircraft? If Elaina's transport was shot down, he needn't care. His deployed aircraft wouldn't be traced back to him, of that he'd made sure. The pilots were expendable.

Professor Goordaiin rose from his chair and walked out of the room. He headed back toward his office and prepared to send the order. Once again, he prided himself in creating The Order of Proper Justice. They weren't a full-fledged military, but they would be enough to secure his legacy. He smiled as he initiated the order.

***

Elaina managed to remain conscious as the shuttle continued its flight. Kyle alternated between checking on her condition and looking out of the windows. He was anxious. Elaina couldn't blame him, as she felt it too. She was a fugitive and Kyle's actions could have made him a target as well. The sentrons unsettled her as they remained quiet and motionless. Had they already alerted The Collective that Kyle was on board? If they had, they didn't act to restrain him. They didn't move at all. Kyle wasn't paying any attention to them either.

Kyle sat on the floor next to Elaina's cot after staring out the window for several minutes. He was clearly tired and on edge. She silently berated him for putting himself in such a difficult position. She wasn't terribly surprised, though. She could tell he found her attractive because she caught him staring more than once. His actions hadn't been dictated by rational thought, but more likely by lust. *That's not fair*, Elaina thought. *I don't really know him. Maybe he really does feel like he needs to protect me for the greater good. Maybe he is as honorable as he claims. Or maybe he isn't. At least I'm safe, and I do appreciate the company.*

Elaina was starting to close her eyes as she felt the need for sleep, which was no doubt a side effect of the medication she was on when Kyle got back up and went back to the window. She looked at him, curiosity keeping her from dozing off. He just stared out the window silently, and in moments Elaina had drifted off. Her sleep was interrupted when Kyle shouted in alarm.

"We're being followed!" Kyle yelled, his voice quavering slightly.

"What?" Elaina asked. She wasn't completely awake and hadn't processed what he'd said.

"There are two aircraft coming up behind us," Kyle said. "They could be Collective Fighter Ships."

"What do we do?" Elaina cried in alarm. She was still strapped to the cot, and she immediately began looking for kind of escape hatch as she struggled against her bonds.

"We're trapped up here," Kyle said. "But if they are Collective Fighters, we should actually be ok. They might just be escorting us to the medical treatment facility."

"What if they're not?" Elaina asked. She was thinking about Professor Goordaiin. There was no way he'd just let her go. Was it possible that he had aerial units?

"I don't think they belong to The Collective," Kyle groaned. "Those aren't human technology."

"Shit! It's Professor Goordaiin!" Elaina cried. "It has to be! That bastard can't possibly know where we are! How did he find us?"

Kyle rushed over to her side. He struggled to release the straps that held her down and then another problem presented itself. There would normally be an escape hatch or even a primitive parachute, but it looked as if neither were intact on this shuttle. It wasn't uncommon for the resources used by humans to be poorly maintained. Funding and staffing for routine maintenance were in critically short supply. It was amazing the transport shuttle could even fly. The Collective had begun focusing all their resources on the sentrons, letting the less critical assets fall by the wayside.

"This is it. We're going to die, aren't we?" Elaina asked, her expression grim. "After everything, we're going to die in this shuttle."

"No," Kyle replied, a look of fierce resolve in his eyes. "I won't let that happen."

"What are we going to do?"

"I'm working' on it."

Elaina heard faint explosions and her panic had been renewed ten-fold. The ships were shooting at them!

"Oh shit!" Kyle yelled as he dove toward Elaina. He collided with her, and both fell to the floor. Elaina's injured arm flared with pain as she hit the floor. Kyle was trying to use his body to shield her. A second later the shuttle shook violently as the blasts from the fighter ships tore through the hull. Elaina felt herself become weightless as the shuttle went into a nose dive. She closed her eyes, bracing for impact.

∗∗∗

Professor Goordaiin listened to the communications between his dispatched fighters. He jumped up from his chair when one of the pilots confirmed they had made contact. The transport vessel had been hit and was plummeting toward the surface! Goordaiin was momentarily filled with joy as his biggest threat had been neutralized. He could finally get back to work! No more needless distractions and no more paranoia. A bonus was the lack of any Collective fighters.

Why hadn't they bothered to protect the shuttle? Had they not had the foresight to send an escort? As if in answer to his question, one of the pilots announced that several aircraft had been spotted heading toward them. It was no doubt the Collective. They were too late, and Professor Goordaiin cared little about the fates of his pilots. It made no difference if they managed to shoot down the Collective's fighters or were shot down themselves.

The voices over the communication channel confirmed their targets and moved to eliminate the threat. There came the triumphant cry of a direct hit and then shouts of alarm as one, and then the other, of the pilots had taken fire and had begun to crash. Well, at least they'd eliminated one of the Collective's fighters. Goordaiin would have preferred all of them eliminated, but the job was done, and all traces back to him had been erased. He could finally relax.

Goordaiin sat back down in his chair and closed his eyes.

A second later his eyes shot open. How could he be so foolish? What if Elaina survived the crash? The probability of survival was incredibly low, but it was not a chance Goordaiin wanted to take. She'd caused him enough grief already. It was also highly unlikely that she would survive long on the surface, but she'd already demonstrated a tenacity he'd never expected from the fragile human race. If she did manage to survive the wreck she could manage, through her seemingly vast pool of luck, to find transport to The Collective's headquarters.

Professor Goordaiin found himself with more than one enticing course of action. He could send his scouts to locate Elaina and eliminate her, or he could have her followed straight to The Collective. He could then launch a strike at the heart of his clandestine enemy before they ever had a chance to react! It was a messier solution to his problem, but he determined that the payoff was worth it. With The Collective out of the way, he would be free to pursue his vision without any more interference.

Goordaiin reestablished contact with his pilots and initiated the order. The woman was to be found and followed. The pilots were instructed to follow her until the location of The Collective's secret headquarters were located. At that point, they would return to the city, and a strike force would be mobilized after they eliminated her. Goordaiin grinned as he sat back in his chair.

Chapter 19

Devin and Ryve continued to make their way through the heart of Houston, wary of any other potential ambushes. They'd elected to move slower than before, scanning every possible hiding place. Houston's ruins were immense, and at times difficult to traverse as entire buildings blocked several blocks and more than once they had to backtrack. Devin was growing weary of walking and struggled to keep his vision in focus. The strike to the head he'd suffered in the ambush was making him feel as if he were in a fog. His head ached, and he could tell his equilibrium was off. He tripped over debris nearly constantly, but Ryve didn't seem to notice.

As the pair trudged through the ruins, they could feel their thirst growing. Dehydration would claim Devin long before Ryve succumbed, but both had become desperate. Ryve's wounds were making him fatigued and only added to his growing dehydration. Devin was starting to feel like he had before the BSS rig and couldn't begin to imagine how he'd ever managed to survive without it. His feet dragged as his legs felt heavier with each step. His throat hurt when he swallowed, and his eyes burned. The blistering sun didn't help.

Devin and Ryve took refuge in any shade they found to replenish their flagging reserves as much as possible. Devin began to regret not making a filtration system for the horse capable of drawing water out of the air as the humidity was growing worse every day. The air felt heavy, adding to the weight of his limbs and amplifying the heat. He felt his face burning under the sun and found himself ducking under any shade he found. He almost wished they'd come under attack again just to distract himself from the misery he was feeling. Ryve had remained quiet, but Devin could tell he was struggling as well. The Trooviians were subterranean in nature, so the oppressive sun had to be wearing on him even more.

Their luck changed when they came upon a rather large puddle of murky water that had been created by a broken water main. Devin used what little energy he had left to run over to the pool of water. He didn't dare drink it, no matter how much he wanted to. He waited instead for his steed, with Ryve still astride, to come up beside him. The headless steed stood stock still at the edge of the water. Devin pulled out the hose where the steed's head should have been and dipped the end into the murky pool. A low whirring sound emanated from his steed as it began to vacuum up the water and processed it through the filtration system. A reservoir on both of the steed's hind legs began filling with crystal clear water, and Devin realized he was starting to drool. Ryve tried to remove one of the reservoirs, but Devin abruptly stopped him.

"Don't remove that!" he shouted. Ryve glared at him. "We need to wait until it finishes. If we take it out now, it'll backfire and eject all the water back out of the hose… I haven't managed to fix that yet."

Ryve grumbled, but he obliged. The massive Trooviian stood and stared impatiently at the reservoir. After a moment, the whirring sound stopped, and the hose retracted back into the horse's body. Devin nodded at Ryve and then began removing the reservoir from the horse's right hind leg. Ryve did the same on the left.

The water was almost sweet as they drank greedily from the containers. Devin felt the cool liquid flow through his body as he gulped down the container's contents. Ryve was already done with his container and had jammed it back into the horse's leg.

"Do it again!" he barked at the mechanized steed.

"Easy!" Devin yelled. He didn't want Ryve to inadvertently damage the horse. "It has to wait before it can do it again!"

"Make it do it again!"

"I can't. The filtration system must purge before it's ready. It needs to recharge."

"How long?"

"Two minutes," Devin said as he lowered his voice. He began to feel uneasy. They were completely exposed as the stood out in the open. This would be another perfect place for an ambush. He was surprised they hadn't been attacked already. He heard metal clattering against concrete in one of the nearby buildings.

"Too long!" Ryve shouted.

"Quiet," Devin said in a hushed tone as he gestured to Ryve to lower his voice. Ryve cocked his head and then began to survey the area. The rifle had reappeared in his massive hands.

"Mine stopped working," Devin said, pointing at the weapon in Ryve's hand.

"Needs to recharge," Ryve growled. Devin laughed involuntarily. The Trooviian's response may not have been intended as sarcasm, but Devin took it that way anyway. Ryve just gave him a confused look.

"Sorry," Devin said once he stopped laughing. "I just didn't realize you were capable of humor."

"I wasn't being funny," Ryve grumbled, but he didn't pay Devin any more attention. His gaze continued to sweep the windows of the nearby buildings. Devin grabbed his own pilfered rifle and began pressing buttons. The weapon emitted a buzzing sound that turned into a whine. He took that as a sign that it was charging up.

"We're not alone," Ryve whispered. Devin's hair stood on end as he broke out in goosebumps. Despite the immense heat, he began to feel cold as a chill crept over him. The air was silent, the only sound coming from Devin and Ryve's heavy breathing. Whatever was around, it wasn't Bandits. Devin had dealt with enough of them to know that they would have begun shouting and screeching when they initiated their attack. They were also incredibly impatient.

A crashing sound emitted from behind them as something was knocked over in a nearby building. Devin and Ryve whirled around to face the noise. Out of the gloom, figures began to appear. They looked human, or rather like the Bandits, but they were quiet and moved at a laborious pace. Devin silently cursed himself. This was perhaps the fifth time he'd ignored his survival instincts since he'd met Deekin and Ryve. He should have known better than to rush straight toward the water. Now he and Ryve were being penned in. On the far side of the pool of water, he could see an opening between two buildings. It had been a road, but the debris blocked all but a human-sized gap. Ryve would be hard pressed to make it through, let alone the mechanical steed.

"Shit!" Devin hissed as he watched the figures approaching. "Wait. What the hell?"

The shapes gained clarity as the first of them walked into the sunlight. It may have been human at one time, but the tumorous growths and mutations robbed it of any semblance of humanity. The creature's head was horribly misshapen and only had a blank patch of flesh where eyes should have been, dotted by tumors. It seemed to be sniffing the air as it approached them. Devin's heart began to thud in his chest. He'd never seen anything like this before. For a moment, he considered calling out. Maybe these things were docile? He changed his mind as the hideous thing forced a strangled cry through its mangled throat and began running.

"Kill them!" Ryve yelled as he took aim. "What you are waiting for?"

"Son of a bitch!" Devin yelled as he shouldered his rifle. More of the things had begun streaming out of the building. Devin pulled the trigger… and nothing happened. He tried to fire three more times before Ryve reached over, flipped a small switch on the side of the rifle, and then began firing his own weapon again. The nearest creature fell in a tangle of body parts. The other creatures ignored their fallen comrade. Devin pulled the trigger again and was relieved, and nauseated, as the creature nearest him nearly exploded at the waist.

The mutant creatures were clumsy as they ran blindly into oncoming fire, tripping over themselves and ramming into one another. The erratic movements made it difficult to line up a shot and Devin began firing wildly, hoping to score a hit. Out of the twelve shots, he'd fired, only half that number hit. Limbs were sheared off, and tumors ruptured, but the creatures barely seemed to notice. One of the things had managed to avoid being shot as it slammed straight into Ryve's chest. The massive Trooviian held his ground as the creature collided with his girth. The creature fell backward and hit its head on the pavement. It didn't immediately get up, giving Ryve enough time to stomp on its chest.

They had killed, or mortally wounded, at least a dozen of the things. The wave of creatures tapered off as the last of them exited the building. How long had they been waiting? Devin took a chance as he looked around at the other buildings. None of the creatures were coming out of the surrounding buildings. They could make their retreat if it came down to that. Ryve was making short work of the creatures advancing on them, but Devin could see that the barrel of Ryve's rifle was beginning to heat up. Devin fired several more shots of his own, but he didn't care to stay in the area any longer.

"We need to go!" Devin yelled. Ryve just nodded in reply as he fired three more shots in quick succession. Then he turned and ran, clutching his wounded side, toward the horse. Devin followed suit and immediately wished he'd acted earlier. He was tired of walking while Ryve rode the horse. At least they'd been able to get water, but both reservoirs had been drained, and they hadn't been able to refill them. They would just have to continue east, then.

Ryve climbed atop the robotic horse and spurred it into motion. Devin ran alongside as they skirted the edge of the filthy pond toward the small opening on the opposite side. He glanced behind him and began running faster. The mutant creatures hadn't stopped their pursuit. Ryve noticed Devin's change in pace and willed the horse to move faster. He began to run ahead of Devin. Devin wanted to yell out, but Ryve yanked him up onto the horse before he'd had a chance. They raced toward the opening.

Chapter 20

As the shuttle plummeted to Earth, the medical sentrons came out of hibernation and sprang into action. Elaina didn't notice that they'd woken up until one grabbed hold of Kyle's jacket and yanked him off her. She reached out toward him, but the other sentron grabbed her and wrapped its arms around her shoulders.

"Execute emergency protocol," both sentrons said in unison. Both robots repeated the phrase as they wrapped their legs around Elaina and Kyle's midsections. Seconds later Elaina found herself encased in a semi-translucent shell. Kyle was similarly encased. They stared at each other as the sentrons continued to repeat the phrase. She wanted to shut her eyes before impact, but she couldn't look away from Kyle's frightened countenance. He was as terrified as she was. She only hoped that the medical units' attempt to protect them was enough. A moment later the shuttle slammed violently into the surface and the pair, still encased by the medical sentrons, bounced around the hull. Elaina blacked out from the force of the impact, as did Kyle.

Elaina couldn't immediately see anything as she regained consciousness, but she could hear the popping and hissing of electricity. Her vision began to return, but she could see little in the gloom. The shuttle must have ended up on its side as light streamed in on only one side. The windows had been blown out, and chunks of glass littered the wreckage. She looked around, searching for Kyle. She found him in the far corner, still encased in the protective shielding, but pinned under twisted metal. He was still unconscious.

The pain in Elaina's left arm returned and threatened to plunge her back into the blackness, but she clenched her teeth and fought through it. She needed to free herself from the protective shell and check on Kyle. She hoped he was okay. Her worries were lessened as he began to stir. His eyes opened and locked onto hers. He began to bang against the shell as he tried desperately to break free. After a moment, Kyle calmed down and began examining the protective casing. The sentron was dead (not that it had ever truly been alive) and would no longer respond to voice commands. The oxygen levels in the cocoon would be depleted in no time, and he would begin to suffocate.

Elaina's own protective casing didn't show any sign of retracting, and she began to worry that it never would. What would the point be, then? If this was the way The Collective intended to rescue crash victims, why would the protective cocoon remain shut? Anger and fear began to flood her senses as claustrophobia began to set in. The very pod that was supposed to save her life was going to become her tomb.

Kyle was finally calm enough to begin searching for any kind of seal or weakness in the shell. He dug out a knife and looked at it. It was luck that he hadn't been impaled on it in the crash. He found what he thought to be a seal and began working his blade into it, hoping to dig the blade in deep enough to pry the shell open. Finally, the blade sank in, and he started to pry, though he made sure to keep from exerting too much force. He didn't want to snap the blade off. The shell resisted for a moment and just when he thought the blade would snap, the shell finally opened. Kyle immediately regretted it as he sucked in the toxic air.

Elaina watched as Kyle began coughing. She hadn't given any thought to the hazardous atmosphere, and apparently neither had Kyle. She watched as he pulled the cloth of his hood up over his mouth and nose. It was no gas mask, but it at least helped him quit coughing. She could see his eyes watering just before he pulled his goggles on. Elaina immediately wondered what she would do if she got out of the protective casing. The hood on her collar was damaged. She had tried to bring it back up, and it made a whining noise but did nothing. Perhaps a mask could be found amongst the wreckage.

Kyle started toward the cocoon holding Elaina and began working at the seal but halted when he saw her gesturing for him to stop. He couldn't hear her, but he realized what she was trying to say when she pointed to her face. He nodded and began searching the hull for any kind of mask. The transport had been for medical purposes so it would make sense that a breathing apparatus of some kind would be on board. Perhaps the pilots had been wearing one, or had one in the cockpit? Why wouldn't they? Transports had crashed before, and The Collective was fully aware of the atmospheric conditions on the surface. Kyle returned to Elaina's cocoon and tried his best to explain that he was going to search the pilots. He didn't want her to think he was abandoning her. The message seemed to get across as Elaina nodded.

Kyle headed toward the back of the hull and squeezed through a jagged hole in the side of the transport that wasn't blocked by earth. He looked around as his head poked out into the open. The landscape was as he had imagined. The terrain was windswept and barren. He could see the edge of what had once been a massive river, but little else. There was no sign of life anywhere. He realized that he'd half expected to see Collective units coming to their rescue.

The transport vessel had taken surprisingly little damage in the crash and Kyle was relieved to see that it hadn't caught fire. It might have even been possible that the pilots had survived. He pulled himself free and ran toward the cockpit, a mixture of hope and dread waging war in his mind. Dread gave way to sadness as he saw the pilots. The front of the transport had completely caved in, pinning both the pilots between a bulk of twisted metal and their seats. Blood filled the cockpit. The pilots were clearly dead.

Elaina tried to remain as calm as possible as she waited for Kyle to return. He'd seemed to indicate that he was looking for a mask for her, but the hunt was taking far longer than she liked. She did her absolute best to fight off the claustrophobia, but the air seemed to be thinning, and the cocoon felt like it was shrinking. Her breathing came in ragged gasps, and her heart thudded in her chest painfully as she began to suffer a panic attack. She nearly blacked out when Kyle reappeared. He was wearing a gas mask and holding another in his hand as he began prying her pod open with his knife. A pair of rifles were also slung over his shoulders.

The protective casing slid open, and Kyle immediately pressed the gas mask to Elaina's face. She grabbed his hand as he held the mask on. He thought she would try to tear it away in her panic, but the touch was almost tender. It only lasted a second and then she was working to pull the straps over her head. She was still struggling to manage the task one-handed when Kyle began to help her. He then helped her tighten the straps and pulled her carefully out of the cocoon. Her wounded arm seemed to be doing better. Kyle felt relieved, though only for a moment.

A fire sparked to life in the hull behind Elaina's cocoon and began to grow rapidly. The pair ran back toward the opening where Kyle had escaped the first time. He helped her out and quickly squeezed himself through. Once they were outside they saw smoke billowing out of the wreckage and flames began to appear. Elaina and Kyle put some distance between themselves and the burning wreck just in case it exploded, though neither of them really expected it too. The pain in Elaina's arm forced her to stop running.

"I didn't see a rescue team!" Kyle yelled. The mask was muffling his voice, though not as much as the cocoon had.

"I'm not sure there's going to be one," Elaina replied, her voice noticeably quieter than his. "You don't have to yell, you know."

"Sorry," Kyle replied sheepishly. "Why don't you think there'll be a rescue team?"

"Professor Goordaiin would make sure if it," Elaina said. Her shoulders drooped as she looked around. She stared upward, hoping to see some kind of ship, but she saw nothing other than the underside of Disc City 9. She hadn't really realized just how massive it was.

"What is it that he's so desperate to hide?" Kyle asked. "Why is he after you?"

"It's because of what I know. I saw what he's really planning, and if The Collective knows…" She was cut off as the transport ship exploded behind them. Elaina and Kyle dove to the ground to avoid flying debris.

They'd gotten far enough away that the heat was minimal, but the threat of an errant shard of metal impaling them was still present. A flaming chunk of steel streaked past Kyle's head when he stood back up. An inch to the left and he would have been decapitated. Kyle dropped back to the ground.

"Holy shit!" he yelled. Elaina echoed the exclamation.

"Somebody probably saw that," Kyle said as he slowly got back up. "We need to get out of here."

"Where are we going to go?"

"I'm not sure, but we can't stay here," Kyle said as he shrugged. "There's no telling' what might have seen that."

"I don't know how far I can go like this," Elaina said, pointing at her injured arm.

"I don't think we have a choice," Kyle replied. "We'll die if we stay out in the open. We need to find shelter."

***

The Collective's remaining aircraft quickly dispatched the hostile Trooviian crafts and began flying low to the surface. They'd seen the medical transport go down and had been ordered to search for survivors. The sentrons on board the medical craft should have deployed their emergency shields over the passengers, but there was no guarantee that the shields would maintain their integrity after the fall.

The ships flew in large spirals, scanning as much of the surface as they could. Moments later, the downed medical craft was spotted. It had erupted in a massive blaze and pieces had been thrown in every direction after it had exploded. Scans of the area failed to show any sign of life. The Collective's search team concluded that the passengers had died in the explosion. It was starting to get dark, and any further search seemed unlikely to produce desirable results. The crafts turned back toward their main base and left.

Elaina and Kyle hadn't seen the aircraft and didn't know a search party had been dispatched. They'd managed to hole up in service tunnel that accessed an old subway station. The dark tunnels offered much-needed refuge from the oppressive sun, but there was no telling what else lurked underground. Kyle hadn't spent time on the surface, as he'd only graduated from The Collective's academy weeks before Elaina and had spent the entirety of his post-graduate time on Disc City 9.

Moments after The Collective's ships had departed more of Professor Goordaiin's Trooviian crafts arrived to investigate. The pilots found the wreck and proceeded to land. The wreckage had finally burnt out and no longer present a risk. The Trooviian search party exited their crafts, along with a pair of Calvoran Scouts, to begin the arduous task of tracking Elaina and Kyle.

They'd been given strict orders to avoid detection. The team split in two, one team staying with the ships while the other team tracked down the fugitives. If Elaina managed to locate another transport, or signal for a rescue, the tracking team would signal their second team, and the ships would be in the air within minutes.

***

The tunnel was black as pitch, making navigation next to impossible. Elaina couldn't even see her hand when she brought it in front of her face. Kyle's goggles had been fitted with night-vision; however, and he led Elaina further down. She'd never been underground and found her claustrophobia rapidly returning. Faint sounds echoed loudly in the tunnels. Her breathing even sounded unnaturally loud down here. Kyle didn't seem terribly concerned, though.

They finally stopped their trek after twenty minutes. The abandoned subway would keep them out of the elements for the night, and the air was significantly cleaner underground. Kyle and Elaina decided to remove their masks and were relieved when they breathed mostly clean air. Kyle elected to build a small fire since the temperature was continuing to drop. He didn't want Elaina to freeze, especially after the wound she'd taken and the medical transport's subsequent crash. The fire provided enough light to ease Elaina's panic.

Elaina huddled as close to the fire as she could. Kyle had tried to give her a respectable amount of space but found himself drawing nearer as the temperature dropped further. After an hour, the pair were huddled against one another, sharing the warmth of the fire.

"Thank you for everything," Elaina said after a period of silence. "I would have died without you."

"I saw you running' from those Trooviians and knew you were in trouble," Kyle answered. "I hate to admit it, but I've never really trusted those things."

"I think the Calvorans are the real problem," Elaina muttered. She went quiet again as she revisited the waking nightmare she'd endured in the Eco-Generator lab. The pain of losing her father, the look in his eyes just before he died, all hit her at once.

She broke down, finally allowing herself to feel grief for the first time since the incident. Kyle felt every cell in his body yearning to touch her, to comfort her. He hesitantly wrapped an arm around her. He was relieved—and a bit surprised—when she didn't pull away.

Elaina tried to explain why she was so upset, but the sobs prevented her from forming a coherent sentence. Kyle just held her as she continued to cry. After a while, she finally calmed down enough to tell him what had happened.

"So, Professor Goordaiin does have an ulterior motive!" Kyle exclaimed after Elaina told him about Goordaiin's plan to use human beings as fuel and his involvement with Disc City 6. "No wonder he was trying to capture you. If The Collective found out, he'd be shut down and replaced. Hell, he'll even be executed."

"My father was always nervous around him," Elaina said sadly, staring into the weak flames of the campfire... "I think he sensed something was off."

The mention of her father caused the tears to flow once more.

"Shhh…" Kyle said as he gently stroked the side of her face. He gazed into Elaina's large brown eyes. "We'll make them pay for what they did. I swear it."

Elaina smiled, though tears remained in her eyes. Kyle slid his hand down her arms and recoiled when she flinched.

"I-I'm sorry," Kyle said. "I forgot about your arm."

"It's okay," Elaina said. "We can't stay here."

Kyle looked around in the gloom. He couldn't see anything approaching, and he began to feel his body fighting to sleep. He was exhausted and knew that Elaina must be as well.

"I think we should be okay," Kyle said. Part of him didn't want to keep moving. He just wanted to sit by her side and talk to her, to forget about everything else. "We need to get some rest, or we won't make it to the Collective."

Elaina opened her mouth to argue but instead nodded. She couldn't deny the fatigue that had begun to set in. The very idea of sleeping was terrifying, but there was truth to Kyle's words. They'd only get so far before their bodies gave out. "Fine," she said at last. "But we can't sleep for long. Just enough to keep us on our feet."

He watched as she began to create a makeshift bed out of debris and—after a moment's struggle—her jacket. Kyle moved to lie beside her, not removing his own jacket. The temperature was continuing to drop, and they would need to huddle close to share their body heat, at least that was Kyle's justification for lying right beside her. Elaina didn't seem to protest. In fact, she seemed to already be fast asleep.

Kyle didn't immediately fall asleep, despite his exhaustion. His mind kept circling around Elaina and how much he wanted to hold her. Would she freak out if he kissed her? Probably, but he wanted so badly to do it. He watched her sleeping form, noting the curves of her body and the gentle rise and fall of her chest as she breathed. His face grew hot with shame. How could he think that way? After everything she went through, how could he entertain the idea of being intimate with the woman?

His internal struggle waged for some time before he finally fell asleep as well.

***

Professor Goordaiin's search team approached the stairwell leading down to the substation. The human woman and her male companion had gone this way, of that the Trooviian scouts were sure. They debated for a moment about descending the stairs. Would they compromise their position if they did so? If the two humans were in the substation and not further down the track, the Trooviians would likely be spotted. One of the scouts elected to do a quick check to determine whether their quarry was lying in wait at the base of the stairs.

The scout slowly crept down the stairs, his superb night vision allowing him to see in the pitch-black darkness of the substation. So far, he saw no sign of the human pair. He ventured further and spied a glimmer of light down the track, flickering in the distance. He surmised that the humans had traveled to the nearest substation from his immediate location. The scout ascended the staircase and waved his companions forward.

Once below the surface, the Trooviian scouts ventured halfway down the track. It had been years since they'd been below the surface and they realized how much they'd missed it. This was their territory. This was where they thrived. The scouts decided to lie in wait, careful to avoid detection.

When the humans decided to move again, the scouts would continue their stealthy pursuit. They were relieved that the orders had changed from a search and destroy mission to a reconnaissance mission.

The Trooviians generally didn't harbor any ill feelings toward the humans, but they had no choice when it came to their orders. Goordaiin would have them eliminated if they disobeyed. Once again, the Trooviians found themselves in the unenviable position of being subservient to the cruel Calvorans.

Chapter 21

The path was narrower than Devin had estimated. It took significant effort for Devin and Ryve to get the mechanical steed through. Ryve tried to follow and got stuck. He must have been claustrophobic because he began to panic, which only served to wedge him tighter, but a moment later he managed to get through.

Devin had an easier time, as he was significantly smaller than the massive Trooviian and the mechanical horse. He was relieved to see that the grotesque mutations that had been in pursuit couldn't make it through. They didn't seem to have the cognitive ability to realize that only one of them could go at a time. The beasts jostled against each other and got so tightly wedged that Devin could hear bones pop and crack like dried twigs. Ryve decided to fire into the throng of wedged bodies, effectively sealing the passage.

"What were those?" Ryve asked, staring at the jumble of mangled bodies, his chest heaving as he regained his breath.

"I don't know," Devin rasped, equally winded. "I've never seen that before."

The pair turned away and continued heading east. Devin took advantage of Ryve's momentary distraction to climb aboard the mechanized horse. Ryve glowered at him but said nothing as they headed away from the courtyard of death. Devin couldn't help grinning, greatly pleased with himself. He feared Ryve less than when they'd first met and no longer worried about repercussion. Ryve may have been irritated with being forced to walk, but he wouldn't shoot Devin in the back. At least Devin hoped he wouldn't.

The broken asphalt was difficult to travel over, the mechanical steed stumbling more than once. Devin took pride in the machine's construction as it expertly corrected itself and adjusted its path to an easier route. It was learning, which Devin had never expected. Scavengers were skilled mechanics, that was undeniable, but Devin was something more. He had an affinity with machines, the depths of which even he didn't understand. Artificial Intelligence wasn't a rare technology, but it was always imperfect. What Devin's steed exhibited was something more. The robot behaved like a real, living creature.

"Any idea where we're going?" Devin asked. Ryve had indicated that he knew where Goordaiin was located, but the exact location was never mentioned. All that had been said was Disc City 9. Ryve responded by pulling a small round disc from his belt and pressed an unseen button. A topographic map was projected several inches above the disc, a bright dot indicating their current location. Devin looked at the projection, noting a small dot labeled Disc City 6 behind them. To the east was nothing for miles and then, on the very edge of the display, a dot labelled Disc City 9. The city was located near the border of Texas and Louisiana, at least two days away by foot, if they kept a rapid pace.

"Wonderful," Devin grumbled. He'd hoped the journey would end sooner.

"We walk as long as it takes," Ryve growled. "We don't stop."

Devin's stomach growled, seemingly in response to Ryve's voice. He hadn't eaten in at least two days and was surprised he hadn't noticed sooner. The BSS rig had made extremely efficient use of the nutrients from his last meal. He would need to eat again soon, though.

"I'm hungry," Devin said. "We need to find food."

"What we eat, huh?" Ryve asked, clearly annoyed. "Dirt?"

"If I starve to death you'll be on your own!" Devin snapped back.

"Fine," Ryve grumbled. "We find Bandit. You eat that."

"The hell I will! I'm not a cannibal you sick sonofabitch!"

"Well, what do humans eat, then?"

"Not other humans!" Devin yelled. He had started warming up to the Trooviian, but the creature was starting to piss him off again.

"Then what?" Ryve questioned. "Millipede?"

"Well," Devin hesitated. "I-I suppose… but that would mean finding and killing one! I don't know about you, but I would rather not take my chances against one of those things. I've seen enough of those monsters to last a lifetime."

"We hunt Millipede, then," Ryve said, allowing little room for argument. His tone was that of finality. Devin began to panic

"Hunt a millipede? Are you insane?"

"You need to eat," Ryve stated matter-of-factly.

"But a Millipede?"

"Not anything else around."

"Yeah, but, a Millipede?" Devin reiterated, his voice cracking. He hoped that Ryve would see the flaw in his plan. Apparently, the Trooviian missed it. Ryve didn't respond. He tucked the holographic map back into his belt and continued walking. Devin threw his hands in the air in frustration and reluctantly followed.

"Shit. I guess we're going hunting."

***

Devin wasn't an expert on the Millipedes so trying to hunt one was proving immensely difficult. He didn't know how to spot their trail since they were primarily subterranean, nor did he know where, or when, they usually hunted. The only thing he could think of was to try to bring a Millipede to him, which put him in harm's way, yet again. That plan didn't sit well with him, so he continued trying to come up with another one. Ryve didn't seem to have much of an idea either.

Devin and Ryve continued their trek east, making their way out of the most congested part of the ruined city. They were closer to the outskirts and travel had grown easier, but they were now more exposed. Devin grew more uneasy with every step, expecting to be ambushed at any moment. Ryve picked up on Devin's unease and opted to carry his weapon at the ready, just in case. Devin followed suit, though his hunger had begun to affect his strength. The rifle felt heavy in his hands, and for one horrible moment, Devin worried that the BSS rig was failing. He quickly discounted this as he wasn't beginning to choke on the fumes in the air, which he was sure would happen if the rig stopped working.

Ryve appeared to be feeling the beginning effects of hunger as well, the front of his rifle dipping lower and lower as they marched on. Either he was fatigued, or he was growing complacent, but Devin doubted the latter as Ryve's body language suggested he was on edge. They needed to eat and soon. If they were ambushed now, Devin doubted they'd be able to fight off their attackers.

"We need to find a better cover," Devin said. "I don't like being out in the open like this."

"Me either," Ryve said. "Not many choices, though."

"Why?"

"Need food," Ryve said. "Food find us."

"And if it does?" Devin asked. "We don't have the strength to fight off an attack. We're going to be food for whatever finds us. Not the other way around."

"We save strength for a fight," Ryve answered cryptically.

"What strength?!"

"BSS help with adrenaline," Ryve said.

"What?" Devin asked, intrigued by the response. "The rig helps with adrenaline? How?"

"Pumps more during the fight and saves energy when body gets low," Ryve answered. "Like battery in rifle." Ryve held up his rifle to punctuate his point.

"Oh!" Devin exclaimed. He stared down at the rig on his chest in amazement. He'd yet to understand the rig's full capabilities. He still didn't like the idea of being ambushed, but he realized that he could use the rig's hidden capabilities to his advantage. Anything that tried to attack would be expecting an easy meal. The advantage could theoretically shift in Devin and Ryve's favor rapidly as their attacker would be caught off guard by an offensive. Devin smiled, and for the first time in his life, he almost welcomed an attack.

Almost.

***

The pair continued to march along the broken asphalt, waiting impatiently for something edible to rear its head. Devin was growing restless as the sun began to set, taking the heat of the day with it. The chill would put them at an even greater disadvantage, but Millipedes typically attacked at night. They could find shelter to escape the cold and still draw a Millipede to them. The last time they had been attacked they'd had a fire burning. It was possible that the smell of smoke had attracted the Millipede.

Devin relayed the theory to Ryve, who merely nodded before searching for a suitable place to bunker down. They'd obviously need a place that could withstand an attack long enough for them to kill the Millipede while simultaneously sheltering them from the freezing wind. Ryve found what had once been an electronics shop that had held up well compared to the buildings that surrounded it. There wouldn't be much inside that they could burn, but Devin began forming another idea.

With enough material, Devin could set up an early warning system from the contents of the old store, so they weren't caught completely off guard. He silently congratulated Ryve on finding the place. Ryve was already checking the perimeter of the building in search of any sign of life or traps, Devin wasn't sure which. When nothing presented itself, Ryve waved him over.

Devin quietly pulled the door open, which was thankfully unlocked, and peered inside. He squinted through the gloom, trying desperately to see anything in the fading sunlight. Nothing moved, and he couldn't see anything lying in wait among the shelves of electronics that had long been outdated. Satisfied that they wouldn't be attacked, Devin quickly brought his horse inside. Ryve followed and shut the door behind them, enveloping them in near complete darkness. Devin stumbled and collided with a shelf of radio equipment when his vision left him.

"What the fuck?" Devin yelled out. "What did you do?"

"Closed door," Ryve said. "Need to block out wind."

"But now I can't see shit!" Devin shouted.

"Nothing else can, too," Ryve hissed. "I make a fire, then you see again."

Devin wasn't thrilled with being blind while Ryve tried to build a fire out of the old moldy instruction manuals. He felt completely vulnerable standing in the open, completely blind. His hearing rapidly heightened to take the place of his hindered sense. The change was disorienting. It was as if the store had come alive. Devin could hear dust settling around him, Ryve rubbing something together to create a spark, and even the constant whir of the mechanized horse's motor. Devin didn't even know that the motor made any noise until now. He'd always prided himself on how silent the horse had been.

The new sensation was frightening at first, but Devin quickly felt fear give way to excitement as he realized this must also be the BSS rig's handiwork. He was enjoying his newfound ability when he heard something very out of place. He heard voices, muffled, above him. They weren't alone in the building.

"Ryve," Devin whispered, though it sounded like he was shouting with his enhanced hearing. "Ryve, we're not alone."

"What?" Ryve said. Devin turned his head in the direction of the

Trooviian's voice. He began making his way toward Ryve, his hands out to make sure he didn't run into anything.

"Someone is upstairs," Devin said. He pointed upward, knowing the Trooviian could see in the dark. "I can hear them. I don't think they heard us, though."

"Bandits?"

"I doubt it," Devin said. The voices were hard to decipher, but he was sure that Bandits were incapable of being quiet. The voices sounded calm. As he continued to listen, he could detect a measure of intelligence in one of the voices' speech pattern. Measured responses and breaks in silence. He wasn't sure how to explain it.

"Then who?" Ryve asked.

"I'm not sure, but I think we should find somewhere else to bed down for the night. I'm not keen on sharing our sleeping quarters with someone else, especially without knowing what they are."

"We stay," Ryve argued. "Best place so far."

"We can find somewhere else," Devin urged.

"No," Ryve growled. "We stay. We find out who here with us."

"Are you fucking insane?" Devin hissed. "You really want to risk walking into a trap?"

"We kill them if they try," Ryve said. It almost sounded like he was smiling when he said it.

"You *are* insane," Devin said, shaking his head. "And I still can't see."

"Then I lead you," Ryve said as if that solved everything.

"And if we end up in the middle of a fight?"

"Voices upstairs have light," Ryve reasoned. Devin couldn't deny the logic. Trooviians were the only humanoid creatures with night vision. The voices hadn't sounded like they belonged to Trooviians.

"Fine," Devin sighed. He readied his rifle and felt Ryve's hand on his shoulder, pushing him forward.

They slowly made their way through the store and reached the staircase in the back. Devin spotted a soft glow above them. Ryve had been correct about the light. They continued forward, silently ascending the stairs. As they reached the landing leading to the next set of stairs, Devin began to feel his anxiety welling up. Even if they weren't walking into some trap things could turn bad very quickly. Whoever was here with them would no doubt respond violently to their sudden appearance.

Ryve didn't seem to have the same concern as he urged Devin forward. Devin tried to resist, but the Trooviian was significantly stronger and pushed him upward anyway. Devin's heart pounded as he drew nearer toward the voices and the glow. He pressed his rifle against his shoulder, getting ready to shoot at the first sign of danger.

As Devin and Ryve reached the second floor, they saw the source of the light and the voices. Devin didn't fire his weapon. He was too confused by what he saw before him.

"Don't shoot," came a distinctly female voice.

Chapter 22

Elaina woke up several hours later. Kyle was still sleeping next to her. She sat up and immediately felt a pain in her stomach. She hadn't eaten in nearly twenty-four hours, and her body had kindly decided to remind her. With everything that had happened the day before she hadn't had time to feel hungry. She'd barely had time to feel grief.

Elaina strained to see in the darkness, the only light coming from the embers left in the campfire. After a moment she grabbed her jacket and began pulling it on with some measure of difficulty. Her frustration grew as she tried to pull her sleeve over her remaining arm. Everything was going to be much harder without the use of her left hand.

Before her injury, she'd been dominantly left-handed. Now she had to learn to do everything with her right. It felt awkward and clumsy. She began to yell out as she struggled, her anger getting the better of her.

"Hey, let me help you," Kyle said softly behind her.

"I can do it myself," Elaina grumbled. Tears were forming in her eyes as she grew more frustrated.

"I'm sure you can," he said as he placed his hands on her waist. Elaina wanted to push his hands away at first, but his touch was having a calming effect on her.

"I can't do this," she said softly. "I can't keep going with just one arm."

"You'll be alright," Kyle said as he rubbed her back to reassure her or comfort her. He wasn't entirely sure which. "The Collective has come a long way with robotic prosthetics. They can give you a new hand."

"I don't know how I would have made it without you," she said. "You came along at the perfect time. I owe you my life."

"You were in a bad spot," Kyle agreed as Elaina turned to face him. "I couldn't let them hurt you. You needed help, and I knew I could protect you. The sentrons helped."

Elaina laughed. It sounded more from frustration than mirth.

"We need to eat," she said.

"You don't have to tell me twice," Kyle said as his stomach grumbled loudly.

"We need food," Elaina said with a chuckle, then her stomach growled as well.

"I think I have some emergency rations in my bag."

Elaina watched as he dug around the pile of his clothes and through the small bag he'd been carrying.

"Well," she said after an agonizingly long moment. "Did you find us some food?"

"Well," he said after a moment. He produced two small pouches. "It's not much, but it's all I've got."

"That should work," Elaina said, though the expression on her face clearly showed the doubt she felt.

"Yeah, I guess," Kyle sighed. "It's not much."

"It's okay," she said. "I'm starving, and any little bit helps."

"Me too," Kyle said as he began opening one of the packages. The mush inside was nearly tasteless, but it contained all the nutrients they'd need for a while. After they finished their food, they gathered up their meager supplies and headed down the subway tracks. The dark was pressing in as they moved further away from the substation.

"We're going to be too blind to go on," Elaina said, already straining to see. "Anything could be waiting up ahead."

"You're right," Kyle said. "I think these rifles have flashlights on them."

Kyle examined one of the rifles while he kept the other slung over his shoulder. He ran his hand along the side of the metal and then along the other side, his finger finding a button. A light clicked on and shone down the tunnel.

"A-ha!" he cried out in triumph. He handed Elaina the other rifle—though she had difficulty carrying it with one hand—and clicked on its flashlight for her.

"I don't know how I'm going to use this," Elaina protested. "It's too heavy to carry one-handed."

Kyle slung his rifle back over his shoulder as he began working on a solution. He draped the rifle's sling over her head, so it was resting across her body, supporting the rifle's weight. Elaina gripped the handle and held it up. The sling helped support its weight significantly. She wouldn't be able to aim very well, but at least she'd be able to keep it pointed ahead of her.

Kyle did the same thing with his own rifle and began to lead the way. The beams from the flashlight attachments cut through the gloom as they marched forward, deeper into the tunnel.

The air felt heavy and thick, necessitating the use of their gas masks, which only served to obscure their vision in the murky gloom. The beams of the flashlights made it, so they could see the tracks and avoid tripping, but little else could be seen. Anything could be hiding in the dark, and the thought made Elaina's skin crawl.

***

"They're moving," the Trooviian scout, Burg, said. She was slightly smaller than the males of her species, but that was where the obvious differences ended. To human eyes, she looked just like the others, but she was lighter in color and slighter of limb.

Female Trooviians made excellent scouts as their eyes were sharper and their skin had the uncanny ability to shift colors to provide camouflage. The males had the ability as well, but with less accuracy.

Burg, who was as low on the ladder as one could get in the Order of Proper Justice, had never seen action. This didn't scare her, though. Captain Grig did, though. He was enormous, even for a Trooviian, and had seen his share of battle. It was well known that he didn't much care for Professor Goordaiin, but he did as his boss ordered without question.

"Pack up and prepare to move out," Captain Grig called out, his voice low. "Their eyes aren't suited for the dark, but they no doubt have flashlights of some kind. We don't want to be spotted."

Several of the Trooviian scouting party began packing up their equipment as quickly and as quietly as they could. The tunnels amplified every sound, and Captain Grig hoped the human pair were far enough away that the sounds wouldn't arouse their curiosity. Humans intrigued Captain Grig. They were a hardy species, despite their frail physiology, and had a knack for survival despite impossible odds. He'd been a lowly grunt when the Trooviians and the Calvorans had first arrived ton Earth. The humans had been slow to trust the alien visitors, and more than once fighting had broken out.

That was until The Human Collective and the Calvoran Council, along with Trooviian ambassadors, had met and come to a truce.

Grig remembered those days. The humans, with their inferior weapons, had managed to kill nearly his entire squad before they were subdued. He'd managed to avoid injury during the initial conflict. He'd admired the humans' tenacity and began working as a liaison for the Trooviians, quelling conflicts without causing massive casualties to either side until the truce was put in place. Small skirmishes still broke out afterward, of course, but Grig had done all he could to calm the people in his assigned quadrants.

The successes of his missions had given him a reputation for diplomacy and helped to escalate his rise through the ranks. Once he reached the higher echelons, he began to realize the Order of Proper Justice was a ruse. They weren't so much a police force. They were a military outfit.

"I don't need to remind the lot of you that these humans aren't to be harmed," Captain Grig said as the Trooviians finished packing. "We are only supposed to follow them and keep them alive, so they can reach The Collective's headquarters. If anyone decides to ignore those orders, you will answer directly to me."

Captain Grig heard some grumbling, but the scouting team all nodded in understanding. He knew some of them had an irrational hatred for humans and had felt it pertinent to address them before someone did something stupid. He did not want to have to explain to Professor Goordaiin why the mission had failed, though he doubted Goordaiin would be too distraught. That wouldn't stop the cruel Calvoran from punishing Grig and his team, but he'd have to wait in line behind Grig himself. Whatever Goordaiin's intentions were, Grig knew it didn't bode well for humans.

"The humans are a quarter mile down the tunnel," Burg said as she came back to the scouting party. She'd been tailing the pair while the rest of the team had formed up.

"Let's fall out," Captain Grig ordered. "Keep a tailing distance of two hundred feet from the targets. We should be out of range of their lights at that distance, but close enough to lend aid should they get into trouble."

With that the scouting party began their rapid march down the tunnels, quickly catching up to Elaina and Kyle.

Chapter 23

The lighting in the room came from an old-fashioned lantern. Devin hadn't seen one in person, though he had seen pictures. The design was ingenious as if it were meant for the volatile atmosphere. The glass bulged outward at the bottom and then tapered off toward the top. The glass was clouded with age, but light still came through.

The figures that were illuminated by the flame were clad in environmental suits, much like the one Devin had worn, but none of these people were wearing masks. The woman who'd shouted out looked to be no older than sixteen, but Devin's attention was not on her. Instead, he was focusing on the imposing figure in the middle of the room.

The man was over six feet tall and looked considerably healthy, compared to the other men and women around him. He wasn't terribly muscular, as he was still malnourished, but his frame (and the suit) made him look massive. The man's face showed the lines of age and Devin figured him to be in his late forties. That alone was enough to set Devin on edge.

Life expectancy on the surface was low, and most Scavengers were lucky to see their late twenties. Anyone older was such a foreign sight that they were often regarded as myth, but the man standing before Devin was very real.

"What do you want?" the man said, his voice coming out in a growl. "And why is *that* with you?"

Devin looked over his shoulder at Ryve and motioned for him to lower his weapon. The Trooviian shook his massive head at first, and then reluctantly obliged.

"We're not here to start anything," Devin said, putting down his own weapon and holding out his hands in a non-threatening manner. "We were just taking refuge inside the building, and we heard voices. Surely you can understand why we would investigate."

"You still haven't answered my question," the man said, narrowing his eyes. He pointed at Ryve. "Why is *that thing* with you?"

"This is Ryve," Devin replied. "He isn't an enemy."

Devin had wanted to say that Ryve was helping him, or that he was a friend, but he couldn't bring himself to say it. Part of him still distrusted the Trooviian. These strangers didn't need to know that, though.

"How do I know you're not its prisoner," the man snapped.

"Do I look like a prisoner?"

"You look like a fool," the man said. Just then he seemed to notice Devin's BSS rig. "Where'd the hell did you get that?"

"Ryve and his partner gave it to me," Devin said, his hand slowly moving toward the hilt of his blade. This exchange wasn't going well.

"But humans can't wear those!" one of the others shouted.

"Well, I am, and I'm human," Devin said with more force than he'd intended. Anger was already beginning to well up inside him. It had been happening more frequently lately, and the thought unnerved him. Devin was typically passive and reclusive, but he'd grown more hostile lately.

"Indeed," the obvious leader said. He walked around the lantern, nearly stepping on a frail-looking man, before walking right up to Devin.

Devin's hand shot toward his blade, but the man was already anticipating the move and grabbed his wrist.

"There's no need for that," he said. "I was just getting a closer look. That gizmo seems to have done you good. You look healthier than any Scavenger I have ever seen."

Ryve had picked up his weapon and pointed it at the man's head, but the man didn't seem to notice or care. He continued to look Devin over.

"Tell your pet to put the weapon down," he said evenly.

"Pet?" Ryve growled.

"Did I hurt the Troglodyte's feelings?" the man asked mockingly as he grinned at Ryve. He had balls, mocking the Trooviian while having a gun to his head. Devin was amazed and perhaps even a little amused.

"It's okay, Ryve," Devin said without looking. "I think."

Ryve snorted but lowered his weapon anyway. His black eyes bore holes into the stranger. He shook his massive, frog-like head and bared his teeth. The man still held Devin's wrist in a grip more powerful than he had expected. It was starting to hurt, and he felt his fingers start to tingle.

"My name is Gerrard Hamaan," the man said as he released Devin's wrist. "The people with me are the last surviving Scavengers in the area. That is until *you* showed up."

"I didn't know there were many of us left," Devin said, his heart rate starting to return to normal now that Gerrard had backed off.

"There aren't, no thanks to *them*," Gerrard said, pointing at Ryve. "Most of our kind were rounded up a while back and shipped off. Those who resisted or fled were killed outright. You can understand my surprise at seeing one accompanying a Scavenger."

"Ryve and his partner were actually out looking for whoever was responsible for destroying Disc City 6," Devin said. Gerrard's face twitched at the mention of the city.

"So, it's true? Disc City 6 is gone?"

"Yeah, unfortunately," Devin said.

"So many people dead," Gerrard muttered, his features downcast. "Who did it? Did you catch them?"

"Yes," Ryve said.

"And? Who in the hell would want to do such a thing?" Gerrard yelled his attention on Ryve.

"It was an agent operating under orders for Professor Goordaiin," Devin said quickly, intentionally leaving out the part about the agent being a Trooviian.

"Goordaiin? Really?" Gerrard asked. He didn't look too surprised. "And why in God's name would he want to do that?"

"We don't know," Devin answered. "But we intend to find out."

"As do I," Gerrard said. "I already wanted to take that Grey down, and now I have even more reason to."

"So, you know who he is?"

"It would seem not many people don't know who he is," Gerrard said. "His name had come up before when the Troglodytes were rounding everyone up. They kept saying he was moving them to better living quarters and had important jobs for them. A complete crock of shit if you ask me."

"From what we gathered, he's got something awful planned," Devin said. "He had sent the agent to Disc City 6 under false pretenses. Said that the people in charge of the eco-generator were building a weapon."

"He intentionally had the eco-generator destroyed? Why the

fuck would he do that?"

"I don't know," Devin shook his head. "My guess is as good as yours."

"Well," Gerrard said as he walked back toward Devin. "I guess it's time we find out."

"How?"

"We're going to storm the city, with a little help from the Bandits," Gerrard said with a sly grin. "The Bandits are a rowdy bunch, and dumb as shit, but they can be manipulated. Give them proper motivation, and they'll work for you. Offer food, and they'll gladly kill anyone you want. Offer them a city, and they'll marshal an army."

"You offered those crazy bastards the entire city?" Devin asked, shocked and even a little terrified. "Why the hell would you do a stupid thing like that?"

"Relax," Gerrard said in a placating manner. "They won't all survive the invasion. Whatever is left over will be taken care of, I assure you."

"You're insane!"

"I'm far from it, actually," Gerrard said. "The Troglodytes and their Grey masters won't expect an onslaught from the Bandits. The buggers have strict instructions to leave all humans alone unless someone gets in their way. If they disobey they know I will kill their 'Chief.'"

"Chief? What are you talking about?" Devin shook his head in disbelief. "The Bandits are disorganized! They *don't* have a hierarchy, and they don't listen to *anyone*!"

"On the contrary. The Bandits have been facing a genocide of their own and have finally gathered the brainpower to organize. It would appear that we have a common enemy and they are ready to take the fight back to the aliens."

"They destroy everything," Ryve interjected. "Disc City 1. Failed experiment. Bandits brought up then break everything. Kill everyone. Bandits not to be trusted."

"What the hell do you know?" Gerrard barked. "For all, we know that was staged to make everyone turn on the Bandits. I don't believe anything you fucking *aliens* say!"

"Please," Devin pleaded, his stomach starting to twist into knots. The situation was quickly dissolving. "You can't do this. There's no way it will work. Innocent people *will* die if you send those psychos up there."

Gerrard just glared at him and then turned away. He almost knocked over the lantern as he strode past. An unlucky Scavenger got kicked in the head when he didn't immediately get out of the way. Gerrard disappeared into a room located at the far side of the room and then reemerged carrying a Trooviian rifle.

"Try to stop me, and you'll die, plain and simple," Gerrard growled, his weapon trained on Ryve. "Help me, and you'll have a new safe haven. It's time we took a stand. Aren't you tired of being treated like shit? We're human, just like those privileged bastards on the cities! Don't we deserve a chance to live too?"

"You're proposing war," Devin said. "You want to send a horde of maniacs into a city full of people – innocent people I may add – and just plan on strolling in after the dust settles? What happens if the Bandits are somehow repelled? The Disc Cities are sure to have some kind of defense system. The Bandits and their primitive weapons are no match for anything the Trooviians and Calvorans have at their disposal."

"That's where you're wrong," Gerrard said, nodding his head toward the weapon in his hand. "The Bandits have been outfitted with Trooviian rifles."

"You crazy bastard!" Devin shouted. "What's to stop them if they destroy the city's resistance? They'll never give the city over to you!"

"I don't have time for this," Gerrard said as he aimed the weapon at Ryve's massive head.

"Wait!" Devin raised his hands. "We'll leave. You don't have to kill us."

"From where I'm standing, you look like an obstacle," Gerrard said. "We can't let you go. You could warn them that we're coming, and he *will* warn them," Gerrard spat, pointing an accusatory finger at Ryve. "Too many lives depend on the success of this mission."

"Do it, and the whole planet dies," Ryve said. "Phoenix One is only hope for all."

"What is the Troglodyte saying?" Gerrard growled.

"Phoenix One is the last-ditch effort to preserve our species," Devin said. "Basically, it's a new planet to replace this one."

"What the hell makes you think we'll be allowed on this new

planet?" Gerrard nearly screamed, his rage boiling over. "They'll just leave us to die with *this* fucking planet!"

"You don't know that!"

"I do!" Gerrard bellowed. "For years, we've been cast out! That ends now! Phoenix One will be ours. Once the Bandits do their job, we will move in and take over the facilities responsible for the project. They'll finish it, and we'll be the first, and maybe the only, ones on board!"

Devin's shoulders slumped, and his heart sank. There was no convincing this madman to abandon his crusade. To make matters worse he and Ryve were going to be the psycho's prisoners. Devin again found himself wondering what had compelled him to stay by Ryve's side. It was out of character for him. It had gone against every instinct Devin had. His future once again looked bleak.

Chapter 24

Elaina struggled to keep up with Kyle. They'd been jogging at a slow pace for close to an hour, the uneven terrain of the subway tunnels preventing them from running. Elaina and Kyle had both stumbled at least twice during their journey. The darkness always felt as though it were closing in. Elaina had even thought she'd heard another set of footsteps behind her, but when she'd looked, she hadn't seen anything approaching.

"There's got to be another terminal up ahead," Kyle said. He didn't know for sure, but he hoped it would help urge Elaina on.

"I certainly hope so," Elaina puffed as she struggled to pull in air. The masks had made their journey even more difficult. "I don't know how much longer I can keep this up."

Kyle looked sadly at the woman he was growing to love. She was undoubtedly a strong person, but she was in bad shape from the Trooviian attacks and the shuttle crash. The fact that she was still on her feet and moving forward amazed him. He doubted that even he could have continued if he'd been in her condition.

"Don't worry about me," Elaina said as she noticed Kyle's gaze. "I can do it."

Kyle hoped so. Now that she was in his life he couldn't imagine being without her. He'd carry her if he absolutely had to. He wished he had some of the sentrons with him. He missed the security their presence provided.

As the pair continued forward, they heard a faint sound. They'd almost missed it, but it had come again and was louder than before. It sounded like something being dragged. Kyle slowed and raised his weapon, the beam from the flashlight on the barrel barely cutting through the gloom. Elaina followed his actions as best she could, but her flagging strength and the weight of the weapon made it difficult to keep the barrel trained directly ahead.

The sound began to grow and multiply as the pair moved closer. Kyle and Elaina stopped their forward progress. Something felt immensely wrong, and dread began to worm through them.

Kyle pointed toward a large piece of concrete that had fallen from the crumbling tunnel ceiling, indicating that Elaina should take cover behind it. Kyle followed as Elaina picked up on his signal. The slab was large enough for the two of them to take cover behind. Elaina poked her head, and her rifle, around the right side and Kyle, did the same on the left.

The sounds continued to grow, and then a shape appeared out of the gloom. It looked vaguely human, but it was covered in lumps from head to toe. It was horribly misshapen, and the face was nearly featureless as it was obscured by massive tumors. More shapes covered in the same kind of tumorous growths emerged from the gloom. So far, the pitiful creatures didn't seem to notice Kyle and Elaina's presence, but they were getting too close for comfort.

The closest of the creatures was almost close enough for Kyle to reach out and touch when its grotesque head turned toward him. A strangled cry issued from the creature's mangle throat, and it lunged. Kyle fell backward and fired his weapon without aiming. The round caught the creature in the stomach, blasting a fist-sized hole through its abdomen. The thing barely noticed. Another round caught it in the chest as Elaina managed to turn and aim her weapon one-handed at the beast.

Kyle's heart pounded in his chest as he scrambled back to his feet and looked around the slab. The thing's kin seemed to have heard the cry and began running toward them. Kyle managed to count a dozen of them before he had to turn his attention toward firing his weapon. He knew that they were about to overrun, but he refused to go down without a fight. If there was a chance, he could buy Elaina time to escape he'd take it.

"Go back!" Kyle yelled. "You need to get out of here!"

"I'm not going anywhere!" Elaina yelled back as she fired shots into the thickening crowd of the mutated creatures. Fortunately, she didn't need to aim as there were so many of the things. She would have been nearly useless if she had to take precision shots.

"There's too many!" Kyle yelled. "You have to go!"

"No!" Elaina screamed. She would hear no more on the subject.

The duo fired continuously into the throng, dropping mutant after mutant, but more always seemed to fill their place. Kyle and

Elaina felt their spirits fall as the twisted things were less than five feet away.

Suddenly the mutants began to fall in droves. Kyle and Elaina looked at each other in bewilderment. Footfalls could be heard behind them, but neither of them dared hazard a glance behind them. A moment later they saw a small band of Trooviians in their peripheral vision.

Elaina's first instinct was to flee. It was highly likely they had been sent by Goordaiin to pursue Kyle and herself. Her suspicion was confirmed when she spotted the emblem of The Order on the Trooviians' uniforms. Kyle hadn't had time to get a better look and had not yet noticed this detail. He was clearly glad for the help, as the swarm of mutants diminished. What had been a tidal wave of twisted, bloated creatures had dwindled to a trickle of maybe two or three at a time.

"We need to run!" Elaina yelled. She could have whispered, and Kyle would have heard her, as the firearms were near silent, as were the mutants. Kyle looked at her, his confusion clearly painted on his features under his mask. Elaina nodded her head toward the Trooviians flanking them. Kyle finally turned to get a better look at their would-be rescuers.

"Oh shit!" Kyle exclaimed as he turned back to face her. They were about to flee when a pair of the Trooviians grabbed them.

"Not so fast," one of the Trooviians, most likely the leader, ordered. He was massive, even by Trooviian standards, and bore an aura of authority. Some of his contingents even backed away as he approached. "I am Grig, Captain of the Order of Proper Justice. As we've just demonstrated, we mean you no harm."

"I highly doubt that," Elaina hissed. She was tired of being chased by the hideous beasts. Trooviians hadn't always made her nervous, but recent events had soured her opinion of the race.

"You must be Miss Perry," Captain Grig said, his voice losing its edge. "I don't blame you for distrusting us. After all, you've been through, I'd be surprised if you didn't."

"What do you want? I'm sure Goordaiin instructed you to execute us," Kyle interjected.

"That was our initial mission, yes," Captain Grig answered. "It would seem he's changed his mind. He wants you followed."

"And why exactly are you telling us this?" Elaina asked. She still wanted nothing more than to get as far away from these things as she could.

"Because what Professor Goordaiin wants would spell disaster for everyone," Captain Grig snapped. "He seeks war, and I've seen far more death than anyone should. His motives, his desires no longer mirror those of everyone else. The survival of our three races is my top priority, but it no longer appears to be his. He has become obsessive, and it is threatening the survival of my entire species, as it is also threatening yours. So, considering this fact, you and I are on the same side."

The Trooviians standing behind Captain Grig began murmuring in their guttural language. None of them seemed to have been aware of this change of circumstance. Kyle visibly relaxed, but Elaina was finding it difficult to trust the Captain. This could easily be a trick. She'd certainly given Goordaiin a lot of trouble, and it was possible that he was changing tactics.

"Why did he want you following us," Elaina asked.

"He knew that you'd be headed to meet with The Collective and he wants to know where their base is," Grig replied. "It is no secret that he intends to wipe them out. To do so would cause another rebellion, which would undoubtedly delay the Phoenix One project and ultimately doom us all. I can't, and won't, let that happen."

The Trooviians had stopped their murmuring and now stood by their Captain's sides. From Elaina's left she saw another, smaller Trooviian appear. She'd never know the Trooviians to employ camouflage, and the development deeply unnerved her. Captain Grig, along with his platoon, holstered their weapons. The mutants had been eliminated or at least deterred for the moment. Kyle followed suit and looked to Elaina to mirror his actions. Reluctantly she did the same.

Kyle stood before Captain Grig and extended his hand.

"Then what do you plan to do?" Kyle asked. Grig just smiled.

Chapter 25

Professor Goordaiin couldn't stay in his office any longer. He was head of the Phoenix One project, after all, and that entailed certain responsibilities. He had to do some damage control -thanks to Elaina. The human woman had caused him quite a bit of grief, but now that she was about to hand over the location of The Human Collective, albeit unwillingly, she finally had some use. She wouldn't be a problem for much longer.

He hadn't heard from the search teams in close to twelve hours, but the radio silence didn't bother him. He figured they were already tailing the woman and her escort, whomever the man was and had no doubt needed to remain quiet. Goordaiin wished he could still reach them telepathically, though. It would help keep him up to speed.

Goordaiin strode gracefully down the tunnel-shaped halls, turning down a section that had been expertly camouflaged to look like a solid wall to any casual observer, and into a large oval room. Inside the room stood three Calvorans.

"Professor," one of the Calvorans said. It was one of the few that had favored the feminine side of its biology, and the voice reflected this.

"Chancellor Vallus," Goordaiin greeted. "Thank you for meeting me."

"I do hope that the incident with the woman has been resolved," another Calvoran said.

"Rectus," Goordaiin nearly hissed. "I'm a bit surprised to see you here."

"I asked Rectus to join us," Chancellor Vallus said.

"I see no need to have *him* here," Goordaiin said, trying his best to sound respectful. "Rectus doesn't hold a position on the Council."

"No," Vallus agreed. "But, I have made him Chief of Security and acting Commander of the Trooviian Task Force. I'm inclined to appoint him as Commander of this 'Order of Proper Justice' that you founded, without permission I may add."

"I assure you that I had good reason to put that together," Goordaiin replied. "These humans are unpredictable. They only respond to a police presence, and I have merely supplied that."

"Your 'police force' killed several human bystanders!" Rectus shouted, his skin turning magenta. "Thanks to *you* we have to deal with a possible uprising, again!"

"The fugitive holds sensitive information that we can't afford falling into the hands of any potential saboteurs," Goordaiin said, turning his attention on Rectus. "Unfortunately, collateral damage occurred in the attempt to apprehend her. You should know better than anyone, *Rectus*, that it can't always be helped."

Rectus recoiled a bit at Goordaiin's statement. He knew the truth of Goordaiin's words and they stung his pride a bit.

"Nonetheless," Vallus interjected. "It has made a mess of things. Tell me, have you succeeded in your search for Disc City 6's saboteur?"

Goordaiin turned his focus back on Vallus. He wasn't prepared to admit that the investigation had not yielded any useful information, nor was he willing to admit that two of his agents had gone missing.

"The investigation is still ongoing," Goordaiin said, mentally preparing a barricade against psychic intrusion. "Any development will be relayed to you directly, Chancellor."

"I hope so," Vallus said. "If The Human Collective is behind it, as you suspect, then we will have to ensure they are no longer a threat to the project. The future of our race rests with you, Goordaiin. I'd rather not be disappointed."

The dropping of Goordaiin's title was not lost on him. Chancellor Vallus was becoming a tenuous ally, and he would have to come up with something tangible for her to act on. She and Rectus were playing into his plan, but any further incident could cause that to quickly change.

The three Calvorans, including one that had remained oddly silent during the conversation, left the room. Goordaiin stood alone in the large oval chamber, contemplating his next course of action. He hoped his search team was carrying out their assignment. They should be sending a report soon, as they were instructed to do every 18 hours.

After a moment Goordaiin exited the room and headed back

to his office. He'd spent a considerable amount of time there since Elaina's escape. He decided to change direction and head toward the lab where the eco-generator prototype was housed. It would help quell his anger and soothe his nerves to focus on the project. Despite all that had happened, he still needed to ensure that Phoenix One was still on track. He needed to ensure that he maintained complete control.

Goordaiin would deal with The Human Collective in time. He'd deal with the Calvoran Council, too. He'd make sure to deal with Chancellor Vallus, and he'd make damn sure to take his time in dealing with Rectus.

***

Captain Grig took the point, along with his lieutenant, and led the way down the tunnel. Typically, Trooviian Captains, much like many human military commanders, stayed as far from trouble as possible. Grig was an exception. He made sure that Elaina and Kyle were in the middle of the contingent, with Trooviians flanking either side and taking up the rear.

The subway tunnel ended abruptly at a cave-in that appeared to have been recent. Elaina and Kyle couldn't figure out how far they'd traveled, but the Trooviians were accustomed to subterranean travel and were adept at judging distance. Grig figured they were near the crash site, meaning they'd travelled east.

"We need to head north," Kyle said after Captain Grig helped them get their bearings. "Maybe we took a wrong turn."

"There was a junction back the way we came," one of the Trooviian soldiers said. "Near where you were camping."

"Then we backtrack and go that way," Captain Grig said, turning and heading back down the tunnel.

None of the Trooviians complained, but Elaina was growing fatigued, and it was starting to show. Kyle could see her steps falter and her body sway unsteadily. They couldn't stop, and they both knew it, so Kyle slung his rifle over his shoulder and put his arm around Elaina's midsection. She smiled up at him in thanks, the support more than welcome.

Elaina groaned when the corpses of the mutants came into view. She'd hoped to never see the mangled beasts again. The bodies had already begun to decay, fouling the air and making it harder to breathe. Elaina was grateful for the gas-mask, even though it did little to filter out the smell. At least she wouldn't be breathing in any of the gasses emitted from the corpses.

The smell intensified when one of the Trooviian soldiers accidentally, or intentionally (Elaina couldn't tell), stepped on one of the bodies. The weight caused the corpse's organs to burst from the hole that had been blasted in its midsection, spilling bile and a myriad of unidentifiable viscera across the ground. The stench was horrific, and Elaina fought hard to suppress the urge to vomit. Kyle hadn't been as successful.

"Dammit!" Kyle shouted as he yanked off his mask. He tried to let loose another expletive, but he gagged on the inhale and vomited again.

"Help him," Grig said without looking. A Trooviian tentatively walked over to Kyle's bent over form and snatched the mask, tossing it into the darkness.

"Wait!" Elaina yelled as she watched the mask disappear. "He'll die without that!"

The Trooviian ignored her as it produced a strange looking object, like a deflated ball, and began placing it over Kyle's head. Elaina panicked, fearing the Trooviian was trying to smother Kyle. It stuck out a massive hand to block her and used its other hand to fiddle with the deflated bag. After a moment, it inflated, and Kyle could stand, his eyes wide with wonder.

"What is this?" he asked.

"Same as mask," the Trooviian said in horribly broken English. "Except better."

"Don't puke in this one," Grig said. Kyle managed to chuckle.

"I'll try not to," he said.

"Good," Grig said, leveling his gaze at the man. "Because it's the only one we have."

Kyle's expression of mirth faded quickly and was replaced by a twinge of fear. At least the globe kept out the smell, which Kyle was immensely thankful for. He put his arm back around Elaina's waist, and they continued forward, quickly leaving the mass graveyard.

***

After what had seemed like an hour they Trooviian contingent flanking Elaina and Kyle finally made their way to the junction and headed north, according to Burg. She'd scouted ahead to ensure no ambushes awaited them and Captain Grig, satisfied with the report, took point once again.

The tunnel was unremarkable. Chunks of concrete had fallen from the roof of the tunnel as it had fallen into a state of disrepair. The subway tunnels had been used less and less until sky-trains, the antigravity equivalent of a subway car, had replaced them. This, of course, was nearly two hundred years in the past. All the new infrastructure had to be abandoned when the need for Disc Cities arose, and the sky-trains never became a common method of public transportation. Houston had been one of the first metropolitan areas to begin implementation of the sky-train, but atmospheric conditions put a permanent hold on the project.

Even though the Trooviians didn't need light to navigate the tunnels they'd switched on their flashlights to aid their human companions. Elaina was grateful after she stumbled for the twentieth time over chunks of concrete and other debris. Captain Grig didn't seem pleased that the flashlights had been turned on, preferring to err on the side of caution, but he understood their necessity.

It was yet another two hours before the small company reached a substation leading back to the surface. Burg headed up the stairwell and quickly scanned the surface. They'd arrived at the northeast side of Houston, but not far enough north. Their goal, Disc City 12, was much further north. Captain Grig wanted to get clear of the Houston Ruins before radioing the second search team for a pick-up. He didn't want to take his chances with the Bandits that no doubt infested the ruins while waiting for the rendezvous.

The initial plan, before Captain Grig deviated from Goordaiin's orders, was to tail the humans until he could get an idea of their general heading. Once that was determined he'd order the second team to bring two transport shuttles to a rendezvous point that would Grig, and his team would secure, with instructions to leave one of the ships behind. That way the human duo would have a way to get to the Disc City that housed The Collective. The second transport would be close by, waiting until the duo managed to "repair" the seemingly abandoned transport and take off.

When Burg relayed her report, Grig gave the order to move

out. They would remain in the subway tunnels for a while longer. Elaina groaned. The flashlights helped, but she was exhausted from her injury and traversing the uneven terrain. Before long she'd need to be carried. Kyle felt the same way, though he still had both of his arms intact.

The tunnel was in even worse shape as they moved further north. There were places where the walls had collapsed, allowing only one Trooviian through at a time. Grig was unnerved by the condition of the tunnel and despised being funneled through a bottleneck. It left them far too vulnerable, and anything could be waiting on the other side.

He growled with anger when he heard a scuttling sound in the distance the moment he squeezed through the debris.

Chapter 26

Devin sat against the wall on the left side of the room they'd entered when they'd met Gerrard. His hands had been bound with a piece of wire. Ryve sat next to him, unbound only because there wasn't a length of wire long enough to secure his wrists. Instead, weapons were trained on the Trooviian. He kept growling whenever one of the impromptu guards shifted their weapon. Devin knew the Trooviian was trying to frighten them, challenging them to make a move. He couldn't figure out why Ryve was taunting them. One panicked guard with an itchy trigger finger would be a twitch away from killing him.

Devin remained quiet and instead focused his attention on Gerrard. The man frightened him. Scavengers were not typically eager for confrontation, so when Gerrard had proposed war it had caught Devin off guard. There was something about the man that seemed off, other than the apparent insanity that seemed to infect his mind. It was the way he carried himself, the confidence in his steps and the way he held his head. It wasn't the attitude of a man who'd spent his life fighting for survival with nothing but scraps and improvised, yet often ineffective, weapons. He carried himself more like a seasoned soldier.

Gerrard was moving about the room with a sense of urgency and had already donned his gas mask. Devin surmised that they were preparing to move out, but he couldn't figure out why. Why would they want to head out at night? The temperature was freezing, and the nocturnal creatures that roamed the wasteland would be more than a match for the small band of survivors. It just didn't make sense.

Within moments Devin was hauled to his feet and led toward the stairwell. Ryve was behind him, still literally staring down the barrel of a gun. Descending the staircase was difficult with his hands bound, but Devin doubted that any of the survivors would be willing to lend a hand if he fell, so he took his time and made his way down as carefully as possible. He smiled when he heard Gerrard complain that it was already taking too long.

The main floor of the now-defunct electronics store was still incredibly dark, but the band of Scavengers carried a pair of lamps, illuminating the gloom. Devin could see enough to know they were heading out the front of the store, rather than from some back door, which also meant they would stumble across Devin's steed. *Not again,* he thought.

The band spotted the steed immediately, just as he feared. It wasn't difficult, as the machine was large and stood out among the debris that littered the floor and the now empty shelves that lined the aisles. The Scavengers recoiled in fear at first, having never seen a machine-like Devin's steed and thus falling back on their ingrained survival instinct. Gerrard didn't react the same way, further reinforcing Devin's suspicions about the man.

"I assume that's yours?" Gerrard asked in a loud whisper, grinning. "Very creative, if I do say so."

"Thanks," Devin hissed. "I worked hard on it, just for you."

Gerrard glared at Devin, picking up quickly on the sarcasm. He glared at Devin for a moment and then chuckled.

"Well," he said, still grinning. "I think I'll take it. For safe keeping. You don't mind, do you?"

Devin knew the question to be rhetorical. Gerrard was going to commandeer the steed whether Devin wanted him to or not. He felt his anger as it grew into a red-hot rage when he continued to dwell on it. All he'd wanted was to find food and keep moving, but Ryve *had* to change their course. Now everything had gone to shit, and Devin was a prisoner, yet again.

Gerrard motioned for the guards flanking Devin and Ryve to continue moving. Devin felt a tentative hand placed against the middle of his back, guiding him out the door and into the open air. The smell hit him again, and he gagged. The Scavenger band, along with Gerrard, all wore gas masks, which they now pulled over their faces. Devin could see a glow on the horizon as he continued out onto the street. Dawn already?

Devin didn't recall blacking out, but everything had become confusing rather quickly, and he supposed he'd lost track of time. He was still getting used to the energy the BSS rig gave him. The temperature of the air was beginning to rise, but the chill had not yet left, and Devin became very aware of his exposed limbs. He began shivering, trying to brace himself against the chill that threatened to permeate every inch of his body.

Gerrard followed the contingent out of the store, sitting astride Devin's steed and looking thoroughly pleased. The growing light of dawn cast a cool blue color on everything, though it looked greener through the tinted masks on the Scavengers. Devin saw the blue, though, and for a moment forgot about the trouble he was in. It was a color he'd seen very little of.

The faint light gave Gerrard's pale skin a deathly quality, making him appear like the vampires of old. Stories of vampires and other creatures that went bump in the night had survived, passed from one person to the next. It was likely that the stories survived to distract from the very real horrors that plagued the surface. Devin stared at the man, an icy chill coursing through him.

Gerrard looked at Devin and caught him staring. "What're you looking at?"

"A dead man," Devin said under his breath. He wasn't sure why he said it, but he believed it.

"What was that?" Gerrard growled.

"I didn't say anything," Devin shot back. Gerrard just narrowed his eyes and then turned his gaze to the east.

"Disc City 9 is that way," Gerrard nearly yelled, making sure he could be heard through the gas mask. "It will take several days to get there on foot. Our *army* has already been instructed to meet us at the halfway mark, where we will begin the final march. The people who cast you out, cast you aside, are now on borrowed time! The Troglodytes and their masters will finally understand their mistake when we descend upon them! It is our time! They plan to leave us here to rot on this forsaken planet while they live happily on a new one! That will *not* happen if we have anything to say about it!"

The small band of Scavengers, spurred by Gerrard's confidence and the hope of a better life, cheered. Devin winced at the noise. They were bringing attention to their location, and Devin shook his head in disbelief. These people should know quite well just how dangerous it was to attract attention. This was stupid, and Devin mentally began preparing for the worst.

A rumble, as if in answer to his suspicions, made its way toward them. Devin felt the ground beneath his feet start to shake as something large was moving their way. He could guess what it was, judging by the source's subterranean approach. He and Ryve had initially set out to find food, planning on luring a Millipede to them.

Their plan, though seemingly abandoned, had worked.

***

Captain Grig aimed down the sights of his weapon toward the sound of the scuttling. It was drawing nearer, approaching from the pitch-black tunnel before him. He strained his eyes, attempting to cut through the gloom to catch sight of what was approaching. After a moment, he wished he hadn't.

The creature was massive, as big around as a bus and twice as long. The head was reminiscent of an insect, but in place of mandibles were lupine jaws. Hundreds of long, sharp legs scrabbled along the concrete walls of the subway tunnel, propelling the massive Millipede toward Grig's position faster than a creature that size should have been able to.

Grig hadn't felt intense terror often during his time with The Order, but he felt it now. He was battle tested and knew that the creature he faced was a threat he would not be able to beat alone. He stood in the tunnel, a tight crevice at his back and a massive insect bearing down on him. Grig knelt, taking a steady firing position and prepared to fight with everything he had until the very end.

Instead, the Millipede slammed into an opening in the ceiling, scratching furiously at the dirt with its forelimbs. The change in direction both confused and relieved Captain Grig. Something had gotten the beast's attention, and he was thrilled that it hadn't been him. The Millipede burrowed into the earth with supernatural speed, disappearing in less than thirty seconds. After a moment Grig managed to exhale a sigh of relief and then signaled for the rest to follow, confident that the danger had passed momentarily. He didn't dare take the chance that the thing had decided to attack his company from behind. It was better to stay together.

***

Devin was surprised that nobody noticed the rumbling, but the noise of their cheering likely masked the sound. They grew quiet, though, when the rumbling intensified. A split second later all hell broke loose.

The band of Scavengers consisted of five healthy young men, several women, a pair of frail older women, as well as Gerrard, Devin and Ryve. Almost every one of them was thrown off their feet when the Millipede erupted from the earth, except the poor bastard that had been caught in the beast's jaws.

Devin tried to focus on the source of the chaos, but the impact of being thrown and the lump on the head he was already nursing was messing with his vision. He blinked and shook his head, trying desperately to get the twin images to merge into one. His vision finally began to clear, but a spray of blood hit him in the face.

Ryve rebounded faster than the Scavenger party and took the opportunity to retrieve his weapon from one of the guards, smashing the man in the face with the butt of the rifle in the process. The Trooviian immediately raised his weapon and began firing at the Millipede. The rounds sizzled from his weapon and slammed into its armored hide, barely leaving a mark. Ryve growled in frustration and continued firing, hoping to find a weakness in the Millipede's natural armor.

Devin wiped the blood from his eyes and saw Ryve standing his ground against the giant insect. Fortunately, the Millipede was still distracted with its meal, thrashing the remains of the man in its jaws and swallowing the pieces. More of the Scavenger party began getting back to their feet, but they weren't prepared for battle. Several tried to flee, but the Millipede was lightning fast and snatched another unfortunate soul in its massive canines.

The screaming was the worst. High pitched and bloodcurdling. Absolute pain and abject horror. Devin felt his stomach tighten as the carnage unfolded before him. He wanted to - no, needed to - get out of the area and as far away from the madness, from Gerrard, and from the Bandit army amassing in the east as possible. That would prove difficult; however, as Gerrard still sat astride Devin's mechanical steed.

Gerrard was operating the machine as if he'd been born on it. He deftly danced out of the Millipede's reach as it lashed out in search of another meal. His attention was on the Millipede completely, offering Devin an opportunity to remove him as a threat, but Devin wasn't a cold-blooded killer. He'd only resorted to violence in the interest of self-preservation. Now, Gerrard wasn't presenting an immediate threat. An obstacle, sure, but not quite a threat.

The Millipede finally turned its attention on Ryve and lunged at him with mind-boggling speed. Ryve had been prepared for the turn of events and immediately dove to his left as soon as the beast turned toward him. The reaction was still almost too slow, the Millipede's mandibles missing Ryve's feet by mere inches. The impact of the Millipede hitting the ground threw Ryve further than his attempted dodge would have, causing him to land roughly on top of his weapon.

Devin managed to shake the dizziness away and reached for his harpoon gun. The previous encounter with a Millipede taught him that the Trooviian weapons were ineffective against the beast's natural armor, but the heavy steel harpoon worked well. He attempted to cut the cable that fastened the harpoon to the barrel with his blade, but the blade was too dull. He would have to part with the weapon once the harpoon found its mark. He'd have only one chance to get a clean shot.

The Millipede reared back in preparation for a second strike. Ryve was still prone, face-down in the dirt and completely vulnerable. He looked up and, upon seeing the beast bearing down on him, closed his eyes in resignation. The Millipede lunged at him, its horrible jaws open wide, but its trajectory was thrown off when something struck the side of its head. Devin quickly let go of the harpoon gun as the Millipede thrashed in pain, an unearthly howl reverberating through its body and bursting forth from its monstrous, lupine jaws. The harpoon jutted from the only exposed flesh Devin could find, the spot where an eye would logically be.

The giant bug thrashed, its razor-sharp legs flailing. One leg lashed out and caught Gerrard across the chest. The impact launched him from Devin's steed and dropped him on his back. Devin gasped and then bolted toward the robot, desperate to reach the steed before Gerrard recovered.

Gerrard lay on his back, the wind knocked out of him. He was lucky that the point of the Millipede's leg hadn't struck him, or he would have been sliced in two. Gerrard rolled, or tried to, to avoid the dangerous appendage, but a sharp pain in his left side halted his progress. He winced and attempted to roll the opposite direction, narrowly avoiding being skewered.

Devin's instincts screamed at him, pulling at him to turn and run from the massive beast. He had to recover his steed. Without it, he would have to stop for rest and would be putting himself into danger. He had to get as far away from Gerrard as possible. Instead of turning, he sprinted straight toward the Millipede, ducking under its flailing legs.

The legs slammed down into the earth all around him, kicking up dirt and more than once knocking Devin off his feet. The impacts shook the ground under his feet as he ran. Devin kept his focus on the robot, and on Gerrard. So far, he hadn't gotten the crazed man's attention, but Devin knew it wouldn't be long. A moment later, as Devin drew nearer, the two locked eyes. Gerrard immediately knew what Devin was planning and started to scramble to his feet. Devin was less than forty yards from the steed, but Gerrard was even closer and would likely cross the distance first if he managed to get to his feet.

The Millipede continued to scream its unearthly scream as the two men fought to reach the robotic horse as though it were the last beacon of safety on earth. Devin pumped his legs faster, propelling himself over the shaking terrain. Gerrard finally got his feet under him and began trying to run, but the pain in his side was making it difficult to breathe or even move. The Millipede continued is furious thrashing as the two men closed the distance.

Devin watched in dismay as Gerrard reached the robotic horse first and began pulling himself on top of it. Devin pulled his blade from his belt as he neared the horse, fully intent on burying the blade in the thief's face, but a wild kick from the Millipede took Gerrard off the horse once again, this time catching the robot in the side and sending it sprawling. Devin dove to his right to avoid the beast's leg as it crashed back down.

Gerrard fell in a heap near a dilapidated building that was little more than crumbling walls and a door. He didn't move. The robotic horse had taken the brunt of the strike and lay nearby, sparking from the deep gash in the metal siding. Devin crawled on his hands and knees to get away from the Millipede, desperate to reach the horse.

He could see the damage his steed had sustained and hoped that it was only superficial. He got to his feet and sprinted up to the robot. Once he arrived by its side, he stared down at it, and his heart began to sink. The Millipede's leg had cut a deep gash in the chassis of the horse, the wiring exposed and severed in some places. It would take time he didn't presently have to fix the damage, and even then, he wasn't sure if it would be functional again.

A seething rage-filled Devin as he shot a glance towards Gerrard's huddled form. He felt the impulse to inflict as much damage as possible to the man, but the feeling also frightened him. It was such an alien feeling for Devin. He'd never actually *wanted* to kill someone. He'd had to, on occasion, but never had he wanted to. The rage, the risk-taking, and the sheer hostility he felt were completely new and unwanted. Where was it coming from?

Devin didn't even realize that he'd begun moving toward Gerrard, blade still in hand.

Chapter 27

The eco-generator prototype hummed as it pumped out a cloud of what looked like green smoke. Professor Goordaiin knew that it was in fact spores of plant life being pumped into the air, searching for somewhere they can settle and begin growing. A thin blanket of moss already covered the walls and floor of the lab, bright green and moist. As the eco-generator continued to work more plant life would spring up, and in no time a full ecosystem would exist in the room. The eco-generator was a success.

Professor Goordaiin, who was not one to show emotion if possible, grinned. "Send me a full report on the eco-generator. It's time to move out of Phase 1 and into Phase 2."

"Yes, Professor," one of the scientists, a hawkish man with beady eyes name Jimmy Swanson, said.

Professor Goordaiin continued to grin as he turned to leave the room. Finally, something was going according to plan. With the eco-generator operational and the framework of Phoenix One ready for launch, it was time to take the project off-world. With any luck his scouting party would also discover the location of The Human Collective's headquarters, thus giving him the ability to rid himself of the last form of real resistance left.

He walked down the halls, a lightness in his steps as everything was finally going his way. The unpleasant business with Elaina had been cause for concern, but no more. He was almost willing to forget about it altogether. Almost. She'd been a thorn in his side, and until she was no longer in the picture, there would always be the chance that she could cause more trouble for him, especially if she reached The Human Collective and told them everything.

Let them find out, he decided. What difference would it make? By the time they were up to speed his troops would be more than halfway to their location. The Collective would have no time to mobilize. It would be quick and easy. Destroy the engines of the Disc City that housed The Collective, and they'd be destroyed. It had certainly worked for Disc City 6.

Everything was going to plan, and soon he'd begin rounding up the "biological material" for the eco-generator. The humans were already serving their purpose exceedingly well and would continue to serve in another, broader capacity.

***

The subway tunnel felt as though it was shrinking, or perhaps it was Elaina's claustrophobia. The rumbling overhead hadn't helped. At any moment, a large chunk of the ceiling could come loose, and they'd be buried alive. It also didn't help that the Trooviian commander had told them all what the source of the rumbling was. The idea of a massive, deadly creature thrashing about just above their heads terrified her. She saw the terror mirrored in Kyle's eyes as well.

Kyle had remained silent and had tried to put on a brave face, but Elaina could see the panic in his eyes. She saw him stare up at the ceiling every time there was a tremor, clutching his rifle tight in his hands until his knuckles turned white. She knew why he was trying not to show that it was bothering him. It may have been a bit chauvinistic, sure, but she appreciated it a little as well. He was holding it together for her.

The Trooviians remained difficult to read. If it hadn't been the change in their posture Elaina would have assumed, they didn't even notice the miniature earthquakes. They continued to stare ahead, weapons trained on the gloom in front of them, prepared for anything that might come out of the dark at the group. She should have felt safer having an armed escort, but after her experiences with the Trooviians, she doubted she'd ever feel safe around them again.

The tunnel quaked again, chunks of dirt and debris falling from the ceiling all around the band. Something major was going on. Maybe two of the creatures were fighting? Elaina shivered when she imagined not one, but two of the monstrous creatures thrashing about, directly overhead. A high pitched, unearthly shriek struck them from somewhere behind them. Elaina jumped, her heart suddenly hammering in her chest so hard and fast that she thought it might just burst through her chest.

The entire squad spun on their heels, weapons trained down the tunnel behind them. Kyle moved even closer to Elaina to help her raise her own rifle. She was bothered by the gesture, but part of her was grateful. She'd have to learn how to function without her arm if she survived the journey. The scream came again, echoing off the concrete walls. It didn't sound like it had moved closer, but the reverberations make it difficult to tell.

The Trooviians listened intently for any further sounds and then started to relax when no more shrieking echoed down the tunnel. Elaina wasn't ready to lower her guard yet, and neither was Kyle. They both stared into the murky darkness, their eyes straining to see anything in the gloom. Elaina exhaled when she realized she'd been holding her breath. She heard Kyle do the same. They continued to listen, but still, there was no sound. The tremors hadn't stopped, but neither had they intensified. Elaina began to relax and turned to continue down the tunnel with the Trooviian escort.

A large crashing noise, not unlike an explosion, thundered behind them. Elaina and Kyle spun around again, followed by the entire Trooviian contingent.

"It's back in the tunnel," Grig said through clenched teeth. "We need to run!"

The squad broke into a run, though their speed was hampered by the uneven terrain, and didn't dare glance behind them. Elaina could hear the scratching, scuttling noise of hundreds of legs on concrete rushing up behind them. Her heart had resumed its furious hammering, and she began to worry that her heart would give out. Kyle stayed by her side, though he certainly could have outrun the entire group.

The scratching noise grew so intense that little else could be heard. The thing had to have been right behind them, but still, they refused to turn and look. Any backward glance would be a risk as any one of them could trip and bring down the rest of the group. The beast would have an easy meal then.

Elaina didn't even look up when the scuttling noise overtook them, coming from directly above. She didn't want to see what was bearing down on them. Maybe, if she didn't look at it, it would just cease to exist. She knew that was a childish thought, but she couldn't help it. She'd been scared before when she was being hunted by Goordaiin's hitmen, but never had she felt such primal terror.

A scream came from the front of the group as one of the Trooviians was snatched up in the Millipede's hideous jaws. The

Millipede had managed to get in front of the group and had reared up out of the dark directly in front of them. None of them had time to react as its vicious maw closed around the unfortunate Trooviian and wrenched him off his feet. The beast used its forelimbs to force the Trooviian deeper into its mouth. The Millipede bit down and severed the poor creature in half right below the ribcage.

Captain Grig bellowed and began firing at the freakish thing's face, hoping to score a mortal wound. The rounds sizzled against the Millipede's natural armor. He didn't stop firing, and more Trooviians took up positions to join in. Round after round hissed and sizzled against the beast as it continued to tear into the corpse, devouring the rest of it. Someone scored a lucky shot and hit it in the mouth as it lunged at Burg. The Millipede recoiled and let out another bloodcurdling shriek.

The reaction was all the group needed. They reacquired their target, focusing this time on the Millipede's jaws. The rounds burrowed into the exposed flesh, and the Millipede howled in pain. It continued to recoil into the darkness, struggling to get away from the onslaught, but the small squad continued forward. The Millipede lunged toward the ceiling to burrow to the surface, but it exposed its underside, and more rounds blasted through. Kyle was growling as he fired relentlessly at the creature's exposed weakness. The rounds slammed mercilessly into the Millipede, eventually cutting the creature completely in half. The upper half disappeared into the roof of the tunnel, leaving the rest of itself behind.

Elaina felt a surge of joy as the creature disappeared. They'd done it! They were still alive! She saw Kyle sag with exhaustion next to her and then saw Captain Grig approach the creature's remains.

Grig was silent as he knelt and plucked something from the mass of gore where the Trooviian had been devoured. It looked to Elaina like some kind of necklace. Grig stood and stuffed the object into a pocket on his vest without bothering to wipe it off. He didn't speak as he motioned for the band to continue their march forward into the dark.

Chapter 28

Devin continued to stalk closer to Gerrard's motionless form, the blade feeling heavy in his hand. Everything about this felt wrong, but something urged him forward. He could feel all the rage he'd been suppressing build and start to overtake him. Devin had never lost control of his emotions in his life, but at this moment he was no longer thinking logically. He didn't even notice the smile that had begun to creep across his features.

Gerrard stirred as Devin approached. He opened his eyes and stared at the Scavenger with the blade in hand, an eerie grin stretched across his face. Gerrard hadn't feared much in his long life, but something about the Scavenger unnerved him. He tried to drag himself backward in a feeble attempt to get away, but his body was racked with pain and his limbs refused to obey.

Devin saw the terror in the man's eyes, and a part of him screamed at him to stop. It was almost as if he was just a passenger and something else was at the controls. He was nearly on top of Gerrard as he raised his blade in preparation. Gerrard closed his eyes, waiting for the blow that would kill him.

The strike never came. Gerrard opened his eyes just as the ground beneath them exploded upward. Devin was thrown several feet away, and Gerrard was airborne once again. In the split second that he hung in the air, he grimaced and tried to mentally prepare for the impact that would surely break his body. He slammed back down and felt several of his ribs break, along with his hip. His right shoulder dislocated at the same time, and the combined pain signals from his wounds caused him to blackout.

Devin bounced hard off the ground and tasted blood in his mouth as he bit into his tongue. He felt several teeth break as well as his chin hit the ground. Dirt filled his nose and eyes, adding to the pain. He could hear the hideous shriek of the Millipede and knew in just a matter of moments he would feel the creature's teeth pierce his flesh. He felt tears welling up in his eyes as he silently berated himself for being dragged into this mess instead of running.

***

The Millipede dragged itself out of the hole and across the broken ground, bleeding profusely from its severed midsection. Internal organs trailed from the hideous wound as it continued to propel itself forward. It moved slowly toward the nearest target, its last possible meal: Devin Slade.

***

Gerrard rolled onto his less injured side and watched as the Millipede inched closer to Devin's still form. He grinned as he waited for the creature to kill the bastard. Gerrard may not walk away from the encounter, but he'd outlive Devin, and that was a small victory. After all the trouble Devin had given him in such a short amount of time, Gerrard was pleased by the idea of him meeting a painfully messy end.

Devin could hear the Millipede's ragged breathing as it moved ever closer. He still couldn't move, and the prolonged wait was agonizing. He wanted nothing more at that very moment than for the Millipede to strike and end his pain. He turned his head to face the creature, blinking the dirt from his eyes. The massive beast was a mere foot away, its jaws dominating Devin's vision. He couldn't bring himself to stare death in the face, so he shut his eyes and turned away, his heart pounding in his chest from the terrible anticipation.

***

The Millipede howled once again as something tore into the gaping wound in its midsection. It could feel blasts cutting through organs and nerves as the intruder moved further inward. A blast tore through its heart, and it no longer tried to move. It lay motionless as more blasts tore through it and the intruder finally burst from its mouth.

***

Devin reluctantly opened his eyes to look at the Millipede again and watched in awe as Ryve emerged from the beast's jaws, drenched in gore. He'd never been happier to see the Trooviian. He continued to watch as Ryve knelt next to him and prepared to lift him off the ground, Ryve's weapon already slung back over his shoulder. Devin groaned as his weight shifted and his wounds flared with renewed agony.

***

Gerrard howled in rage when the Trooviian carried Devin away. It wasn't fair! The Millipede was so close! Gerrard laid his head back and ground his teeth in a mixture of rage and pain. When he opened his eyes, he spotted the robotic steed off to his right. The Scavenger may not have been killed, but the robotic steed would be a nice consolation prize. He doubted Devin would get very far without it, especially now.

Grinning, Gerrard began crawling toward the robotic horse.

***

Devin struggled to remain conscious as Ryve carried him away from the Millipede's remains and the remains of its victims. He could see the bodies of several Scavengers who'd been following Gerrard strewn about. He strained to see through the growing haze induced by the concussion to spot signs of life. Not every person in Gerrard's party was dead. In fact, Devin could see several of them carefully wandering toward the fallen, still wary of the Millipede. He couldn't blame them for being overly cautious. He had been the same way for much of his life, until recently. Maybe the blow to the head from the Bandit attack had scrambled his brains? He couldn't explain his dramatic shift in personality any other way.

The Millipede had done an incredible amount of damage in just a short span of time. The encounter couldn't have lasted more than five minutes from start to finish, but to Devin, it felt like it had spanned an entire day. The people who'd been at the epicenter of the Millipede's eruption were sprawled several feet away. Most of them, at least half a dozen, were clearly dead as their necks had been broken from the violent flight or their skulls crushed when they landed. Others were struggling to move their broken bodies, and Devin began to doubt they would survive long.

The Scavengers who'd been fortunate enough to be further away from the Millipede's initial attack hadn't come away unscathed.

Many would bear hideous new scars from the encounter if they survived. Out of the thirty people in Gerrard's group, half still stood. Devin continued to scan the surrounding area to spot Gerrard. He hoped the crazy bastard was dead. A moment later, his heart dropped. Gerrard was once again astride the mechanical horse, bruised and bleeding, but alive. Devin felt the rage building again just before he lost consciousness.

***

Gerrard watched from his perch as his people attempted to regroup. The attack was a massive setback, but all was not lost. Some still survived, and none of his army was nearby. He doubted all the Bandits would survive their march toward Disc City 9. They would have to contend with the wildlife that remained, as well as the unforgiving climate. Still, the army was large enough to afford the inevitable losses.

The survivors of the attack did their best to tend to the wounded. Without proper medical training and equipment, the most they could offer to the critically wounded was an easy, nearly painless passing. Those that hadn't been critically injured didn't have much of a chance as well, but at least they'd last a little while longer. That was fine with Gerrard. The losses weren't something he'd wanted, but he was still alive – albeit barely- and so were at least half his contingent. That would be enough to help him take control of Phoenix One.

Scavengers will no longer have to fight to survive and live off scraps. They'd no longer be subjected to slave labor. Gerrard wondered how long the Calvorans would survive as the new labor force. Those he allowed to live, that is. The fragile creatures would likely drop like flies from the strain. How nice it would be to finally turn the tables on the miserable, pompous bastards.

Chapter 29

Elaina and Kyle sat toward the back of the Trooviian scouting party while Grig took stock of their losses. Only one Trooviian fell to the Millipede, but the loss still weighed heavily on the seasoned warrior. Elaina could see, through the Trooviian's body language, that he took responsibility for the tragedy. His shoulders were slumped, and he snapped at more than one Trooviian who'd dared question what he was saying, though Elaina couldn't understand a word of their native language.

Kyle was tending to Elaina's injured arm while she sat silently. Her arm had been well treated by the Sentrons, but she figured Kyle was just trying to stay occupied instead of dwelling on what had been happening. The Millipede was something neither of them had ever seen before, and the monstrosity had absolutely terrified both of them.

Kyle had frozen in place—a fact that shamed and infuriated him—during the creature's initial appearance and it wasn't until one of the Trooviians smacked him on the shoulder that he finally began firing at it. Elaina had frozen as well, but she didn't have a clear shot at any point in the attack, so that was just as well. She was still trying to process what had happened in the last couple of days.

Minutes later, the Trooviian scouting party formed up and began their march once more. The mission hadn't changed. They still needed to get Kyle and Elaina to the transport ship as soon as possible so The Collective could be briefed. Grig had grown surer of his decision with every step. It was as if he'd walked out of a fog and could see everything clearly for the first time in months. He wasn't a stranger to the telepathic powers of the Calvorans and figured that Goordaiin's influence over him had faded with the growing distance.

Several hours passed as they continued down the ruined subway tunnels, their progress diverted more than once due to blocked passages and excessive debris. Elaina was already taxed from the events of the last 48 hours, compounded with the Millipede attack and her amputated arm, and she was struggling to stay standing. Kyle tried his best to help her, but he was exhausted as well. They would have to stop before too much longer.

"Please tell me we're getting close," Kyle called out.

"We shouldn't be far now," Captain Grig called back. "We are just looking for a way back to the surface. The transport shuttle and the second team are close by."

"How far?" Kyle asked.

"Can't say for sure," Grig replied. "Like I said, we need to find a way back to the surface. The last platform was completely blocked off, and there's supposed to be another one about a mile ahead of us."

"We need to rest, then," Kyle said. At that moment, Elaina collapsed to her knees.

"I can barely feel my legs," she said. Her face had begun to pale.

"We're almost there," Grig argued. "We can't stop now."

"We *have* to," Kyle snapped back. "Unless one of your people wants to carry us the rest of the way."

This caused an eruption of grumbling from the Trooviians. Apparently, they weren't too thrilled with the prospect, as Kyle had expected. Captain Grig raised a fist to silence them.

"Fine," he conceded. "But only for a moment."

"A moment should be all we need," Kyle said. He didn't really believe it, but there was no use arguing any further. Elaina needed help, and Kyle wasn't far from collapsing himself.

***

Grig had only intended to stop for a minimum of five minutes, but when he tried to rouse Elaina and Kyle, they ignored him. He could see that Elaina was not well. She could no longer sit up on her own, and her eyes were closed more often than not. Kyle wasn't doing much better. He continuously attempted to stand, but he began to waver within seconds and had to sit back down. Exhaustion had set in, and Grig knew enough about humans to know that pushing them further would kill them.

Five minutes turned into thirty. Elaina had fallen asleep completely, and Kyle dozed off for minutes at a time. The Trooviians, Grig included, were growing restless. They were at home underground, but the appearance of the mutants and the Millipede had made them extremely cautious.

The wildlife on their home planet had been dangerous as well, but the Trooviians had been used to dealing with them. The Millipedes on Earth were far more dangerous, though. They didn't emit a pheromone that the Trooviians could detect. The horizontal slit on their face, which humans had assumed was the equivalent of a nose, was, in fact, a specially evolved sensory organ that picked up unique pheromones and electrical pulses. Since the Millipede was a completely foreign organism in which the Trooviians had nearly no contact with, their sensory organs hadn't been able to adapt. They had spent enough time around humans, however, and had already adapted.

After nearly an hour Grig had had enough waiting. He issued orders to his company and approached Kyle directly. Kyle had fallen asleep, and it took a moment, as well as some less than gentle jostling, to rouse him. He grumbled and tried to turn away from the invasive Trooviian, but Grig grabbed ahold of him and lifted him easily to his feet.

"We have to go now," Grig insisted. Kyle detected a note of fear in his voice.

"How long have we been out?"

"Almost a full Earth-hour," Grig replied. "We can't stay any longer. The rendezvous point may already be compromised."

"Okay, okay," Kyle said as he turned to face Elaina. She wasn't nearly as pale, but she still didn't look well. "I think we are going to have to carry her."

"Fine, I'll do it," Grig said hastily, already moving to scoop her up. The Trooviians agitation and impatience were not lost on Kyle.

"What is it?" he asked.

"I'm not sure," Grig answered in a whisper. "One of my scouts have gone missing. He was supposed to do a perimeter check, and he hasn't returned. I don't think we're alone, again."

"Shit!" Kyle gasped a little too loudly. The other Trooviians looked over at the pair and immediately increased their pace.

Grig hadn't intended to get them riled up. Doing so could do more damage than harm. As with most sentient creatures, increased agitation could sharpen the senses, but too much would irrational panic and simple warnings can be missed. It was too late, now. The Trooviian scouting party was scrambling about like ants. They had to move out immediately.

Grig hefted Elaine onto his shoulder and carried his rifle in his left hand. Kyle followed immediately behind as they raced down the tunnel, surrounded by the rest of the Trooviians. They weren't proceeding with caution any longer. It looked more like a stampede than an organized group.

Kyle couldn't help feeling that they were merely running away from phantoms conjured by the heightened anxiety. He didn't care, though. He would much rather get out of the tunnels than stay in the dark. The tunnels had begun to feel like a tomb.

***

The Trooviian scouts had miscalculated the distance to the next platform. It took longer than expected to reach their destination, but they, fortunately, arrived without incident. Light began to filter from the top of the stairs. It was literally the light at the end of the tunnel. The contingent began to relax, and some of them even felt a bit embarrassed by their panic. It didn't appear as though they'd been followed.

Elaina had woken up during their haste and had immediately joined in their panic, though she didn't know exactly why. Captain Grig's pace had made her journey immensely uncomfortable as she bounced on his shoulder with every step. She wanted to tell him to put her down, but her legs still felt weak. Instead, she endured the less than dignified ride. She felt embarrassed that she was being carried and couldn't even bring herself to look at Kyle, who always stayed a step behind the racing Trooviian.

Kyle didn't care that Elaina was being carried over Captain Grig's shoulder like a captive. If it meant keeping her alive, he could care less. He saw the embarrassment on her face and silently made a note to alleviate it later when they had time to relax. She needn't be embarrassed. He didn't pass judgment on her or her condition, and he wanted to make sure she knew it.

Grig finally lowered Elaina to her feet when they arrived at the platform. She was still shaky, but she could remain standing. Kyle came up to her and offered his arm to her. She took it, reluctantly, and let him guide her toward the stairs. Her face felt hot with embarrassment, even though she knew it was ridiculous. She found she cared quite a bit about how Kyle perceived her. She didn't want him to think she was weak and helpless, but that was pretty much all he'd seen since they'd met.

The Trooviians positioned themselves in front of and directly behind the pair as they ascended. The light was blinding, and the first Trooviians out faltered. Elaina and Kyle collided into the back of the nearest one as it stopped. Fortunately, the Trooviians behind them noticed and didn't add to the collision.

"Why are we stopping?" Kyle called.

"Can't see," came a reply from up ahead. "Too dangerous to continue until eyes adjust!"

How long could that possibly take? Kyle continued to try to push forward as his frustration grew. They needed to get out of the deadly tunnels, and he didn't want to waste any more time. The Trooviian in front of him refused to budge for a moment longer, and then thankfully began moving once again. Kyle let out a small sigh of relief.

A scream from behind shattered the relative calm. Kyle twisted to see behind him, but he couldn't see past Captain Grig, who'd followed directly behind. Grig had turned as well, straining to see what had caused the outburst. Another scream erupted from below, and then the entire contingent of Trooviians began forcing their way forward. The Earth's hidden horrors had once again found them—of that Grig had no doubt.

Chapter 30

Professor Goordaiin made his way once again to the conference room to address the Council. Now that the Eco-Generator was fully operational, the fuel source would need to be harvested. After the justification he'd previously given, he doubted he'd meet much resistance. For the first time since the incident with Elaina, he was at ease. So, what if he hadn't heard from his scouting party? None of that would matter much longer. Phoenix One was about to enter the second phase, and everyone – The Human Collective included- will be focusing all their efforts on completing it promptly.

The conference room was overflowing with a mixture of apprehension and excitement. Goordaiin hadn't been specific in his instructions for them to assemble. He merely stated that they were back on track. All eyes were on him as he entered, and he had to muster all his will to prevent his emotions from showing on his skin. He couldn't show them his elation. He had to remain in full control and play on their emotions, rather than allow his own to interfere.

"My fellow councilmen," Goordaiin began, his arms opening wide as he addressed the room. He realized, immediately afterward, that it likely came off too flamboyant. He'd need to reign it in.

"When we last convened I had the unfortunate task of breaking the news of Doctor Peterson's death, but I also had the pleasure to inform you that the Eco-Generator had passed its trial. After closely monitoring it I am confident in saying that it is a success. We are now ready to take Phoenix One out of phase one and into phase two."

The bubble of excitement burst as the weight of the words finally took hold on the council. The Calvoran members flashed a bright blue as they expressed their pleasure, and the Trooviians began to hoot with excitement. Goordaiin had to refrain from showing his disgust from the Trooviian display. Such uncivilized beasts. How he despised the Calvorans' dependency on the creatures, nearly as much as he despised being near the Humans.

"There is one thing I must mention," he continued after recomposing himself. "As previously stated, the fuel source for the

Eco-Generator must be obtained, and the most useful source is the biological material contained within the humans' bodies. We will need to begin harvesting the Bandit population quickly if there is to be any chance of sustainment once the generator is installed."

The excitement died down as he finished his statement. The Trooviians simply stared stupidly while the Calvorans began to shift toward a green hue. They were nervous about the proposition, understandably so, but it wouldn't be hard to sway them.

"If we begin harvesting humans, even if it *is* just the Bandit population, we'll be risking a confrontation with The Human Collective," one Calvoran stated. "The Collective has already made it quite clear that further attacks on humanity will be met with force."

"I am aware of this, Vallus," Goordaiin retorted, intentionally dropping the Calvoran's title of Doctor. "And what I am proposing is not violence. As far as The Collective is concerned, we are merely escorting the Bandits to safety while keeping them separate from the main populace. If you study the schematics for the Phoenix One station, you'll notice an entire section dedicated to containment in the event of a quarantine. We will convert part of that section to a 'farm' as the humans call it."

"Have you already cleared this with The Collective?" Vallus interjected. Goordaiin wasn't entirely comfortable with lying to another Calvoran but wasting time could easily spell disaster.

"I have," Goordaiin replied. The rest of the council looked at one another. "So long as the Bandits are not treated cruelly, or 'inhumanely' as they put it, we are authorized to move forward with their evacuation and subsequent relocation."

For a moment, everyone stared at Goordaiin, watching him closely. He knew they were looking for some sign of deceit. Some hint that he could be lying. He remained stone-faced and denied them any emotion that would sow seeds of doubt. When no betrayal of his features was forthcoming, the council nodded in approval and agreed to proceed. Goordaiin smiled as he exited the conference room.

***

Goordaiin allowed himself to relax in his living quarters. The space was sparsely decorated and lacked much in the way of furniture, save for a chair that resembled a floating egg. Calvorans slept, but, unlike their Trooviian counterparts or Humans, they slept in a seated position. It was more akin to meditation than to the sleep nearly every living creature experienced. The Calvorans had evolved past the need for REM sleep as their brains were more efficient.

As he sat in his chair, Goordaiin closed his beady eyes and slipped immediately into a meditative state. It had been more than 24 hours since he last "slept" and he knew his body would need to refresh itself. He would need to be sharp and in prime operating condition for the next 48 hours, at least. Extracting the Bandits, and inevitably dealing with the Chancellor, would be no easy task. Perhaps he should remove the Chancellor, as he had every other opposition he'd faced.

Then, of course, there was Rectus. It was no secret that the two Calvorans hated one another, though few knew exactly why. All that was presently known was Rectus had led an attack on a human settlement during the earliest days when the three species had tried to work together. The intent, as far as everyone knew, was to quell the rebellious uprising without inflicting casualties. What happened, instead, was a wholesale slaughter of one of the last surface-dwelling communities. Rectus had overseen the Calvoran task force then. The Chancellor saw to it that he was removed from the position.

What nobody really knew; however, was that Goordaiin had encouraged the attack. He'd gone so far as to fabricate a story of weapons manufacturing so that Rectus would respond with devastating force. The plan, at the time, had seemed to be entirely Rectus's. He'd perceived the reports from his scouts as such and acted according to what he'd believed, that the human settlement was a massive threat.

In truth, the settlement had nearly no way to protect themselves and never could manufacture weapons. Goordaiin had wanted it removed completely after he had relieved Richard Dawkins as President of the Phoenix One Project. Any further ties to the man had needed to be severed, which Goordaiin ensured by having the settlement exterminated. Any family that could potentially stake claim to the project had died that day, and it was Rectus who had to deal with the fallout.

Goordaiin prided himself on his exceptional psychic abilities. It was nearly unheard of for one Calvoran to completely control another. It was especially unique that a Calvoran could replace or modify the memories of another, but Rectus's mind was weak by comparison. Rectus hated Goordaiin, but even he didn't know exactly why.

Chapter 31

Elaina fought to ascend the stairwell as the Trooviians pressed against her. The rear element was fighting forward with a desperation she'd never seen from the usually stoic beings. Their girth threatened to crush her as she found herself directly in the center of the throng. Once again terror welled up within her as her lungs fought for oxygen. Despite trying to help her, the Trooviians were surely going to kill her.

Elaina's vision started to narrow to pinpoints and unconsciousness was drawing near when she felt someone grip her hand and pull her forward. She knew that, though she couldn't see anything, Kyle was trying to pull her free. He was risking his life for hers yet again, though she knew he'd never complain. She knew without a shadow of a doubt that he'd risk death for her at every opportunity. It was in the way he kept looking at her, though he probably thought he'd been able to hide it. The truth was, the man was an open book.

Kyle may have had no problem sacrificing himself, but Elaina felt guilty about it. If he died because of her, she'd never forgive herself. With humanity diminishing it had become necessary for everyone, even children, to become self-sufficient and act in accordance with preserving the species. There was no more time for courtship, leisure, or selfish pursuits.

It was everyone's responsibility to aid in protecting humanity, but Kyle's actions had been in contradiction to this mentality. His death would only detract from humanity's chance for survival, but this didn't appear to matter to him. He'd done what most people had no time for—he'd fallen in love.

The grip of darkness released its hold as Elaina finally came free from the chaos. She sucked in a large intake of oxygen and felt Kyle's arms around her as he guided her upward. She could still hear the shrieks and howls of the Trooviians behind her, but she had no idea what was happening. It didn't seem as if anyone really knew.

***

Captain Grig acted against his instincts and pressed his way through the crowd toward the rear element. The chaos was uncharacteristic of his squad, and he was intent on discovering the cause. He could see the look of panic in the eyes of his companions and could detect the pheromones they were releasing as terror overwhelmed them.

As he descended, he saw the human couple struggle to free themselves. He grabbed Kyle around the waist once Elaina was in his grasp and pulled both free. Kyle gave him a quick nod in thanks and immediately turned his attention on Elaina. Grig left them as he pushed into the pressing bodies of the Trooviian scouting party.

Grig saw immediately what had caused the mass panic as he finally made his way to the rear. Several of his scouts were covered in tumorous growths identical to the ones that had enveloped the poor souls they'd encountered earlier in the tunnels. How the growths had occurred, and how rapidly they'd grown, confounded him. The poor creatures flailed in agony and panic before finally dropping to the ground.

He was about to turn and ascend the stairs when the infected Trooviians began to twitch. It wasn't the Trooviians that were twitching, though. The growths appeared to be moving on their own, forcing limbs to move. It was then that Grig began to understand the true nature of the tumors. They weren't tumors at all. Something alive was moving beneath the surface.

To his horror Grig watched the infected scouts climb clumsily to their feet and advance. They were blinded by the masses that had covered their flesh, but they seemed to be relying on their other senses to track him. Grig backed up as they advanced, trying his best to keep his distance. He felt hands on his shoulders drag him back as his fellow Trooviians attempted to pull him to safety.

The Trooviian that had helped Grig turned just as the nearest infected creature closed the distance. The growths on its body exploded and swarms of fat, black insects crawled over Grig's savior, burrowing into any exposed soft tissue. The Trooviian clawed at his face in a mixture of agony and panic as the parasitic creatures dug into his eyes, his nasal slit, his mouth and every other orifice. The flesh began to swell and bulge as more of the invasive creatures made their way inside.

Captain Grig, having heard enough of the terrified Trooviian's screams, drew his weapon and fired. The blast blew the poor creature's head apart, and the body tumbled down the stairs, landing with a wet slap at the base. Grig bellowed orders to retreat as the second infected Trooviian stepped over its fallen companions and continued its advance. Grig was determined to prevent the same fate from befalling the rest of his company.

Chapter 32

Devin groaned in agony while Ryve worked on the Millipede's carcass. None of the Scavengers had dared venture near the beast, despite it being very dead. The Trooviian carved large slabs of flesh from the beast and stuffed the gooey pieces into a large bag that he'd pulled from one of his many pouches. Devin could see the viscera oozing through the bag. The sight was enough to make him gag, though the smell was far worse.

The smell permeated everything. It was the smell of garbage left in the sun for days, accelerating decomposition. The pungent, yet slightly sweet, smell of rot gave Devin pause. How in the hell would he bring himself to eat something that smelled so foul? He was hungry, but he doubted he'd ever be hungry enough to eat the foul-smelling globs of flesh. Ryve didn't seem bothered by the smell, though. He just kept hacking away at the corpse and stuffing the chunks into the bag, seemingly oblivious to the stench and the liquid oozing through the bag.

Instead of watching Ryve work, Devin opted to search once more for Gerrard. Ryve had only carried Devin a short distance from the carnage, but he'd already lost sight of the madman. He wasn't sure if he was unnerved by the man's disappearance or disappointed that he couldn't watch the crazy bastard die. *Holy shit*, Devin though. *Where the hell did* that *come from? What is going on with me?*

A glint of light caught Devin's eye, and he immediately focused on it. There Gerrard sat astride the mechanical steed. It didn't seem as if Gerrard had spotted him yet, but he was completely exposed, and it wouldn't be long. He tried to move, but his limbs felt as if they weighed tons and the effort alone produced agony. He was certain he'd broken at least a few bones. How Gerrard survived, Devin could only guess. The repeated strikes from the Millipede should have, theoretically, killed the man. As if in defiance, Gerrard sat up straight in the saddle.

Ryve finally finished butchering the carcass and strode back toward Devin. He nearly called to Ryve to stop as the horrendous stench grew more potent, but he knew the Trooviian would at least feign ignorance. Ryve knew more of the common tongue than he let on, of this Devin was certain. There'd been hints during their short time together, and the Trooviians increasing proficiency with the language only served to confirm his suspicion.

"Why are you making face?" Ryve asked as he crouched by Devin's head.

"It... "Devin began, but the smell caused him to vomit. "It-it stinks!"

"Not so bad," Ryve grunted while raising the bag to his face. He appeared to sniff it, glancing sideways toward Devin as he did so. Devin vomited again. Ryve let out a chuckle. The bastard was enjoying this!

"I'm not eating that!" Devin finally managed, though he tried to breathe as little as possible.

"Tastes better than smell," Ryve said. Devin arched an eyebrow as he tried to understand what the Trooviian meant. "Tastes good."

"I doubt that," Devin snapped. He couldn't stop the small smile that had begun to creep over his face. "You eat it, then."

To his horror, Ryve reached into the sack and pulled a gummy chunk of flesh from within. Without hesitation, he popped it into his mouth and began to chew. Devin could even swear that Ryve was making sounds of pleasure as he ate!

"Ugh! What the fuck?" Devin shouted just as more bile rose in his throat. He was no longer hungry. "You bastard."

"Come," Ryve said as he scooped Devin up and draped him over a massive shoulder. "We leave this place. Find Disc City 9. Find New Haven and kill Goordaiin."

"Yeah, right," Devin grumbled. "How are we going to do that? I can't even walk."

"Rig help," Ryve said, tapping the back of Devin's. "Heal soon."

"Not soon enough," Devin muttered, but already the pain in his limbs had seemed to lessen. The BSS rig still astounded him.

"Only Goordaiin needs to die," Ryve said as he trudged on. "Others don't need to die. Must warn them of Bandit army."

"That is probably the only thing we agree on," Devin replied. "Gerrard is nuts and who knows what he has planned. Getting

Bandits to march for him sounds loony as hell. How do they plan on taking over a flying city? With some goddamn rope?"

"Trooviian weapons have long range," Ryve said. "Made to fire shorter range. For safety. Dampener."

"Oh," Devin said. He couldn't think of anything else to say. The Bandits would likely fire at the underside of the city if they could figure out how to adjust the weapons. He doubted it would take them long, as they had a similar affinity for machines. They had been Scavengers at one time, after all.

"Many die," Ryve continued. "Phoenix One project fail. All will be doomed."

Once again, Devin found himself agreeing with the massive alien. *Shit*, Devin thought.

Chapter 33

Grig had only truly felt fear a handful of times during his life. Each time had been in the face of seemingly impossible odds. This time, however, his fear was borne from the hideous nature of the parasites that had already consumed two of his men. Never before had he seen something control another organism so completely. The humans had a term for such a creature, though the origins of the mythological being differed. Zombies, they'd called them. No such creature had ever actually existed, but the fear had been global and passed from generation to generation.

It seemed that zombies, in some form, truly did exist. This frightened Grig more than anything else. He'd been personally subjected to some form of outside control since he had begun working for Goordaiin, but he'd managed to maintain some degree of autonomy and individuality during this time. Many of his actions had been dictated by orders that he'd been compelled to follow, but he had at least been aware of it.

What was happening to the infected Trooviians was something they'd never witnessed before. During the time they'd spent on Earth, they'd never run across such a creature. The atmosphere had made research expeditions impractical, so it was very likely there were life forms nobody knew about, but most of the larger ruins had been investigated and nothing like this had ever been seen.

The remaining infected Trooviian extended its hands toward Grig, grasping blindly at thin air. He wanted to retreat. To turn and flee as far away from this abomination as possible, but Grig knew he'd be condemning more of his team to a fate worse than death. He quelled his fear as much as possible and held his ground. He still held his rifle at the ready, but he had hesitated to pull the trigger. He'd know the Trooviian personally. He'd was Grig's nephew.

The husk of Grig's kin was dead, in a sense, and was now a puppet for another. He had to remind himself of this repeatedly as the Trooviian advanced.

The zombie Trooviian's fingers brushed the barrel of Grig's weapon, and he fired in response. The blast tore through the extended limb and through the lower half of its face.

"Rest easy now," Grig said in hushed tones before turning away and following his team up the stairwell and into the harsh light of the sun.

***

Kyle was the first to emerge from the subway stairwell, his heart still pounding in his chest. He put one hand up to shield his eyes from the glare and pulled Elaina along. He'd had to sling his weapon to protect his vision, a decision he already detested. They were sitting ducks, and he was in no position to launch a counter-attack if the situation dictated.

He braced himself for the impact of some kind of archaic weapon, but nothing happened. As his vision adjusted, Kyle began to take in his surroundings. They'd stepped out onto a wide street, choked with the decayed remnants of vehicles long dead. The ruined buildings pressed inward as some had toppled into one another at one time. Among the congested road was massive chunks of rubble from buildings that no longer stood proudly.

There were simply too many places to hide.

"I don't see anything," Elaina said. Kyle turned his attention from the decrepit city to face her. Her face was pale, and she looked exhausted, dark rings surrounded her eyes.

"Neither do I," he replied. He crouched down as he ventured forth, hoping to create as small a target as possible as he made his way quickly toward cover. His weapon was back in his hands, ready for the first sign of danger.

"We must move," came the gravelly voice of a Trooviian. "Too many enemies below."

"And possibly more above," Kyle shot back. "I refuse to rush headlong into another shit-storm if I can absolutely help it."

"Spread out and find cover," Grig commanded as he exited the subway tunnel. "Our friend has it right. To stand out in the open is to invite death."

Elaina moved with some measure of difficulty to rejoin Kyle's side. She heard the heavy footsteps of their Trooviian companions, though she found no comfort in their presence. Kyle only hazarded a quick glance toward her before looking through the weapon's scope, scanning for any movement. Even in that short glance, he'd seen the exhaustion in her face, accompanied by fear.

Elaina's condition only enraged Kyle, and he found himself hoping something would pop out from the many crevices so that he had something to shoot. He knew where the fault lay, but he still wanted to take out his anger on anything nearby. His training and his measured demeanor had been cast aside as something more primal took over.

A chunk of debris fell from one of the derelict buildings before him, and he fired without hesitation. It was only after that Kyle realized there was no threat. He heard the Trooviians growling their displeasure. His hasty reaction could very easily have given away their position.

"We move north," Grig ordered. "The rendezvous point is only a mile away. Keep your eyes open - and don't engage unless you make a positive ID of an enemy."

Kyle knew Grig added that last part in response to his hasty actions. He winced, suddenly feeling very stupid. He knew better. Fortunately, it didn't appear as if they'd been seen. Everything remained quiet, save for the occasional clatter of debris falling from the crumbling buildings.

"I don't like this," Kyle said as Grig joined him where he hid. "Something feels wrong."

"Paranoia," Grig responded. "It's to be expected. Everything seems like it's going to explode after dealing with combat for any length of time. You're still primed for a fight."

"It seems way too quiet," he retorted.

"What exactly did you expect?" Grig asked. "The surface is barely habitable."

"I'm just used to the constant noise of people," Kyle said. "I've never been to the surface."

Grig just grunted as he scanned their surroundings once more.

"Looks clear," he said after a moment. "Advance carefully. Keep your eyes open."

The contingent moved as quietly and as swiftly as they could from cover to cover. Elaina struggled to keep up, her strength waning. The injection she'd been given had slowed the effects of the toxin, but she needed more medical care and soon.

They continued toward the rendezvous point at an agonizingly slow pace. Kyle understood caution, but Elaina didn't have a lot of time. They couldn't afford to drag their feet. The look on her face confirmed his concerns.

The congested roadway opened into an intersection, the buildings pulling further back and exposing the party. There was less debris here, which meant fewer places to hide. It was the perfect spot for an ambush.

Grig sent his scout, Burg, ahead. She used her natural ability to camouflage to hide her advance, but Grig and the others scanned their surroundings all the same. She used the scope of her weapon to scan the buildings staring vacantly back at her. She switched over to the thermal setting, looking for any heat signatures. Finally, satisfied that nothing was near, she signaled to the rest of the party.

Captain Grig took point, followed by Kyle and Elaina. They made their way across the intersection at a brisk pace, still uneasy about being so exposed. Grig half expected a battle cry or something to jump out at them, but nothing happened. When they made it to the other side, he allowed himself to relax. The rest of the contingent followed suit.

That was a mistake.

***

Devin and Ryve raced east toward Disc City 9, desperate to reach the city before Gerrard's army.

"What are we going to do?" Devin asked. "We can't stop an entire army by ourselves."

"No," Ryve said in agreement. "Need to warn city."

"What about Goordaiin?"

"City more important," Ryve said after a moment's pause. "Make safe, then deal with Goordaiin."

"Great," Devin replied.

They ran at a pace slightly faster than a jog, remaining silent for several miles. After escaping the ruined city, the landscape had opened into a barren wasteland. They wouldn't be able to take cover from the glaring sun, but they would see anything coming toward them.

It was nearly midday before the pair stopped, and the heat was already intense. Devin, even with the aid of the BSS rig, was gasping for air and his throat felt as dry as the ground beneath their feet. Even Ryve seemed out of breath.

"We can't maintain this pace," Devin gasped. "We need cover."

"Can't," Ryve grunted. "Need to warn city fast. Need time to get ready."

"I get that, but I doubt Gerrard's army is running at the same pace that we are."

"Can't take risk," Ryve replied, shaking his massive head. "Don't know strength of his army or ability."

Devin sat down on the ground as his legs began to give out. He was dehydrated and his steed, along with their water supply, was still in Gerrard's possession. Ryve didn't move to lift him back on his feet. He was struggling with dehydration as well.

"We'll be no good to the city dead," Devin said after a moment. "We need water, at least."

"Where water?" Ryve asked. He held his arms out wide, pointing out their surroundings. "All dry."

"I – I don't know," Devin said as he bowed his head. "Maybe underground."

Ryve just stared at him for a moment and then turned away. Devin watched as the Trooviian crouched on his haunches and began working at something, but he couldn't see what exactly.

"What the hell are you doing?" Devin called out after a moment.

"Digging," grunted Ryve. "Need water. Need to dig."

"The fuck?" Devin asked as he stood up and approached the hunched Trooviian.

Ryve had already managed to dig a relatively large hole in the short amount of time. Devin watched in awe as he watched Ryve work. He knew that the Trooviians were a subterranean race after talking with Deekin, but he hadn't known how adept they were at burrowing. Ryve's massive hands slammed into the soil and then scooped out large handfuls of earth. He worked quickly and easily as if it were as normal as breathing.

"Wow," Devin was all he managed to say. He couldn't think of anything else.

Within moments Ryve's hands struck clay and mud. He worked more furiously until he exposed a small puddle of filthy water.

"There," Ryve said. "Water."

Devin gestured toward the water, inviting Ryve to go first. The Trooviian turned and lowered his face into the growing pool. Devin watched as Ryve drew large gulps of water into his mouth, straining dirt and other flotsam with his teeth.

After a moment Ryve stood and gestured toward the pool, mud covering his mouth. Devin hesitated a moment as he stared at the Trooviian, then shrugged and approached the filthy pool. It was better than nothing, he concluded.

Devin lowered his lips to the pool of lukewarm water, the taste of dirt immediately filling his mouth as he drew water in. He gagged and then tried again. It tasted terrible, but he persisted until his throat no longer felt like sandpaper. He stood and wiped the mud from his face.

The pair looked at each other and then resumed their rapid trek toward Disc City 9.

***

Out of the shadowed doorways of buildings seemingly abandoned stumbled more of the mutated zombie-like creatures. Within moments the entire party found themselves surrounded by the wretches, advancing slowly and remaining eerily silent.

"I don't understand," Grig shouted. "This area should have been cleared! Where's the other team?"

"Another team?" Kyle yelled over his shoulder, eyes wide in panic. "What other team?"

Grig didn't respond. He took aim and began firing. He knew what would happen if the writhing masses got too close. The rest of the team followed suit, firing at any of the things that got too close.

"What other team?" Kyle yelled again, this time keeping his focus on the zombie-like bandits in front of him.

"We had two teams," Grig said as he fired again. "One to follow you and another to meet up at the rendezvous point after you took off in the shuttle. We were supposed to follow you to the Collective."

Kyle turned to face him. He'd already known they were supposed to be followed, but he hadn't known anything about a second team. For all he knew, the other team could still be under Goordaiin's control. It started feeling too much like a trap. Perhaps that had been the plan all along.

"What are you doing?" Elaina yelled as she tried to get Kyle's attention.

"When were you going to tell us?" Kyle demanded. His face was growing red with rage, a vein throbbing in his temple as he fought to keep his temper under control.

"Didn't think it necessary," Grig said brusquely. "Exposing ourselves to you already went against the plan. The other team is under my control. They report to me."

"That's what you fucking think!" Kyle hollered. He'd turned completely around to face Grig. Now his weapon was trained on the Trooviian. "But you don't actually know that!"

"Stand down, human!" Grig bellowed. "Now is *not* the time!"

Kyle opened his mouth to respond, but a cry from one of the Trooviians caught his attention. The mutant beasts had gotten too close and dragged one of the Trooviian soldiers to the ground. It was immediately infested with the same parasites that controlled the mutants, and within seconds the Trooviian began to convulse violently.

Grig didn't give the doomed soldier a chance to turn. He fired a round into the Trooviian's head and then fired several more shots in quick succession, dropping the beasts that were swarming over the body.

Kyle spun back toward his original firing lane and resumed shooting. His hands began to cramp as he fired, and he finally began to ease up. The beasts were reduced to a few stragglers, but the immediate danger had passed, or so he thought.

Elaina had been trying her best to fire her weapon one-handed, but her arm gave out, and she slumped to her knees from exhaustion. She still looked terribly ill. She was barely coherent and hadn't noticed one of the fallen Trooviians approach her.

Kyle tried to cry out to get her attention, but Elaina was unresponsive. The Trooviian moved blindly towards her huddled form, nearly upon her when Kyle finally snapped out of his state of panic and fired. The Trooviian fell backward, colliding with another that hadn't been paying attention.

The parasites immediately vacated the corpse in search of living flesh, and the Trooviian screamed. Kyle fired again, ending the poor creature's agony. Elaina finally looked up and began fighting to stand once more.

Kyle's eyes widened in alarm as Elaina lifted her weapon directly at him. He didn't even have a chance to speak before she fired. He heard the hiss of the round as passed by him and struck its target—another one of the grotesque beasts had been sneaking up behind him.

"Stop worry about me so much," Elaina said through clenched teeth. "You're going to get yourself killed."

The remaining members of Grig's team moved away from their dead to avoid possible infection. They'd lost almost half of their team in a span of only a few minutes. Several Trooviians had to be executed before they became a danger to the rest of the group. That was the hardest part for the survivors to handle.

"We must move," Grig said after a moment of silence. "I don't know what happened to the second team, but we have to assume that they aren't waiting for us at the rendezvous point. We don't have much time before it is overrun."

The group nodded solemnly and began to move out. Grig, without saying a word, lifted Elaina gently over his shoulder and followed, with Kyle at his side.

Chapter 34

Professor Goordaiin roused himself from his meditation and left his chamber. It wouldn't be long now. The Eco-generator was in its last phase of testing and would be prepped for installation within a few hours, barring any unforeseen complications. He doubted that there was much to worry about. The combination of Calvoran, Trooviian, and human technology had seemed to work symbiotically with each other. The Eco-generator worked better than anyone had expected.

The hallway leading to the lab housing the eco-generator was quiet. The laboratory building wasn't exactly bursting at the seams with inhabitants, but today it was even more barren than usual. Goordaiin took notice but put it out of his mind. Who cared where everyone one of the human scientists had scurried off to? His security force had been guarding the exits around the clock ever since Elaina escaped, and he wasn't concerned that anyone was conspiring against him. It wouldn't be in the three species' best interests to incite a coup anyway.

The door hissed open as Goordaiin approached, revealing what looked like a dense forest within. The eco-generator had been working hard, and the results were astounding! The repairs it had needed had put the eco-generator on standby for several hours. Goordaiin had been worried that its pause in function would lead to an utter collapse of the ecosystem it had begun to create. There had been some decay, but the moss like substance had proven resilient. Now, only an hour after the eco-generator resumed its function, the entire room had exploded with life.

"Breathtaking," Goordaiin said aloud as he strode into the portal to another world. "It's ready."

"Professor," a lab coat-clad man said. "The generator's output is far greater than previously anticipated. I fear that it will try to spread out of control, and some of the technicians have said they've seen things moving in here."

"Well, of course they did," Goordaiin said, dismissing the man's complaints. "The generator is working just as intended. Did your technicians fail to understand the meaning of 'ecosystem?'"

"No, sir," the man said quickly. "It just makes them nervous. Who knows what is living in here, and what may be dangerous."

"I fail to see the problem," Goordaiin hissed as he finally turned to face the whining pest. "Unless the organisms in here perceive some kind of threat, it is highly unlikely that they will be a danger to any of us. I don't understand what you expected to happen when the eco-generator did as it was designed. Did you think the floor would sprout vegetables and small animals prepped for slaughter? It's a fully functioning, self-contained, ecosystem. Now, enough of your mewling! Prep the eco-generator for installation. The first segments of the Phoenix One structure will be departing the surface within the next twelve hours, and that eco-generator *must* be on board. Is there any confusion with those instructions?"

"No, Professor," the man sighed. "I will get the technicians started on dismantling the eco-generator for transportation."

"None of them had better damage anything," Goordaiin growled. "Or they will be the next to be fed to the machine. Do I make myself absolutely clear?"

"Yes, Professor."

"That includes you," Goordaiin said over his shoulder as he turned to exit the room.

***

Moving the eco-generator was no easy task. The massive machine had to be disassembled piece by piece, and even then, it took specialized machinery to move the parts to the cargo shuttle. Half of the crew that had spent the first few hours disassembling and moving the eco-generator would be accompanying the machine to the launch pad, where they would work without a break reassembling the hulking machine.

Professor Goordaiin's warning had been relayed to every member of the moving crew before they ever got started. The crew at the launch pad had been briefed as well. As if to ensure the safe handling of the valuable machine, the crews were under constant watch by Trooviian guards. This made many of the workers intensely uncomfortable since everyone had heard about the assault only several days earlier. Maybe the Trooviians hadn't meant to kill any civilians, but relations amongst the three races had been tense for some time, which was only made more strained as of late.

"Projected departure in forty-five minutes," a voice called over the loudspeakers.

The workers, who'd already been moving at a hurried pace, sped up frantically. Since the launch pad was underground, it was safe from exterior disturbance, but the timing had to be precise. The storms had become more frequent and more violent. A window of thirty minutes was projected by weather teams where launch would be best achieved. Nobody could afford to waste time.

The eco-generator was prepped and fully assembled with less than five minutes to go before launch. The hurried pace made everyone nervous about inadvertently damaging the machinery, but they knew they had to work fast. The Trooviian guards' tireless surveillance made the situation even more unnerving.

***

The countdown began as the crew departed the launch pad, retreating behind large viewing panels so they could watch the launch. The spire, which is what the massive piece of the Phoenix One framework looked like, was flanked by nearly a dozen transport vessels.

Rocket power had long since been phased out as more advanced technology took its place. Cleaner, more powerful propulsion engines were outfitted on each of the transports. These engines were the most powerful models designed and manufactured, solely created to launch the Phoenix One framework beyond the atmosphere. The transport vessels were a part of the framework itself, which would later serve as a propulsion system for the "planet" when it was finished.

The large blast door over the launch pad began to retract, dirt and debris immediately falling inside. Nobody in the viewing chambers could see the opening above, the detritus the only indication that anything had changed at all.

The countdown reached zero and the transport vessels kicked on their engines, spouts of hazy blue discharge flowing around the base as the spire began its ascent. Everyone held their breath, praying that nothing went wrong with the launch, as the massive spike moved slowly upward.

***

Devin and Ryve heard the rumbling first, quickly followed by the quaking of the ground beneath their feet. Ryve immediately looked north, and Devin followed his gaze. The sight that met his eyes didn't even register at first. When he realized what he saw he let out a gasp and dropped to his knees.

In the distance, many miles to the north, a large gleaming spike rose from the horizon. It rose almost as slowly as a sunrise rises at the start of a new day. It continued to move skyward, a seemingly endless shaft of metal growing from the earth.

"My God," Devin finally managed to whisper, once he remembered to breathe. "It's enormous."

"Only one piece," Ryve said.

As if to punctuate his point, the rumbling grew even louder, and the ground shook so violently that neither of them could remain upright. At several points on the horizon, more spires began to sprout from the surface. Devin feared for a moment that the simultaneous launches would shake the planet apart. How ironic would that be, to be destroyed by the very thing they'd been building to save them?

Devin and Ryve watched in silence as the spikes moved ever higher.

***

Elaina, Kyle, Grig, and the rest of the Trooviian scouting party dropped to the ground when the ground first began to rumble. Elaina and Kyle stared at each other. The launch had begun, and they were still on the ground, the Human Collective still unaware of Goordaiin's nefarious plan. To make matters worse, the quakes grew in number and intensity, shaking the buildings so violently that many began to crumble and fall.

Chunks of debris scattered as buildings that had stood for over two centuries finally crumbled to dust. The scouting party would have stayed where they were if it weren't for the chunks of concrete and other materials raining down around them.

It took every ounce of effort they could muster to stay upright as they tried to navigate the destruction falling all around them. A massive block of concrete, with large exposed lengths of rebar jutting from almost every side, slammed down and tumble directly toward the party. The last Trooviian in the group had been too slow. The massive rock rolled right over him, pinning him to the rebar spikes. His body was pinned to the rolling chunk of death as it continued past, impaled by the rebar spikes.

"Run!" Grig bellowed as they advanced. The group was already running, but he hoped his command would spur them on faster. The rendezvous point was not far ahead if it remained. He fought the panic that welled up inside him as he let his worries run rampant.

"Holy shit!" Kyle yelled. He was pointing toward the horizon, obscured by what buildings remained. The entire group gasped as they saw the gleaming spikes that rose above the ground. Yet, despite their shock and awe, they ran.

***

Gerrard wasn't the first to notice the rumbling. He heard cries of alarm coming from his group, rousing him from his intermittent bouts of unconsciousness. It wasn't until he realized he was awake that he noticed the ground had begun to shake.

"Shit!" he barked. "They started the launch already!"

"What does this mean?" one of the grouped called out in distress.

"It means that we need to move faster!" he yelled.

Gerrard knew his agitation wasn't helping to sooth his group, but he had been fighting against death with one mission in mind. He still intended to accomplish that mission. So, what if the launch had begun? The disc cities had transport shuttles for the populace when it was time to leave the doomed planet behind. It just meant that they would have to work faster to take Disc City 9.

Gerrard had a penchant for being strangely optimistic at the most unlikely of times. Where others in his position would panic at the prospect of failing their mission, Gerrard found a silver lining. With the spires in space, there would be less opposition aboard the disc cities. The launch had, in effect, made the assault much easier than it would have been.

Exhaustion began to overtake Gerrard once again, his body rebelling against him as organs were likely beginning to fail. He was quickly running out of time. He wasn't even sure he would live long enough to see the assault.

Gerrard could see the spires in the distance as his vision began to cloud over, but then something else caught his attention. Slowly a smile crept over his features.

Gerrard wasn't looking at the spires when they reached the apex of their initial launch, nor did he seem to notice when the engines on the transport vessels kicked into overdrive and the spires shot skyward in a blur of motion.

His gaze, instead, was on a group of Trooviians huddled by a transport ship, oblivious to his presence. He might just live long enough to see his assault on Disc City 9 after all.

Chapter 35

Elaina was struggling to stay conscious. Her injury and the poison that had accompanied it were taking their toll. Despite this, however, she still managed a cry of excitement when Grig stopped and lowered her to the ground.

Before them, somehow virtually untouched by the debris scattered about, was the transport shuttle that Grig had said would be there. Finally, they would be able to get off the surface and away from the hell it had become.

Grig seemed less excited. He began looking about frantically. They were finally on the northeast side of the ruins, in the outskirts, and he'd been expecting to see his other team. He doubted that the ghoulish creatures that had been within the ruined city had survived the destruction and he doubted that they'd overtaken his team.

The other shuttle that should have been nearby was nowhere to be seen. Maybe they'd bugged out when the city began to crumble. It wasn't terribly unlikely. The will to protect oneself was strong and would likely overtake even the most loyal of people, but he knew his team. They would have waited until they saw their Captain before departing.

The others in Grig's scouting party began to search the surrounding area as well. Kyle couldn't figure out what they might be looking for, but he knew something was off.

"What is it?" Kyle asked.

Grig didn't answer. Instead, he waved his as if to dismiss the question. This only made Kyle even more uneasy.

It wasn't long before Grig found something that could tell him what had happened to the second team. Blood splattered the ground in some places. This wasn't what had gotten Grig's attention. His focus was on the communication device his Lieutenant had been carrying.

"They were ambushed," Grig growled as he walked back toward Kyle, communicator in hand. "Their shuttle is gone. So are their bodies, and their weapons, and their BSS rigs."

"Oh," Kyle said. He couldn't think of anything else.

"We need to leave," Grig commanded as he made his way to the remaining shuttle. "The mission still stands, and it seems that it has become even more vital that we get Elaina to The Collective. Out there, somewhere, is a well equipped group of savage assholes and I don't want to be around if they decide to come back."

Nobody responded as Grig pressed the buttons on the panel by the passenger door. The shuttle door hissed as it slid open. He didn't hesitate as he proceeded inside. Kyle, with the help of one of the other Trooviians, carried Elaina on board the shuttle. Within minutes they were strapped in and prepped for takeoff.

Elaina was toward the back of the shuttle in the cargo hold, where they'd set up an impromptu medical bay. There weren't any sentrons on board, much to Kyles dismay, but there was some first aid equipment. It wasn't much, but it would be enough to keep Elaina stable until they reached The Collective.

***

The initial take off wasn't bad. Elaina hadn't even noticed at first. She was barely conscious, and her mind was seemingly a million miles away. She was thinking about her father, Dr. Peterson, and their time working in tandem. All that time he'd been unaware of her heritage. Had he known, things may have been different.

It may have been harder, though. He'd regarded her as an assistant and had treated her as such. He had been respectful and open to her suggestions. He had also been willing to allow her to take risks that he probably wouldn't have allowed had he known she was his daughter.

Elaina felt sorrow begin to overtake her as she began to recall her father's final moments. Her heart ached as she replayed his violent death. It was the look on his face that threatened to break her completely. It was as if, in those final seconds, he finally remembered who she was.

"Holy fucking shit!" she heard a voice cry out.

***

Kyle had been gazing out of the viewing port as they traveled toward the coordinates of The Collective, which he'd been careful to relay to the shuttle pilot. The worst had seemed to finally be behind them. He was starting to feel more optimistic now that Elaina was going to get the care she needed. It had almost been too close. Any longer and she may not have made it.

He wasn't really paying attention to what lay beyond the protective glass. The landscape looked as condemned as he expected. No plant life. The ground scorched by the sun and ravaged by powerful storms.

If Kyle had been paying attention, he would have seen the army of people in the distance. It wasn't until he heard one of the Trooviian passengers gasp in shock that he finally noticed what had begun unfolding beneath them.

As they continued overhead, Kyle could see several columns of people marching onward, flanked by vehicles that had no right to exist. The vehicles were scrap heaps on wheels, but the somehow moved steadily onward and didn't fall apart under their own weight.

The shuttle's altitude wasn't terribly high. They'd only been flying for fifteen minutes and had slowly begun to ascend. It was only because of this that Kyle could tell the army consisted of Bandits.

"Holy fucking shit!" he cried in alarm. Among the contingents, he could make out Trooviian weapons, and several were wearing a harness of some kind. He surmised that the harnesses, while seemingly impossible, were BSS rigs like his Trooviian counterparts wore. What had surprised him the most was the apparent order to their march. There was a level of discipline that he'd thought impossible for Bandits to achieve.

"Where the hell are they going?" he asked. The question had been meant rhetorically, but Grig answered.

"Disc City 9 is in that direction," Grig said as he pointed toward the horizon. "There's really no other reason for an army of any kind to march in that direction.

"They mean to take the fucking city?"

"It appears that way."

"They're even crazier than I thought!"

"It's not impossible," Grig said. "Hell, it's not really even improbable. Those weapons are capable of firing accurately over long distances, with some modification. Bandits have proven to be rather tech savvy so I wouldn't be surprised if they've already made the adjustments. If enough shots hit the engines, the whole City will come crashing down."

"Why would they try something like that?" Kyle asked, though his attention had traveled to Elaina. She'd begun to stir, and he found himself worrying that her condition was deteriorating. "They've never tried that before."

"Your guess is as good as mine," Grig replied, shaking his head. "But whatever their plan is, we need to inform The Collective immediately."

***

Goordaiin watched in delight as the spires launched skyward. Finally, he would be able to get off this doomed planet. The success of the Eco Generator and the completion of phase one of the project all but guaranteed his place at the top of the pecking order. Chancellor Vallus wouldn't be able to do a thing about it. She'd be reporting to him, and Rectus would serve as his plaything.

It had been some time since he'd heard anything from his scouting party, and he was starting to grow uneasy. Everything else had fallen into place perfectly, but Elaina and The Human Collective could still potentially derail everything.

Goordaiin reached out along one of his many psychic strands, hoping that Captain Grig was within his range. The thread was thin, and he wondered if he would be able to continue along. He didn't want to risk the potential blowback if the link broke while he was on it. It wouldn't harm him, but it would effectively stun him for some time.

He traveled further along the psychic link tentatively until he found what he was searching for.

Grig was just barely within his range, but it was enough. Goordaiin allowed himself to enter the Trooviian's mind, watching through the creature's eyes.

***

Kyle had a hard time shaking the image of the Bandits marching in unison. It had deeply unnerved him. He had been trying to find any way to distract himself and finally settled upon the display near their pilot. It was ticking away as the coordinates continually changed.

Something was mesmerizing about the way the digits shifted from one to the next.

He was watching, his mind still wandering, and nearly missed the coordinates that he'd been looking for.

"Here!" he shouted. Kyle was staring out the viewport and was oblivious to the glare he'd drawn from the pilot.

Grig moved forward along the rows of seats in the roomy cockpit toward the viewport. He couldn't see anything of note.

"What are you talking about?" Grig growled. "We don't have time for this!"

"The Collective's headquarters are supposed to be right here," Kyle said, scanning their surroundings. "I don't understand. Where are they?"

"Are you telling me that we came all this way for nothing?" Grig nearly bellowed as he leaned in toward Kyle's face. The hostility took Kyle by surprise.

"These are the coordinates I was given," Kyle replied. "Every agent has them."

Grig was about to slam his fist into the human's head when he caught the movement of a potential strike coming. Grig realized his fist still hung in the air and, after a moment of confusion, lowered it. Was he really about to kill the man? Where had that come from?

In front of the shuttle, a shape began to lower through the clouds. It looked very similar to the disc cities but significantly smaller.

"Is that it?"

"It is," Kyle replied.

***

Goordaiin nearly leaped out of his seat when he saw what Grig saw. There, before him, was the location of The Human Collective. They were the final loose end, and now he knew right where they were. He almost let the flood of emotions overwhelm him. Instead, he opened his eyes and turned toward his desk.

He spoke to his second in command, a Calvoran by the name of Floos, and gave the order he'd been waiting to give.

It was finally time.

Chapter 36

Devin watched the fragments of what would eventually become the framework for Phoenix One as they ascended into the heavens. He would have watched until the last of them disappeared, but he once again remembered the threat marching toward Disc City 9. How he and Ryve would beat the Bandits there eluded him, but he was determined to try.

They resumed their jog across the hardpan toward their destination, still invisible on the horizon. The sun had reached its apex, and the heat was unbearable. The terrain had once been home to a forest, but all that remained were the bleached bone-white trunks that had been left behind. None of the skeletal forms provided much of a refuge from the intense glare.

Sweat poured down Devin's face and stung his eyes as he struggled to keep up with Ryve. The massive creature seemed to be flagging as well, but its endurance was incredible. Devin figured Ryve would be able to keep up the pace for another three miles at least, but there was no way Devin would last that long.

"This won't work," Devin gasped as he slowed, his hands clutching his side. "We'll never make it."

"Need a faster way," Ryve agreed. He scanned the barren wasteland with his massive eyes. "Need a shuttle."

Devin looked around and raised his hands in confusion. "Where are we going to find something like that? There's nothing out here!"

"Hmm…" Ryve began. Devin just stared at the Trooviian, waiting for something more. "I make a call. You act like prisoner. Take a shuttle to Disc City 9, and to Goordaiin."

Devin stopped, in part due to exhaustion, but also because he had to hold back the rage that had begun to well up inside him.

"Are you fucking serious?" he nearly hollered. "You're just *now* coming up with that idea?"

"Now in range," Ryve replied simply. Devin shook his head and began jogging to catch up.

The pair found a particularly large tree trunk to huddle under, though the shade was minimal at that time of day so that they could catch their breath. Ryve took that moment to make the call to The Order's dispatcher. Devin didn't understand anything Ryve said as he spoke in his guttural native language, and once again felt a wave of apprehension wash over him. What if Ryve had planned this all along to get him to come peacefully? Devin doubted it, after everything they'd experienced and Ryve's supposed hatred for Goordaiin, but the thought still nagged at him.

The conversation took longer than Devin expected. This only served to aggravate his anxiety, and he began considering making a run for it. Forget Disc City 9 and Gerrard's army. It wasn't as if the upper class would listen to anything he had to say, and even if they did, they'd likely cast him aside afterward. He struggled with the idea of abandoning all those people, but his survival instincts told him to turn away from them and save himself. A week ago, he very well may have, but he'd come this far.

He'd see it through, Devin decided. A small part of himself nearly screamed in protest, but he chose to ignore it just as he had been almost the entire time he'd been with Ryve. He wanted to trust that Ryve wouldn't betray him, though he knew it wasn't an impossibility. He also wanted his horse back, and he knew right where it would be.

"We wait here," Ryve said after he finished his call. "Shuttle on its way."

"Fantastic," Devin grumbled. "And how do you want me to act as your prisoner?"

"Put on these," he said as he held out metal handcuffs.

"Shit," Devin said, his head dropping along with his shoulders. He had no desire to be restrained again, but it was necessary to sell the illusion. If it was an illusion, that is. "Fine. Just don't make them too tight. We may need to fight, and I really don't want to be vulnerable if that is the case."

Ryve placed the cuffs at Devin's wrists, and a moment later a band of cabling snaked out and around both wrists before retreating into the rest of the assembly. The cabling began to cinch down, and Devin started to panic as they continued to tighten. He'd nearly resigned himself to the fact that he'd been betrayed when the cables stopped constricting and he found he could still wriggle his hands free if he needed to.

"Keep hands in cuffs," Ryve said. "Only take off if we have to fight."

Devin smiled. He felt more than a little relieved that Ryve hadn't lied, as far as he could tell.

***

They waited for twenty minutes in the blistering heat for the shuttle to arrive. The craft looked like a small, silver bus with wings and bright blue exhaust ports in the rear. Devin stood with his hands behind his back while Ryve stood by his side.

"Here goes nothing," Devin muttered.

"Quiet," Ryve hissed.

The side of the shuttle opened inward to reveal a pair of Trooviians dressed in the uniform that Ryve wore. The uniforms identified them as soldiers of the Order and the familiar instinct to flee washed through Devin as he watched them approach. Every fiber of his being wanted to turn tail and run as far away as possible, but he knew that doing so would only get him killed.

These soldiers no doubt believed that Devin was responsible for the destruction of Disc City 6 and would not hesitate to fire if he tried to flee. He fought his instincts and let Ryve lead him forward. As they walked, he felt Ryve press something into his left hand.

Devin's breath caught in his chest when he finally realized what the object was. It had been the remote to his BSS rig! But why now? Why did Ryve decide to start fulling trusting him now, right at this moment? Was it because it was inevitable that they would both make it to Disc City 9 now? He had to assume that was the reason. No other answer was forthcoming.

Ryve stopped as the Trooviian pair flanked Devin and then led him toward the shuttle. He glanced over his shoulder and saw Ryve following close behind. The sight of his friend – is that what Ryve was to him now? – walking behind him, keeping an eye on his captors.

"Sit," one of the Trooviians said once they climbed aboard the shuttle. Devin quickly obliged and sat on a seat as close to the back of the shuttle as possible. The air inside was nearly thirty degrees cooler, and he felt himself relax a little. The cool air felt nice on his sunburned skin.

Ryve sat in one of the seats in front of him and turned to face him. "We land and let them take us to Goordaiin. We only attack after. No funny stuff."

Devin stared a moment and then grinned, matching the massive toothy grin on Ryve's face.

Chapter 37

The Human Collective Government's reception of their wayward agents could only be described as tense. The officials were happy to see their people alive and well—for the most part—but the appearance of the Trooviians aboard their floating headquarters was unnerving at best. Never had any other race been aboard the micro city—most of whom didn't even know where it was.

Kyle opted to stay by Elaina's side as Grig's soldiers wheeled her out of the shuttle. He stared at her and found himself once more transfixed by her beauty. He hated seeing her injured, though that was really the only condition he'd ever seen her in and was ready to do whatever was necessary to help her.

The pilot and Captain Grig were the first to disembark from the shuttle and the "welcoming party" immediately trained their weapons on the pair. Grig didn't so much as blink, knowing full well what to expect upon arrival. The pilot was less stoic and uttered a low growl. Grig placed a hand on his pilot's shoulder to calm him.

"Relax," he said in a low tone. "We're guests here. No need to do anything rash."

This seemed to help placate the agitated Trooviian.

The rest of the crew followed close behind, with Kyle and Elaina taking up the rear. Weapons were immediately lowered at the sight of the human pair. The tension was still there, so heavy it was nearly palpable, but at least nobody was at immediate risk of being shot.

A man in his late forties with silver, clean cut hair and trimmed beard stepped forward to greet them. He wore a suit and looked more like a political figure than a Collective Agent. Kyle figured this man to be the Director of the Human Collective Government, Richard Clavin.

"Agent Mathis," the man said, immediately focusing his attention on Kyle. "I wasn't aware that you would be accompanying Agent Perry. I recall giving strict orders for you to stay aboard Disc City 9."

"Sir," Kyle began. "I know, but there were too many enemies around to let her out of my sight. The Sentrons are effective, but it still wasn't enough to make me feel comfortable about leaving her alone with them."

"I'm sure," Director Clavin said, coolly. "That still does not dismiss the fact that you disobeyed a direct order."

"If I hadn't…" Kyle began, but Director Clavin cut him off.

"In this case, however, I would be remiss if I didn't admit that your disobedience was rather fortuitous." He looked over at Elaina as she struggled to remain conscious.

"I suppose if you hadn't," he continued. "She wouldn't be here with us right now. Consider yourself lucky, Agent Mathis."

"Thank you, sir," Kyle said stiffly.

Clavin turned and gave an order for several officials to escort Elaina inside the compound and straight to the medical facility. He was aware that she had information that was time sensitive, but it would be useless if she were dead before she could share it.

"I imagine Agent Perry relayed her information to you," Clavin said as he turned back to face Kyle. "Is this correct?"

"Yes, sir," Kyle replied. He was still wary of the man and half expected to be punished for his insubordination. He was certain that he wouldn't get off clean.

"Follow me to my office. We'll discuss what she told you there."

***

It had only taken a few minutes for Kyle to share what he knew had happened in the laboratory on Disc City 9. He wasn't a direct witness, but Clavin was comfortable with accepting his rendition of the events that had occurred.

"It would appear that my instincts about that damn Calvoran were spot on," Clavin said after Kyle finished speaking. "I always figured there was something off about 'Professor' Goordaiin."

"That's not all, sir," Kyle interjected. "We also spotted a large contingent of Bandit forces marching toward the city."

"What?" Clavin asked with an expression of disbelief plastered across his features. "Bandits? Are you sure? Those brainless bastards don't do anything together!"

"I know what I saw," Kyle replied. He'd expected Clavin to be skeptical. He had been himself when he'd first seen the marching party. "They're Bandits. And they appear to have gotten their hands on Trooviian weapons. Captain Grig believes that they intend to shoot Disc City 9 down before launching an invasion."

"How is this even possible?" Clavin asked rhetorically. "They've never shown any indication of organization. Someone must be leading them, but I can't begin to fathom how."

Kyle remained quiet as he stood in Director Clavin's chambers. Where the laboratory on Disc City 9 had been brightly lit with white walls, the walls of the Collective were a dark brown and even black in some areas. The whole office had an ominous feel to it as the desk was a dark granite and the bookshelves were nearly black. In fact, almost every piece of furniture was black or dark hues of blue and brown. Even the lighting seemed to be absorbed by the darkness of the room. He wondered how anyone would be comfortable in such a dreary looking office.

Clavin had turned away from Kyle to gaze at a large screen on the wall, displaying what appeared to be shifting images of the Collective Headquarters perimeter, his hands clasped behind his back.

"I would like nothing more than to see Goordaiin go down in flames," he said without turning to face Kyle. "But we need to protect as many human lives on board the city as possible. I'm going to send you with a battalion of soldiers to secured Disc City 9. You know approximately where the Bandits are, and with any hope, we can intercept them before they reach the city."

"Understood, sir," Kyle said.

"One more thing," Clavin added. "I want you to apprehend Goordaiin. Make sure he doesn't flee. I want to watch him atone for his crimes personally."

***

Goordaiin left his office and headed toward the now vacant lab where the Eco generator had been. The door slid open silently and he half expected the room to be devoid of life, but the ecosystem that had been created had become self-sufficient. Small insect-like creatures buzzed around the large room, settling upon brightly colored flora. Since there was no natural light in the room, the plant life was almost entirely breeds of fungi and moss.

Goordaiin gasped when he saw something small and furry scamper among the mossy carpeting. It was spectacular!

He watched in silence as the room continued its activity, completely oblivious to his presence. He allowed himself to feel elation as he gazed at the room. Everything had gone as planned and soon the Human Collective Government would no longer be a problem. Thanks to Elaina, he knew where they hid, and fighter crafts were speeding toward it at that very moment. Goordaiin expected to hear about the destruction of the micro-city within the next thirty minutes.

His focus was broken when he heard footsteps behind him. He turned around and came face to face with Chancellor Vallus, with Rectus by her side.

"Professor Goordaiin," she said firmly. "Who sanctioned the dispatch of our fighting force?"

Goordaiin found he couldn't speak. For once he was unable to think up a convincing excuse. How could he have been so stupid? He let his emotions dictate his decision making, and now he was stuck. The presence of Rectus only made him grow angry and even less clear headed.

"Professor Goordaiin," Vallus continued. "You did not have the authority to send those fighters away. You have overstepped this time, and I cannot look the other way. You are hereby under arrest for your infraction and sentenced to confinement to your quarters until a formal hearing can be scheduled. You do not, nor have you ever, have command of our military. I allowed you to keep your security force only because it helped police the city, but they are now under Rectus's command."

"Chancellor," Goordaiin began. "I fail to see the problem here. Phase one is a success, and phase two will be starting immediately. Shuttles will be taking personnel to their designated space stations within the next few hours. I merely employed the fighter crafts as a method to protect our shuttles as the launched."

"I don't care why you did it," Vallus hissed. "That was not your place. Congratulations on the success of phase one, but you are still under arrest."

Rectus strode forward and took Goordaiin by the arm in a

firm grip, a ghost of a smile on his lips as he escorted Goordaiin out of the room.

Chapter 38

Devin remained quiet for most of the flight. It had been so long since he'd been on one of the disc cities and the idea of revisiting an area—despite the city being different—that had been nothing but unpleasant for him in the past deeply unnerved him. He tried to sleep, but rest was elusive despite how tired his body felt. The rig did a magnificent job of keeping him going, but fatigue was inevitable, and it was finally setting in.

He finally spoke when he saw Ryve grow anxious.

"What's wrong?" he asked.

"We're close," Ryve replied. "We find Goordaiin soon. Then we kill him."

"The city is huge! How do expect to find him?"

"Linked," Ryve said, pointing to his head. "Works both ways. Find him that way."

"Linked," Devin asked, not quite understanding what Ryve meant. "Do you mean telepathically? How?"

"Calvorans do it," Ryve said. "They don't know we know. Don't know we can do it back."

Ryve was grinning again. Devin allowed himself to smile. The Trooviian's excitement was nearly infectious, but another thought occurred to him.

"So, we kill this Goordaiin," he said, his voice nearly a whisper. "Then what? Won't we be arrested, or killed? We're talking about murder."

"Doesn't matter," Ryve said firmly. "Goordaiin must die."

"It *does* matter," Devin hissed. "I don't want to die. You never told me this would be a suicide mission!"

"You don't have to follow," the Trooviian said. "Gave your freedom back."

Devin shifted the remote the BSS rig in his hands. That explained why Ryve gave it back. He could put as much distance between him and this madness as possible after he escaped from his captors, that is. That was another hiccup in this whole plan, but he had a feeling Ryve had planned for that as well. Devin nearly made his decision, but the thought of leaving Ryve to die unsettled him. The Trooviian was as close to a friend as he'd ever had. Abandoning him now felt wrong, dirty even.

"No," Devin said simply. "I'll go with you. We've come this far."

"Good," Ryve said, that large toothed smile on his face once again.

***

They arrived at the docking station fifteen minutes later. Devin was immediately surrounded by Trooviian soldiers, and he felt another moment of panic. He hoped Ryve had a plan because fighting their way to Goordaiin seemed like an incredibly stupid idea.

Devin's weapons had been confiscated by Ryve before the shuttle had picked them up and he still carried them. Devin couldn't see any sign of worry in the Trooviian, which comforted him a little.

Even though the trip hadn't taken long, the sun was already beginning to set. It had been later in the day than Devin thought, which confused him. He'd been using the sun to gauge the time of day for most of his life. How had he misjudged it now?

His captors led him off the shuttle and into the aggressive wind that blew across the dock. Grit whipped into his face and eyes, stinging his skin and effectively blinding him. Devin's captors seemed to take notice and used their bodies to shield him. He may have been a prisoner, but he was no good to them dead.

Ryve strode up behind him and slid a spherical helmet over his head like a bubble. It wouldn't protect the rest of his exposed torso, but at least he could see again.

Ryve spoke to one of the guards as they walked. Devin had only spent a short amount of time with the Trooviian and still didn't understand a word of their language. If he survived this endeavor, he might take the time to learn it.

The Trooviian that was conversing with Ryve was growing agitated. Whatever Ryve was saying was not sitting well with the soldier. After a moment and more growling in their guttural language, the two ceased their conversation, and Ryve walked over to stand by Devin's side.

"I tell them I deliver you myself," Ryve said. "Said it specific request by Goordaiin."

"Oh, and they believed you?"

"Said order given to Deekin," Ryve said, his voice trembled slightly at the mention of his dead friend's name. "Said Deekin gave order to me before he died. Deekin respected officer, so they believed me."

Devin nodded slightly, noticing that Ryve's grasp of the English language had improved significantly.

The soldiers walked with Ryve and Devin for a while longer, until they started to near the Hub, as the main science center was called. Ryve and Devin continued toward the building, noticing briefly as the soldiers turned and walked away.

"I give weapons back when we're inside," Ryve said. "You take off handcuffs inside too."

"If you say so," Devin replied. He felt his heart rate increase as his anxiety grew. He'd fought for his life more in the past few days than he'd had for most of his life, but he still wasn't comfortable with the idea of battle.

The doorway slid open to reveal a brightly lit chamber. Devin saw a series of protective suits hanging on the walls and guessed they were in a decontamination chamber of sorts. He'd seen them a few times when he'd been dragged onto the Disc Cities to perform maintenance.

"Put this on," Ryve said as he handed one of the suits to Devin. "Help blend in. You stand out."

Devin grabbed the suit and nodded in agreement. It made a fair amount of sense to him. He would definitely stand out dressed only from the waist down and sporting a BSS rig on his chest. His sunburned skin would likely give him away, but he'd take any precautions necessary to lessen the chance that he'd be detected.

The suit felt more comfortable against his skin than his protective clothing ever had. It was as if he'd stripped off a layer of burlap and had slid into a silk robe. The suit stung his damaged skin for a moment, but it stopped once he had zipped it up completely. He noticed a slight bulge around the collar and began to prod at it when Ryve grabbed his hand.

"No," he said. "Makes helmet come out. Will hit helmet you're wearing and break your neck."

"Oh," Devin said as he quickly dropped his hands. "Thanks."

They were about to step through the next doorway when he remembered the bubble-like helmet. He doubted anyone else was wearing one indoors and figured he'd stand out like a beacon if he walked around still wearing it.

"Good idea," Ryve said.

"So," Devin said as they stepped out of the decontamination chamber and into a brightly lit white hallway. "Where's Goordaiin?"

***

Goordaiin seethed as he paced around his office. How could he have been so stupid? Of course, the bitch would notice the fighter crafts launch. It was obvious in hindsight. He'd been too rash, allowed himself to get too excited.

"Shit," he hissed. "Shit! Shit! Shit!"

He'd screwed up. He knew this, and it infuriated him. For so long he'd been at least one step ahead of everyone, and then he had gone and messed everything up. At least they didn't know about the fuel for the Eco generator as the method of extermination it was. He'd done a good job selling the council on that aspect, at least.

Goordaiin wanted to see the extermination of humanity personally, save for a few kept around to feed the Eco generator, but it appeared he'd see it from the inside of a cell if he didn't think quickly. It wouldn't be hard to manipulate Rectus into releasing him, he surmised. It was dealing with the Chancellor that hung him up.

He continued pacing the room when he heard footsteps out in the hallway. *Here comes Rectus,* he thought. *I guess it's now or never.*

The door slid open, but it wasn't a Calvoran standing in the doorway.

Chapter 39

Kyle donned his flight suit, which didn't look very different from the protective suit he already wore, though it was reinforced with fibers made with alien alloys mixed with Kevlar. It also didn't have a helmet built into it, either. It wasn't necessary.

The suit felt heavy as he began walking to his ship. All around him on the docking station he could see men and women in identical suits climbing into their personal fighter crafts and going through their takeoff routines.

Kyle's craft looked just like the rest. It was sleek, black and almost completely devoid of ridges, like a bullet train, except for the wings that jutted out at either side at the rear. He walked beneath the ship and found the entry portal. It slid silently open, and a clear tube lowered from within. He allowed the tube to envelop him and then felt himself become weightless as it drew him inside.

"This is fancy," he remarked. "I wonder what else this thing can do."

The interior was small and lit with an array of lights across the instrument panel. He could see out of the viewing port at the front of the cockpit, figures, and numbers displayed over the glass. He stood until a seat folded out of the floor beneath him. He sat and immediately decided he would never get up again. The chair was immensely comfortable.

A helmet hung overhead, which Kyle promptly slipped over his head.

"Agent Mathis," a voice said in his ear.

"This is him."

"My name is Ford. I will be your liaison with headquarters. I will also help you if I can, but the flying and fighting will be up to you."

"Thank you," Kyle said flatly.

"Have you flown a battle fighter before? Specifically, the

A776 model?"

"Do virtual reality flight simulators count?" Kyle asked.

"Oh shit," he heard Ford mutter. "Well, it's a good thing these crafts are mostly self-automated. You can still mess up and get yourself killed, though. I'm going to try to talk you through as much as I can."

"I appreciate that Ford," Kyle said. He knew Ford hadn't intended for him to hear the expletive and chose not to let him know. He found it amusing.

Kyle went through the startup procedures from his memory of the simulators and had almost done it on his own. Ford had to interject when he was about to press the afterburner switch, which would have been disastrous.

"Well, not bad so far," Ford said. Kyle could pick up a hint of sarcasm. "Once the docking doors open you'll be clear for takeoff."

Kyle watched as the massive, sleek door in front of his craft began to lift upward into the ceiling. He was ready to take off right away, his hands shaking with anticipation and more than a little anxiety. He waited until Ford gave him the go ahead and nearly shot out of the docking station like a bullet.

"Well, I don't think you needed to take off *quite* that fast," Ford said.

"Sorry," Kyle said sheepishly. He eased back on the throttle, which was controlled by a lever at his side. The ship began to slow to a more reasonable speed.

"Your mounted weapons are guided by the HUD on your viewing port and by the angle of your helmet," Ford said. "Basically, you look at your target and the weapons will shoot at it."

Kyle moved his head around to look at his surroundings and heard a mechanical whirr around him. "Cool," he said.

"The trigger is on each of the hand controls, which also controls the pitch of your craft," Ford continued.

Ford went on for several moments, pointing out necessary functions that Kyle would likely need. There weren't too many, to Kyle's relief, which made the craft easy to pilot. He tried a few barrel rolls and even went in a reverse loop, going end over end. The craft responded intuitively to his hands as they manipulated the control handles.

The practice gave the rest of the crafts a chance to catch up and fall into formation. Kyle just had to follow as they sped off toward their destination. The craft fell into formation with the others on its own. Ford hadn't been exaggerating when he said the craft was almost self-automated.

He stared ahead at the horizon as the sky grew a deep indigo color, a sliver of orange at the very edge. Night had fallen, and that would put the Bandits at a disadvantage. Kyle was perfectly okay with that. He'd take any help he could get.

****

The squadron of fighter ships flew noiselessly toward Disc City 9 like phantoms. Fitting, Kyle felt, as they were going to be harbingers of death.

"We have contact," a voice said over the speaker. "My HUD picked up life signs only a few miles ahead. We'll be right on top of them in just a couple minutes."

Kyle felt his hands tingle as his anxiety grew. It almost didn't seem fair to fire on an enemy who couldn't see you. He pushed the thought out of his mind as reminded himself of the Bandit's target and the destruction they were planning to bring.

They were flying in a staggered formation, spread horizontally across the sky. Kyle could see blasts of light as the nearest crafts began opening fire on their targets below. In seconds the sky lit up with flashes of light lancing toward the ground, answered by long lines of light from the weapons below.

Kyle's HUD was flashing with figures, and displays of what he surmised were vital signs as it picked up target after target. He saw a clump of Bandits who had turned and were focusing their attention on the crafts above. He pulled the trigger on the left control and a massive ball of light rocketed toward the ground. Mere seconds later the group of Bandits had been incinerated, as well as those within a ten-foot radius.

"Holy shit!" Kyle exclaimed.

"That was the rocket pod," Ford said. The voice nearly startled Kyle. "Your craft only has two, which are normally for… ahem… larger targets."

"It was certainly effective," Kyle replied quickly. "I'll remember to leave that trigger alone, though."

The crafts flew in large concentric rings around the battalion of Bandits below. Within minutes the HUDs of the crafts no longer picked up signs of life.

"Was that really it?" Kyle asked in disbelief. "I swore there'd been more."

***

Gerrard swore as he saw death raining down in the distance. It had been smart of him to have a battalion break off and march in a slightly different direction. The main bulk of his fighting force had gone undetected, but the arrival of the fighter ships was cause for concern.

"How the fuck did they know we were coming?" he yelled. He sat astride the mechanical horse, his body almost completely back to one hundred percent. He felt younger than he had in years and he attributed it to the BSS rig strapped on his chest. He'd been wary about putting the alien tech on his body, but he'd seen that Scavenger, Devin, wearing one.

The Trooviians that his group had stumbled upon didn't have time to react before they were cut down. Gerrard almost lost his temper when he thought all the rigs had been damaged, but they'd found several that had come away unscathed. He selected one for himself and the others he gave to men he decided to appoint as his lieutenants.

The trip had been slow and painful at first, but as the rig did its work Gerrard have felt better after every passing moment. Devin had tried to kill him, as had the fucking Millipede, but he wasn't going to go down that easily. He still had a part to play and was determined to see it through.

In the distance, directly ahead, he could see the faint lights of Disc City 9 high in the air. They were close. He hoped they would at least have enough time to open fire on the city's engines before the fighter crafts showed up.

***

Kyle circled the area, letting the craft's computer search for life signs, but there was nothing left alive below. They'd been efficient and swift. He doubted that had been the entirety of the Bandit army, but the results lessened his worry. It wouldn't take long to eradicate the rest of the threat when they finally came upon them.

"Disc City 9 is straight ahead and a little to the right," a voice said over the speaker. "Looks like these guys didn't know exactly where they were going."

"I don't think that was all of them," Kyle chimed in.

"What are you talking about? There were almost a hundred of the filthy bastards!"

"I saw three times that number earlier," Kyle said. "On my way to headquarters."

"Then where the fuck are they?"

"I think these guys may have been a diversion," Kyle said, dread growing within. "There's really no other reason for these guys to have been off target like this."

"He's right," came another voice, female this time. "My systems are picking up more signs to the south."

"That must be them," Kyle said. "How far away?"

"They're almost directly below the city."

***

Gerrard stared upward at the underbelly of Disc City 9. He'd halted his army short, to keep them from being crushed when the city came down.

"There she is," Gerrard said with a massive grin. "On my signal, fire."

His lieutenants relayed the message across ranks. He waited for one of his lieutenants, a scruffy looking man with one eye, to confirm that the message had been sent before giving the signal.

Gerrard pointed his commandeered Trooviian rifle skyward and fired. The beam of light struck a moment later, hitting one of the many engines keeping the city aloft.

Seconds later the air was filled with flashes of light, and miniature explosions as the rest of his army opened fire. Two engines were destroyed within seconds, with two more rapidly failing.

"They don't even know what hit them," Gerrard cackled.

***

Kyle's heart dropped as he saw the blasts lancing upward toward the city. He had to hope they could intercept the Bandits before the city was dropped completely. He found the afterburner switch, which he'd almost hit by accident earlier, and flipped it. His ship rocketed forward at incredible speed, the force pressing him deep into his chair.

"Oh shit!" Kyle yelled out, but the sound was almost ripped from his mouth. He knew he said the words but didn't hear them.

He managed to flip the switch before he overshot the Bandit army's location. The craft slowed significantly, and Kyle found that he could once again draw breath. He could see more fighter crafts join him in his peripheral vision, but his eyes were locked on the plethora of targets flashing across the viewport. He didn't hesitate.

Lines arced toward the ground, cutting down close to thirty enemies in seconds. The other fighter ships had followed suit, and soon death rained from above.

The city had begun to descend toward the ground, not quite in a free fall. Several platoons decided to turn their attention on their aerial attackers.

The weapons worked with horrifying efficiency. Kyle saw several fighters plummet after taking several shots. He had to shut off the speaker system as he heard the screams of the dying coming through. He felt his ship shudder as one of the Bandits' shots struck the underside, and his craft immediately initiated evasive maneuvers. Kyle struggled to keep his attention on his targets as his ship rolled and dipped.

More fighters were falling around him as the other platoons turned their focus skyward. Kyle had been confident at the start that this would be a quick and easy fight. He could now see just how badly he'd underestimated the enemy. If they managed to emerge victoriously, it wouldn't be without suffering heavy losses.

Another blast struck the side of his craft as he circled back around toward the throng of savage warriors. Alarms began to go off in the cockpit as pressure started to vent from the hole that had been opened in the ship's flank. Red lights flashed, but Kyle ignored it. If he were going to go down, he'd take as many of the bastards out as he could along with him.

∗∗∗

Gerrard seethed at the arrival of the ships. He knew they'd be on top of them quickly, but he'd hoped the damage to Disc City 9 would be enough by then. With the city grounded his troops could use the buildings as cover. They were still too exposed as the ships flew overhead.

"Don't take your focus off the city!" he hollered. "Split your attention! The city must fall!"

He could tell his message had been relayed as several platoons turned and began firing at the engines of the city once more.

Bandits were being cut down all around him, and he almost felt pain at their loss, only in that he'd have a smaller fighting force to take the city. He heard a sizzle as a blast struck directly to his left, far too close for comfort.

"Come on," he implored at the descending city. "Drop you fucker!"

The city was no more than a hundred feet off the ground, the engines kicking up massive plumes of dust. Gerrard estimated touchdown in less than a minute. He hoped his army could hold out for that long, but their situation looked grim.

He began to move toward the city as it came down, flying across the ground on the mechanical horse. He was determined to make it on board the floating city. It wouldn't necessarily be a lost cause, then.

The city hit the ground with a massive, resounding crash. More dust billowed from beneath it, creating a miniature dust storm. Gerrard squinted his eyes against the stinging particles as he advanced.

∗∗∗

Kyle watched in despair as the city crashed to the ground. All was not lost, yet, but it would be over quickly if the Bandits managed to infiltrate the city. He continued his flybys, firing at anything he could see, but he could feel his controls growing stiff as power began to drain. He wouldn't be able to stay in the air for much longer.

"Ford," Kyle said, trying his best to keep his voice calm.

"Can you relay a message for me?"

"I-I suppose," he said. "Who for?"

"There's an agent in the medical wing," Kyle explained. "Her name is Elaina Perry. Could you tell her… I tried. And, that I love her."

"Ok, Agent Mathis. I'll tell her."

His ship was flying dangerously close to the ground when he saw the figure dashing toward the edge of the city. The crazy bastard looked like it was riding some kind of animal, moving at a frenzied pace trying to evade the fighter ships.

Kyle wrenched the controls toward the figure. He made it his personal mission to make sure nobody entered the city while he still lived. The ship struggled to respond to his directions, and he could see the ground rapidly coming up to meet him.

"Fuck," Kyle said. "Well, here goes nothing."

***

He was so close he could see the edge of the city. Gerrard was maybe thirty or so strides away when he heard the crash behind him. He didn't dare look. The steed continued forward, and Gerrard felt heat at his back, then a blinding flash of light.

He was dazed and blinded. When his vision returned, he realized he was airborne.

And he was on fire.

Chapter 40

Ryve and Devin moved at a hurried pace down the maze of hallways. Devin had no idea where they were going, but Ryve seemed drawn as if he were being led by a divining rod. He turned and moved without hesitation. Devin struggled to keep up with the Trooviian.

Ahead they saw a Calvoran walking directly toward them. Devin glanced at Ryve, looking for any sign that this was the Professor Goordaiin he'd spoken of. Ryve didn't even seem to notice.

"Who are you?" the Calvoran called.

"Ryve, of the Order of Proper Justice," Ryve called out. "Escorting prisoner to Goordaiin, on his orders."

"Your prisoner doesn't appear to be restrained," the Calvoran said as they came upon it. "In fact, he looks armed."

Ryve tried to speak but seemed frozen in place. Devin stared at his friend, confused by the sudden change in behavior.

"What are you doing?" he asked. Ryve didn't respond.

After a moment Ryve seemed to relax. The Calvoran stood and stared at them. Devin expected the alien to strike them down or call for reinforcements, but it didn't do a thing. After a moment, it spoke.

"I'd think a Trooviian would realize the folly of trying to deceive a Calvoran," it said. "I know what you are thinking. It's as plain as if you had spoken your intent aloud."

Ryve reached for his weapon and Devin mirrored him.

"There's no need for that," the Calvoran continued. "I mean you no harm."

Devin looked quizzically at the alien. Why, if it knew why they were there, was it not trying to stop them? Was it some kind of trick?

"My name is Rectus," the Calvoran said. "I am the general of the planetary army. You have nothing to fear from me. You're here for Goordaiin, yes?"

"Yes…" Devin said after a moment's hesitation.

"Good," Rectus said, a small smile on his thin lips. "He's no friend of mine. I'll take you to him."

What was going on? Ryve looked as confused as Devin was. They looked at each other in silence, shrugged, and then followed the Calvoran down the hall. They might make it out of this crazy mission alive.

They had been walking for at least five minutes when the ground seemed to fall out from under them. Ryve crashed down on his face, Devin on his back. Rectus had managed to remain standing, though he was bent over almost completely, his hands on the floor to steady himself.

"What the hell was that?" Devin gasped.

"The city," Rectus said. "It's falling."

***

Kyle saw the rocket pod hit directly behind the figure on the animal just as his ship slammed into the earth. His head bounced off the instrument panel with enough force that he heard something in his face crack. The pain was intense. His face felt like it was on fire.

He blinked, trying to clear his vision. Through the haze, he saw the figure fly through the air, the creature it was riding destroyed.

"Well," Kyle coughed. "That's one bastard who won't make it to the city. What the fuck was he riding?"

The question hung in the air for a moment before he blacked out.

***

Gerrard landed with a painful crunching sound. His limbs felt as though they were on fire, which was probably because they were. He knew without looking that he'd broken many bones in his body, again.

The fire continued to eat away at his flesh, sizzling as the flames reached fatty tissue. Gerrard screamed out in agony. It wasn't fair! He was so fucking close!

Gerrard tried to roll his body over to stifle the flames. His limbs screamed in protest, but he managed to turn over completely before blacking out. He came to only seconds later. His skin still felt as though it were burning, but he no longer felt the intense heat of the fire. Maybe he'd survive this if he was lucky. But to what end? How much could the BSS rig repair?

He heard screams as people ran about in panic. He looked around as best he could and saw people running from burning buildings. He was in the city, that much was for certain. He'd accomplished part of what he'd set out to do. If only he could move so he could see the rest of his plan come to fruition.

***

Elaina had been in surgery for the better part of eight hours, and the anesthesia hadn't worn off when she was moved to recovery.

The attending nurse came into her room when she'd gotten a message that was meant for Elaina. She tried to rouse Elaina from her slumber, but it was no use. Another hour, maybe, and Elaina would probably wake up.

"I'll come back in a bit," the nurse said, though Elaina didn't hear her.

***

"You need to hurry," Rectus said as they got to their feet. "The city is under attack, and I am positive Goordaiin will use the opportunity to flee. I can't join you, though. I have to marshal our army and defend the city!"

Ryve nodded. Devin looked at the Calvoran, puzzled. What was this thing talking about? The ground shook again, and he was broken out of his thoughts. Well, the city was falling, that much he could tell.

"Fuck," he shouted. "Gerrard! That crazy bastard is attacking the city!"

"You know who is attacking us?" Rectus asked in an accusatory tone. "Why haven't you warned anyone?"

"I thought he was dead," Devin retorted. How? How had the psycho survived?

"What can you tell me," Rectus implored. "Hurry, there isn't much time."

"He had an army," Devin began, halting as the ground shook violently. "Bandits, he said. Armed with Trooviian weapons."

"Bandits? Really? That will only spell disaster if the enter the city. Go, I must make sure they don't get in. Goordaiin is just down the hall. He's locked in his office." With that Rectus hurried past them down the hall, back from where they'd come.

"He's right," Ryve said. "Goordaiin will try to escape. Can't let him."

"Lead on, big guy," Devin said.

They ran down the hall, struggling to stay upright as the floor shook. They came upon a closed door, a name written in alien symbols on the front. Ryve didn't hesitate. He opened the door and walked in. Devin followed closely behind.

"Who the hell are you?" the Calvoran asked when they entered the room. After a moment, the Calvoran's facial expression changed, as did the hue of its skin. It had taken on a purplish color. "You. You were one of the Trooviians I sent after the fugitive. Why hadn't you responded? I had figured you were dead."

"Deekin is dead," Ryve growled. "Tor dead too. My brother. Your fault."

"Who?" the Calvoran, who Devin assumed to be Professor Goordaiin, asked.

"My friend. My brother. Dead."

Ryve tried to continue forward but stopped as if blocked by an invisible wall. Seconds later he began clutching his head. Goordaiin had taken the opportunity during their exchange reestablish the psychic link. Ryve was helpless.

"That's a shame," Goordaiin said, his skin fading to a lighter shade. "Casualties are sometimes an unfortunate risk…"

Goordaiin didn't finish his sentence. He doubled over, clutching his stomach. A small trail of smoke snaked through his fingers. He looked down at his stomach and then to the Scavenger that had accompanied Ryve into his office.

Devin had raised his rifle and fired. He hadn't thought about it. To be honest, he hadn't even planned on shooting the Calvoran. He had intended to let Ryve exact his revenge, but an uncontrollable rage had consumed him, operating his limbs on its own without his direction.

Ryve shot Devin a look before approaching Goordaiin, who'd fallen to his knees.

"You… you can't do this," Goordaiin gasped. "I'm the director of the Phoenix One project. I-I'm in charge! You work for me!" Goordaiin pointed an accusatory finger at Ryve.

"No more," Ryve said, indicating on his shoulder where the patch for the Order once resided. "I quit."

Goordaiin tried to stand, his legs trembled beneath him. Devin aimed for the Calvoran's head, ready to fire, but Ryve had beat him to it.

Ryve clasped both sides of Goordaiin's head between his hands and lifted him upward.

"You die now," Ryve hissed through clenched teeth right before lowering Goordaiin to chest level.

The floor gave way beneath them, and Ryve dropped Goordaiin to the ground. Goordaiin mustered as much psychic energy as was possible and threw it at the Trooviian. The howl of pain and rage brought a smile to his face. The beast had tried to kill him—had nearly succeeded—but now he had the upper hand. He wouldn't allow the creature to get the best of him again. Goordaiin continued the psychic assault and watched as the Trooviian grabbed its head in agony.

Another shockwave shook the building and sent Goordaiin crashing to the floor once again. As he tried to stand, he saw the Trooviian sit up and shake its head. The damn thing was resilient, he had to give it that, but it wouldn't be enough. An idea came to him as he fought to stand before the Trooviian and its human companion could get to their feet.

Goordaiin dashed out of the room and down the hall. He knew exactly where he wanted to go. The chaos outside would not offer him any safety, but perhaps the budding ecosystem in the Eco-Generator room would.

***

"Where'd he go?" Devin called out once he and Ryve regained their footing.

"Not sure," Ryve said as he rubbed his massive temples. "Went left after leaving room, I think."

"It's better than nothing," Devin said as he headed for the door. Ryve followed right behind him.

"Link not broken," Ryve grumbled. "Just weakened. Can still find him."

"Oh good," Devin replied. "Then let's get this bastard, for Deekin and Tor."

Ryve grinned and nodded in agreement.

They raced out of the room and down the hall where Ryve believed Goordaiin had fled. Where he was going, Ryve wasn't sure. The exit of the building was the opposite direction.

The hallway wound and twisted like a massive snake, but Ryve kept moving. Devin hoped his friend was able to track the Calvoran and wasn't just guessing. They still needed to get out of the building before the tremors shook it apart and buried them.

***

Goordaiin pushed open the door and gasped as he took in the sight before him. The ecosystem had grown exponentially since his last visit. It almost looked like the forests on his homeworld. The air was thick with humidity and an earthy smell. Large swathes of moss-covered nearly every surface, with large columns that must have been plants jutting from the floor. The once open room was now congested with plant life and the further into the room Goordaiin went, the harder it was to see.

It was breathtaking. The Eco-Generator was working far better than he had ever expected. Perhaps the chaos and the destruction would bear fruit after all. If the chancellor was killed in the confusion, he might be safe and remain in control of the project. Hell, if the chancellor was dead, he might even be appointed as the replacement. How perfect that would be!

He heard footsteps coming down the hall and immediately made his way deeper into the room. The Trooviian may be superior in size, and the human may be with him, but Goordaiin had his superior intellect. They wouldn't be able to harm what they couldn't see, and he would have ample time to obliterate their fragile brains. Perhaps he'd leave them coherent enough to understand what was happening to them when he loaded them inside the generator. Let them feed the machine. Goordaiin grinned wickedly as he awaited their approach.

***

Devin was immediately stunned when he saw the blanket of green covering the room. He'd never seen anything like it. How was this even possible? Ryve seemed to be just as taken aback as he gasped at Devin's side.

The magnitude of what they were seeing was distracting, and Devin could have continued taking it all in, but Ryve nudged him and growled. Devin knew what that meant. They still had Goordaiin to deal with.

The moss seemed to be dampening sound as the room was deafeningly quiet except for a low humming coming from somewhere within the chamber. Devin searched intently for any sign of movement, any sign of the Calvoran who no doubt was hiding somewhere within.

"Come out!" Ryve bellowed though the sound dampening effect of the room made it barely audible.

"We need to be careful," Devin called out. "He could be anywhere in here."

Devin's head felt as if it were about to explode as an immense pressure seemed to press in from nowhere. He dropped his weapon as he brought his hands to the sides of his head. There was nothing physically pressing on his skull, but the pressure was still growing. Panic gripped him as the pain grew so intense that it effectively blinded him.

Ryve saw his friend clutch his head and knew immediately that Goordaiin was nearby. He wanted to help Devin, but he knew there was little he would be able to do. All he could do was kill Goordaiin before Devin's brain imploded.

He aimed and fired his weapon at the columns nearby, hoping that Goordaiin was behind one of them and would be blasted in the process. Plant life and debris exploded around him and filled the air, making it even harder to see. He glanced over at Devin to see if the onslaught had ceased, but it hadn't. Goordaiin was still alive.

***

A column exploded right next to where Goordaiin crouched. He feared for a moment that the next shot would hit him, but nothing struck him. The Trooviian missed every shot. The air may have been choked with detritus, but in his mind's eye, Goordaiin was able to see the room unhindered. The Trooviian had only succeeded in making it easier to see it. It was standing stupidly out in the open.

Goordaiin wanted to continue his psychic assault on the human, but the Trooviian was far more dangerous. He'd need to eliminate it first.

His focus shifted from the prone human to the far larger creature, and he began his assault anew. He watched in satisfaction as the Trooviian howled in pain and dropped to the ground, writhing in agony. This was just too damn easy!

A sound, barely audible in the mossy room, caught Goordaiin's attention. He wanted to investigate the sound, but he had to maintain his focus on the Trooviian.

The sound came again, a faint rustling that set his nerves on edge. He knew without a doubt that there was more than plant life in this room and he remembered the furry shape he'd seen during his last visit. What had the thing been and was even something he should bother concerning himself with? It had appeared quite small at the time, though size didn't always mean much. Often the smallest creatures were the deadliest. But he was so close! A moment more and the Trooviian would be little more than a quivering pile of tissue lacking the intellect to do more than keep its organs functioning.

He focused harder, and his grin grew wider. He could see the human struggling to stand, but the damage would have been enough to at least stall him for a while longer. There wasn't anything he would be able to do to save his friend. Goordaiin would be done with the Trooviian and could focus his attention on the human within moments.

Once again, the sound came, closer this time, but once again Goordaiin chose to ignore it. An instant later he wished he hadn't as something large slammed into his back and knocked him prone. He felt the weight of something large pressing down on him and the breath from whatever it was warm on the back of his head. He tried to buck and throw it off his back, but he could barely even breathe beneath the weight.

Goordaiin flailed his arms uselessly just as the creature lunged toward his head, clamping his skull in its jaws. His eyes grew wide with shock as the jaws snapped shut and crushed his head as easily as an egg.

***

Devin rubbed his eyes furiously as he tried to understand what he was seeing. The mental attack had made him dizzy and blurred his vision, but he could make out a large mass huddled over something flailing beneath it.

He blinked and saw, just as his eyes focused, a very large and hairy creature bite through Goordaiin's head. He saw the beast's jaws coated in bluish blood mixed with grey as the Calvoran's skull erupted.

"Get up!" Devin hissed at Ryve, though he could see his friend still writhing in pain. "You have to get up!"

Ryve continued to clutch at his head, though his grip was beginning to lessen. Devin knew it would take a moment to recover, but they didn't have a moment. The thing that killed Goordaiin would most likely turn its attention toward them. It wasn't as if the Calvoran would make much of a meal.

"Get up!" Devin yelled again, panic causing his voice to crack. "Get up damn you!"

Ryve groaned as Devin tried to haul the far larger Trooviian to its feet. He shook his head, trying desperately to relieve the pressure that had built up within. He could see the creature that was feasting on Goordaiin's corpse, and he forced himself to his feet. He stood, but his legs refused to hold his weight, and he fell back to the floor. Ryve heard Devin shouting for him to get back up, but his body didn't want to cooperate.

He heard a deep growl and saw Goordaiin's killer look over at them. The creature was unlike anything he'd ever seen. It was covered in fur, and he could tell it was quadrupedal, but his mind struggled to make sense of what he was seeing. The thing's head was vaguely like that of the giant Millipede's, but it was far smaller, and its jaws opened sideways. The eyes were milky, and there were far too many of them. Ryve counted, twelve at least. What the hell was this thing?

Ryve didn't have much time to ponder the question as the beast began its advance toward him. He mustered all his strength and climbed to his feet. As he glanced around, he could see the door to the hall was not far behind, but he doubted he'd make it before the beast caught him. He'd have to try, though. If anything, he'd be able to hold it off long enough for Devin to make it to safety.

"Go," he said as he stared at the creature stalking toward him. "You go. I will be behind you."

"What?" Devin cried out. "What the hell are you talking about?"

"Go!" Ryve bellowed. "Now!"

Devin turned and sprinted toward the door. The sudden movement got the creature's attention and ignited its hunting instincts. It sprang toward him, but Ryve's massive fist collided with its side, knocking it off course. The beast turned its dozen eyes on Ryve and snarled.

Ryve couldn't look to see if Devin had made it out of the room. He had to keep his eyes on the hideous beast and hope that his friend had managed to escape.

The creature readied itself to strike, leaning its weight on its haunches in preparation to jump. Ryve had seen other creatures behave similarly and hoped he could time his actions right. The beast launched itself toward Ryve with blinding speed. Ryve swung both of his fists clasped together at the creature. His timing had been off by a fraction of a second and, instead of hitting the thing in the head, struck its neck. The blow was enough to send the creature sprawling, but it also threw Ryve off balance, and he fell.

The creature was stunned for a moment, but Ryve was certain it would reorient itself quicker than he'd be able to stand. His only hope was to bear crawl toward the doorway as fast as he possibly could. With hesitation, Ryve began propelling his girth on all fours. He heard the beast scrabble to its feet and begin thudding toward him. The creature was gaining on him, but he was near to the door. Just a little further and he would clear the doorway. It likely wouldn't be enough, but maybe he'd have time to shut the door on the creature.

Ryve scrambled through the doorway and felt a stabbing pain in his calf as the creature bit him. He howled in pain and fear as the creature tried to haul him back into the room. The thing's teeth were tearing through the muscles in his leg as it yanked on the limb.

He fought with every ounce of his being against the pull of the creature's vicious jaws. He looked up in time to see Devin rush toward him and slam into the door. The door swung shut on the creature's head with a sickening crunch, and Ryve managed to free his leg.

"Let's get the fuck out of here!" Devin yelled as he helped his friend unsteadily to his feet.

Chapter 41

Kyle regained consciousness but wished he hadn't. His body hurt all over, and he could smell smoke. He shook his head to clear the fog that flooded his mind and tried to move. His limbs felt as though electricity was arcing through them, while simultaneously burning. He screamed in pain and almost blacked out a second time.

He could hear nothing besides the crackle of sparks and flames around him. He couldn't hear the signs of battle or the screams of the wounded. It was completely silent. Kyle felt claustrophobia begin setting in as he realized he was trapped inside a burning vessel. On the surface. Where the fumes were explosive.

Through gritted teeth, he moaned as he tried to move again. Once again, his arms screamed in protest, but it was at that moment that he couldn't feel anything below the waist. He expected his legs to be in intense agony as well, but he felt nothing.

"Shit!" he gasped. He didn't want to look down, fearing that the entire lower half of his body was gone. He was partially correct. When he finally looked down he saw blood everywhere, his legs (what remained of them) were intermingled in the pool of blood. The crash had forced the internal components of the ship upward, crushing his legs between the floor and the instrument panel.

"Oh fuck," he cried out. "I'm dead."

Kyle closed his eyes as he braced himself for the explosion he was sure to come. He waited long moments in horrified anticipation, but he heard no explosion. A moment later he heard a loud hissing sound followed by banging on the outside of the craft.

"Help!" he screamed, though it came out barely louder than as if he were speaking casually.

The banging sound resumed in earnest. A moment later Kyle heard a crashing sound, which he took for an explosion for a split second, and then voices.

"Anyone in here?" a voice called out.

Kyle cried out again, but his rescuers had already found him.

"Jesus," one of the voices said. "This guy's in bad shape!"

"He'll probably never walk again," said another. "If he survives, that is."

"Don't worry pal," the other voice said next to Kyle's head. "We're going to do all we can to help you. Just don't move."

Kyle wanted to respond, but he lost consciousness once again.

Epilogue

The days that followed were filled with stress and fear. Rectus had managed to marshal his army just before the Bandits attempted to enter the city. The losses were far worse than anyone would have expected. The Bandits fought with a level of organization nobody was prepared for. Everyone aboard the floating cities had assumed the Bandits to be mindless savages, but the attack on Disc City 9 proved that assumption false.

Rectus used the security force founded by Professor Goordaiin to search the city for any possible infiltrators. It was a slow process. The plan for phase two was to have the populations of every Disc City board shuttles and launch. They were supposed to dock at the space stations established around where Phoenix One was to be built.

Most of the cities followed this plan, at Chancellor Vallus's behest. Disc City 9 would have to wait, though. They couldn't risk stowaways on the shuttles. After a week Vallus ordered the evacuation of the city, satisfied that the Bandits who'd managed to infiltrate the city were eradicated. The shuttles prepared for launch as every survivor of the city was led aboard.

Goordaiin's remains were found in his office after the attack. Vallus initially wanted his murderer apprehended but abandoned the idea at Rectus's request. He argued that the time spent would be a waste and potentially detrimental to the safety of the city's residents. He knew who had killed Goordaiin, of course, but he made sure to block that information from Vallus's probing. Better she didn't know.

Devin waited for the aftermath of the battle before he set out in search of Gerrard and, with luck, his robotic horse. He spent several hours scouring the ruins before he found what remained of his steed. Fury, once again, threatened to overtake him as he searched frantically for Gerrard. Ryve eventually decided that they'd spent enough time digging through corpses and wanted nothing more than to finally rest. Devin relented, but only because Ryve picked him up and dragged him away.

Devin and Ryve were later permitted to board the shuttles as well, though Devin was initially denied access because of his status as Scavenger. Ryve threatened to tear the soldier's head off if he didn't let them pass. After a call to his superiors, the soldier waved them past and continued checking the passengers. Devin was awestruck by the size of the shuttle. Each section had been designated as living quarters for the residents, with a main chamber for them to sit during takeoff.

Devin couldn't believe he was leaving the planet. Never had he dreamed he'd see anything other than the barren wastes of planet Earth. Ryve may have caught him crying, though Devin wouldn't admit to it.

The rig he wore was a matter of discussion when he had first been brought on board. Everyone had been led to believe the system to be incompatible with human biology. It was another of Goordaiin's lies, they concluded.

Devin was glad they let him keep the BSS rig, though there wasn't much use for it anymore. He couldn't ignore the mood swings that he kept experiencing, though. Could it be due to the rig? Devin put it out of his mind and settled into his seat, preparing himself for takeoff.

Elaina managed to survive her wounds. It had taken an immense amount of effort to cleanse the poison from her system, and there was a significant portion of her damaged arm that had to be removed. Necrosis had begun to set in, and the medical staff feared that it would enter her bloodstream.

She woke up in a hospital bed several days later, an IV tube in her arm and sensors monitoring her vitals. She wondered in her doped-up state if all that had happened was merely a dream. It wasn't until she looked at her left arm that she knew it hadn't been. Attached to what remained of her limb was a prosthetic arm. She tried to open and close her left hand, and the hand had responded instantly! It was as if she'd never lost the limb.

Elaina would have to resign herself to the fact that it was a robotic limb, but she could live with it. Her thoughts suddenly turned to Kyle. Where was he?

A nurse came to check on her and Elaina immediately began her barrage of questions, most of which had to do with Kyle. The nurse, to her credit, was patient and waited for Elaina to finish her interrogation. The nurse filled her in on as much of what had happened as she could, but she only knew so much.

There had been an assault on Disc City 9. Elaina had been worried about that, but she wasn't all that surprised by the news. She nearly jumped out of her bed when the nurse told her Kyle had gone with a fleet of fighter ships to stop the attack. This caused Elaina to begin her questioning anew. All the nurse knew was that the fleet had suffered grievous losses, but the attack had been repelled.

Elaina lied back on her bed and closed her eyes. She was thankful that they had been able to save Disc City 9, but she was still horribly unhappy. She knew nothing about Kyle's condition, or if he was even alive. What upset her most was that she didn't know if Goordaiin was still alive or in custody. The nurse knew nothing about it.

Several hours later she was visited by Director Clavin. The man looked tired, as though he'd been awake for days. He told her more about what had transpired at the site of Disc City 9. He told her that her warning had saved the lives of many. If she hadn't come all that way to deliver her message, the city might very well have been lost. She took a small measure of relief at the news, but that still didn't answer her more pressing concerns.

Kyle was alive, Director Clavin assured her. He'd been badly injured and would never walk on his own legs again. It took an extensive amount of surgery just to ensure he wasn't completely paralyzed. In time, it was possible that he would be fitted for prosthetics, but his road to recovery would be a long one.

Elaina cried, though part of the reason was due to the joy of hearing Kyle was alive. His injuries upset her, but she decided she'd help him on his road to recovery in any way she could. It was her fault he was in the condition he was in. If he hadn't followed her, he would have been perfectly fine, assuming he wasn't killed in the assault of Disc City 9.

The last bit of information made Elaina sit up in her bed, which resulted in her immediately blacking out from the blood rush.

Goordaiin had been killed, though nobody knew by whom. His body had been found in his office, his skull crushed and a hole in his midsection from a Trooviian weapon. Elaina didn't care who had killed him. She was just happy he was dead.

Clavin left her alone after a while but promised he'd be back to check in on her.

"I guess we did it," a weak voice said in the bed to her right. She couldn't see who it was because the privacy curtain obstructed her vision, but she knew the voice.

"Kyle?" she asked, her voice taking on a noticeable tremor.

"I'm still here, baby," he said. "You're still stuck with me."

Gerrard had awoken to find himself buried under a layer of dirt and rubble. The only reason he hadn't been crushed to death was that a beam had prevented the rubble from falling on top of him. His body ached, but the pain was no longer as intense. He looked down at himself, expecting to see his body in ruins, but was surprised to see that he was completely intact. His skin looked raw and bruised, but he could move his limbs.

As Gerrard crawled from beneath the rubble, he noticed that the device in the center of his BSS rig was broken. It sparked intermittently, but his current state meant it was still functional. Maybe he'd replace it if he found another. Maybe not. It really depended on whether it continued to function as he expected.

He snuck toward the center of the city, where he guessed the shuttles would be. He may not have been successful in his attempt to take the city, but he wasn't dead yet. It wasn't over. He waited until everyone was on board the last shuttle before slipping inside. A guard tried to stop him, but a broken neck put an end to that obstacle.

Gerrard crept along the maintenance section of the shuttle and found a place to secure himself for launch. It wasn't over. Not yet. He had more to do, and now he had plenty of time to do it.

Devin sat back and let the force of the launch press him into his seat. He felt a measure of fear as they took off, but that was eclipsed by the happiness that he felt at being alive and no longer on Earth.

His past was behind him, and, with luck, a brighter future lay ahead.

ABOUT THE AUTHOR

Chase MacLeod is an American author. He received his Associates Degree in Information Systems Technology Management from Ashford University in 2016. He currently serves in the United States Air Force and lives in Northern California with his wife, two children, and four pets.

As an independent author, it is through word of mouth that we can reach a larger audience. Please leave a review where you purchased this book. Thank you!

www.ingramcontent.com/pod-product-compliance
Lightning Source LLC
Chambersburg PA
CBHW061611100726

47898CB00002B/612